AVALANCHE ON THE MOUNTAIN

WATCHDOG MOUNTAIN DIVISION
BOOK 6

OLIVIA MICHAELS

FALCON IN HAND PUBLISHING LLC

By Falcon in Hand Publishing

Cover by Syneca Featherstone

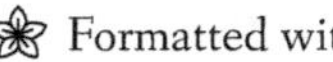 Formatted with Vellum

This one's for The 'Guy' at the Hiring Fair. 36 years, and going strong.

ONE

Ben Massey was driving the backroads to Lyons from setting up his stall at the Renaissance Faire when he spotted the broken-down Honda Civic. The little sedan sat canted on the shoulder, hazards blinking in the last light of a warm, late-summer Sunday evening. He eased his truck to a stop behind it, keeping enough distance that he wouldn't box the driver in and turned on his own hazards. His military training kicked in automatically—scan the area, check for threats, assess the situation before committing.

The driver's door opened and a woman stepped out and looked at him warily before giving him a nervous smile. She kept glancing past Ben down the road toward Sedalia like she expected someone to come roaring up behind her.

Ben killed the engine and took a breath. This part never got easier—the approach. He knew what he looked like climbing out of his truck. Six-seven, two-forty of solid muscle, shoulders that barely fit through most doorframes. He'd learned young that his size scared people, especially women who'd been hurt before. And this woman's body language screamed hurt.

He opened his door slowly, making sure she could see him

coming. When his boots hit the pavement, he deliberately hunched his shoulders, making himself smaller. Old habit. Didn't always work, but it was worth trying.

"Hey there," he called, keeping his voice soft and his hands visible. "Looks like you could use some help."

Ben's chest tightened as he drew closer. Her face was a mess—mascara streaked down her cheeks, eyes red and swollen from crying. But it was the look in those eyes that got him. Not just worry. Terror.

"I'm fine, thanks," she said too quickly. Her hands twisted together in front of her, knuckles white. "Triple-A is on the way."

Ben stopped a good fifteen feet back, giving her space. "That's good. How long did they say they'd be?"

"Um..." She glanced at her phone, then her gaze went back to Ben. "Twenty minutes."

He glanced at his watch, then at the empty road stretching in both directions. "I can wait with you, in case they're late. It's getting dark."

She hesitated, and Ben could see her weighing it—stranger danger versus the very real problem of being stranded on a lonely stretch of road. He knew she was contemplating which scenario was the bigger risk and he couldn't blame her.

Some women would rather face a bear than a strange man my size. Or any size for that matter.

He slouched a little more. "I'm Ben Massey," he added, hooking his thumbs in his belt loops so his hands were visible but not threatening. "I'm heading back up to Lyons. Coming back from the Ren Faire."

That got a flicker of interest. Her gaze dropped to his shirt—a plain black tee—but his leather apron was visible through the truck's windshield, draped over the back of the passenger seat. He wished he'd kept his kilt on instead of changing back into his cargos. It always seemed to be less threatening to women.

"The Renaissance Faire?" she asked, her voice a little steadier.

"Yeah." He grinned as he nodded. "I'm a blacksmith." Then he gave her a full smile, going for as friendly and non-threatening as he could. "I spend my summers making chainmail, forging swords, shoeing horses, and selling jewelry to tourists. Very normal guy stuff—well, if you're a guy in the fifteenth century, I suppose."

The corner of her mouth twitched. Not quite a smile, but close.

"I'm good with more modern machines, too. I could take a quick look at your Civic, if you wanted me to. Might be something simple."

The woman glanced at her car, then back to Ben, a contemplating expression on her face. "I'm Shelly," she said finally. "And... okay. If you could just look, that would be great."

Ben approached Shelly and the Honda like he was gentling a spooked horse—slow movements, lots of space, no sudden gestures. He rounded the car on the passenger side opposite of her and stooped when he got to the hood, making himself smaller again. She relaxed a fraction.

"Would you pop the hood for me, please?"

"Sure." Shelly leaned inside and pulled the release. Ben lifted the hood and immediately spotted the problem. The serpentine belt was broken. He looked closer.

His jaw clenched.

Shelly came around and stood next to him, looking at the engine. Ben took in a deep breath and kept his expression neutral. Now was definitely not the time to scare her.

"Did your battery die while you were driving? Is that why you pulled over?" he asked.

She looked surprised. "No, that's not why, but the car wouldn't start after I pulled over, so I think it is dead. Would that make the car start vibrating?"

Ben tried to keep the alarm out of his eyes. "Vibrating as you drove?"

"Yeah. And it got really hard to steer. I had to really wrench the wheel. I thought maybe I was getting a flat, but the tires all look full. Is it just a dead battery?" She looked hopeful. It broke his heart.

"It wouldn't cause the car to vibrate." Ben went around the Civic, checking each tire. Like Shelly said, they were full with no signs of punctures or slow leaks. Then he tested the lug nuts. All were loose, enough that the tires probably started wobbling as she drove. Ben straightened slowly, his mind already cataloging the damage and what it meant. Combine the loose lug nuts with what he found under the hood, he could come to only one conclusion.

This wasn't mechanical failure. This was sabotage. And considering the damage done, someone wanted this woman dead.

"See? The tires are good," Shelly said. "So...maybe the battery just needs a jump?"

Ben turned to face her, gentling his expression even though rage was building in his chest. He kept his voice level and calm. "It's a little more than a dead battery, Shelly. The lug nuts on the tires are loose. I can tighten those easy." He walked back to the hood and pointed at the serpentine belt. "But, the serpentine belt's broken, too. That's why you can't start the car. The belt charges the alternator so if it slips or breaks, the battery dies and it can affect the power steering."

Shelly's eyes widened. "Oh, so that's why the steering felt off. Would it cause the car to vibrate, and maybe that's why the lug nuts are loose?"

Ben kept himself from flinching. She really had no idea how much danger she was in and that horrified him.

She went on. "I don't suppose you have an extra serpentine belt? I'd love to be on my way sooner rather than later." She glanced toward Sedalia again.

Ben shook his head. He didn't dare tell her that if she hadn't pulled over, her engine might have overheated and seized. Or worse, one of the tires could have sheered off. He took one more look at the belt. Yup—it had been partially cut and then tore the rest of the way.

Dear God. She's lucky to be alive.

"Can I ask you something, Shelly?"

She tensed. "What?"

"Is someone after you?"

Fresh tears spilled down her cheeks and she pressed her hand over her mouth, trying to hold back a sob. She nodded.

"It's okay," Ben said softly. "You're safe right now. But I need you to tell me what's going on so I can help you properly."

"I can't—" Her breath hitched. "I can't go back. I can't."

"You don't have to." He kept his voice steady, soothing, the same tone he used when shoeing a nervous horse.

"The belt didn't just break by itself, Shelly. It was partially cut. And your car was vibrating *because* of the loose lug nuts. You're lucky you didn't lose a wheel. This wasn't an accident. Someone sabotaged your car."

She swallowed, hard. "Oh," she whispered. "Oh, God."

Shelly swayed, and Ben instinctively reached out to steady her, then stopped himself. Too fast. Too close. She needed space.

Instead he said, "Why don't we sit in my truck? It's cooler in there, and you can tell me what's happening."

She looked at his truck. He hoped she saw it the right way—big, safe, with tinted windows that would hide her from anyone driving past. Then she looked back at him. Ben watched her making the calculation again—trust the stranger or wait for whoever sabotaged her car to come looking.

"Okay," she whispered as she wiped her eye. She wrapped her arms around her torso as she walked to the truck. Ben opened the passenger door and stepped back, giving her room to climb in. She moved stiffly, like her whole body hurt, and when she settled into the seat she wrapped her arms back around herself. He left the door open so she wouldn't feel trapped.

Ben walked around to the driver's side and climbed in, leaving his door open too. He set his keys on the dashboard where she could see them. The cab smelled like leather, metal, and the incense that permeated the Faire. Shelly took a shaky breath.

"His name is Dex," she said finally. "Dexter Morrison. He's... we've been living together for six months. It was great right up until it wasn't." She tucked a lock of long, brown hair behind her ear as she gave Ben a quick, sad smile and shrugged her shoulder.

"What did he do to you, Shelly?"

She flinched. "It started small. Yelling. Throwing things. Then he started grabbing my wrists when we argued. Last week he pushed me into a wall." She touched her ribs carefully. "He accused me of cheating on him. I told him I wasn't, I would never do that, and then I caught him spying on me whenever I left the house. We fought about it last night. I told him to stop it and this morning I told him I was moving out." She covered her mouth as she stared at her car. "Now... now I get why he gave me this scary smile and said go ahead, see how far you get."

Ben's hands tightened on the steering wheel.

"He must have done it last night while I was sleeping," Shelly said. Fresh tears tracked down her face. "I have a friend up in Denver who said I could stay with her." She shook her head. "I can't get her into trouble, too."

"Then let me take you to the police."

Shelly's shook her head wildly. "I can't file a report against him. They won't believe me."

Ben's jaw clenched so hard his teeth ached, but when he spoke he kept his voice soft and gentle. "Why wouldn't they believe you?"

Shelly looked at him then, her eyes flat and hopeless.

"Because he's a cop."

Everything clicked into place. The sabotage. The confidence that he could hurt her and get away with it. Dex Morrison was betting his badge would protect him.

Ben pulled out his phone. "Change of plans. We're not going to the PD."

"Where—"

"There's a place called Watchdog Security in Lyons. They have safehouses for situations exactly like this. I'm taking you there tonight."

"I don't have money for—"

"You don't need it." Ben was already texting Kyle McGuire. "These are good people, Shelly. They'll keep you safe while you figure out your next steps."

His phone buzzed almost immediately.

> Bring her in. I'll have a safehouse ready. I'll also call George.

Ben showed Shelly the text. "See? You're not alone anymore."

"Who's George?"

"George is the sergeant for Lyons PD and a good friend. He'll know how to handle Dex."

She read it again, her lips trembling. "Why are you helping me?"

"Because you need help." Ben said it like it was the simplest thing in the world. Because it was. "And because men like Dex Morrison count on women being too scared to ask for it. We're going to prove him wrong."

Shelly's lips trembled, but this time when she cried, it sounded like relief.

"Thank you," she whispered.

"Is Triple-A really coming, or was that to get me back on the road?"

"No, they're really coming...Wait, I think that's them," she said, looking in the passenger side mirror. Sure enough, a tow truck was coming over a rise in the road.

"Then you talk to them while I get your things into the truck, then we'll get you to safety."

Shelly nodded as the tow truck passed them and pulled off in front of her Civic. "Thank you again."

"Don't mention it."

They got out of the truck and Shelly approached the tow truck. The driver took one look at her smeared mascara and gave Ben the stink eye.

"You all right, miss?" he asked, never taking his eyes off Ben, which Ben thought was just fine given the circumstances.

"I am now." Shelly turned to look at Ben. "This man's an angel for stopping to help."

Ben felt his cheeks redden. "I w-wouldn't go that far."

"Well, you are,"

"Th-thank you." He cleared his throat. "You give him your info while I load up your bags."

Embarrassed, he opened the trunk and took out two large duffel bags while Shelly gave the driver her information. He carried them to the truck while the driver tilted the flatbed then hooked a winch cable to the front of the Civic. Ben was walking back toward Shelly when a cop car came over the ridge and slowed down.

Shelly froze.

Ben reached her side. He stood between Shelly and the road, blocking her, ready to throw her to the ground if the son of a bitch decided to shoot. He felt the weight of his gun in his cargos' pocket, hoping it wouldn't come to that.

At least not here.

"Is that him?"

"I don't know," Shelly answered in a high-pitched whisper.

"If I tell you to get down, get down."

Shelly nodded.

The cruiser slowed further, rolling past at five miles an hour. Two cops stared blank-faced at them. Ben stared back. The cop nearest to him flinched and looked away.

That's right, you sons of bitches. Keep going.

Oblivious to the danger, the tow truck driver waved out his window as the Civic climbed the tilted deck. Once the cruiser passed the tow truck, it sped up. They watched it grow smaller, Shelly trembling at Ben's side.

"Was it him?" Ben asked again.

"N-no." She swallowed. "A couple of his buddies though."

Ben nodded once. "We'll take a different route. Just in case." He looked down at Shelly. "Hey."

She didn't move, just kept staring at the disappearing cruiser.

"I need you to look at me, Shelly."

She looked up at him.

"You're safe with me. I swear it to you upon my honor." The words from his favorite book, *Sword of Embers*, flowed off his tongue. Words spoken by the hero, a knight trying to claim his rightful throne. He thought it must have been the influence of the Ren Faire. Ben felt every inch the nerd he was.

The words did the trick though. Shelly gave him a wistful smile and nodded.

"I believe you," she said.

The hydraulics stopped humming as the Civic was loaded into place. The driver got out to secure the wheels and told Shelly she was free to go. Ben walked her back to the truck and held the door open for her, then got in.

As they pulled onto the highway, Ben caught a glimpse of Shelly in his peripheral vision. She'd stopped crying. Her hands were still shaking, but her jaw was set with something that looked like determination.

She was going to be okay. They'd make sure of it.

And Dexter Morrison? He was about to learn that not everyone was afraid of badges.

On the drive to Watchdog, Ben kept the conversation light even as he kept an eye out for any rollers in his rearview. He asked about Denver, about Shelly's friend, about anything except the man who'd hurt her. Shelly relaxed incrementally, her voice evening out as they got closer to Lyons.

The Watchdog gates opened before Ben reached them and he pulled through without slowing as the truck made its way up the winding road to the main office. Kyle was already waiting in the parking lot. The former SEAL looked every inch the professional—tactical pants, dark polo with the Watchdog logo, and an expression that said he'd seen this before and knew exactly what to do.

Beside him sat a gold-and-black mottled Lab who looked like he was about to vibrate out of his skin, wanting to greet the visitors but too well-behaved to leave Kyle's side. Camo was Kyle's former military working dog, and now his and his wife Arden's constant companion.

"You must be Shelly," Kyle said as she climbed out of the truck. His voice was gentle but confident as he fixed his ice-blue eyes on her. "I'm Kyle McGuire." He gestured at his dog. "And this is my boss, Camo. Welcome to Watchdog."

Shelly grinned and knelt to pet Camo, who melted under the attention. "Aren't you a good, good boy," Shelly told him, looking more relieved than she had since Ben met her.

Good move, Kyle.

Shelly gave Camo one last ear scratch and stood. She glanced at Ben, then back at Kyle. "Ben said you could help me."

"We absolutely can." Kyle gestured toward the building. "Let's get you inside and we'll talk through everything. The safehouse is all ready for you."

Kyle and Camo flanked Shelly. Ben followed them in, catching Kyle's eye. The look they exchanged said everything—cop abuser, sabotaged car, scared victim. Kyle gave a slight nod. He understood what Ben was about to do.

Inside, Kyle led them to a quiet office and closed the door. Camo settled himself in the corner closest to Shelly. The dog had a protective streak that rivaled any bodyguard.

"First things first—you're safe here," Kyle said. "Our facility is secure. Second, I've already contacted Sergeant George Williams with Lyons PD. He's a good man and he'll get this sorted."

"But Dex is a cop," Shelly said. "Won't they protect him?"

"Not if I have anything to say about it," a new voice said from the doorway.

Ben turned to see Sergeant Williams. Behind him stood Ben's best friend, Shane.

And beside Shane stood a woman who never failed to take Ben's breath away.

Charlie King.

Her gaze met Ben's, and like clockwork, he forgot to take his next breath until she looked past him at Shelly, her expression all-business.

"Ma'am, I'm George Williams," he said, stepping into the room, Charlie and Shane following. Charlie was shorter than Shane by a couple of inches, but at over six feet, she stood taller than George. Ben noticed her stooping ever so slightly as she glanced at the officer, as if to make herself smaller.

Ben's heart clenched with sympathy. He knew exactly how that felt.

"Kyle filled me in," George continued. "I want you to know that badge or no badge, Dexter Morrison doesn't get a pass for hurting you."

Shelly's eyes welled up again. "You believe me?"

"I do," George said simply. "And we're going to make sure he can't hurt you again." He turned to Charlie. "This is Charlie King. She's the best bodyguard here at Watchdog and she's gonna keep an eye on you." He nodded at Shane. "Shane Foti here's not half bad, either," he said with a smile.

Ben watched the tension drain from Shelly's shoulders. She'd been carrying the weight of this alone for so long, convinced no one would help her. Now she was surrounded by people who would.

Charlie smiled warmly as she reached out to shake Shelly's hand. "You're safe with me, Shelly. I swear it to you upon my honor."

Ben drew a quick breath in surprise.

Did she just quote...?

Behind Charlie, Shane smirked at Ben with a look in his eyes that said *See? I told you so*. Shane had served with Charlie in the Navy as SWCCs. A few months ago, he'd called out Ben's crush on her, and gave Ben some intel on Charlie for him to use to get over his nervousness and finally ask her out. Intel that Charlie herself had just confirmed—she was also a big fan of the *Legends of BattleLore* series.

I owe Shane lunch.

Kyle caught Ben's attention and jerked his head toward the door. Ben followed him into the hallway.

"Good work bringing her in," Kyle said quietly. "How'd you find her?"

"Broken down on the side of the road. Soon as I saw the look in her eyes, I knew something was off." Ben scrubbed a hand over his face. "Bastard sabotaged it. Wanted her stranded. At best."

Kyle's expression darkened. "And dead at worst. Morrison's going to regret that."

"Yeah, he is." Ben glanced back at the office where George was taking Shelly's statement. "A couple of Morrison's buddies rolled by in their cruiser, undoubtedly hoping to find her in the ditch. God only knows what they would've done if she'd been alone. She needs serious protection until Morrison's in custody."

"Already handled. I don't like to pick favorites, but George wasn't wrong when he said Charlie's the best. Shane's on standby if we need extra security, and no one's getting into the safehouse here. Morrison won't get within a mile of her." Kyle clapped Ben on the shoulder. "You did good, brother."

Ben nodded, but his jaw was still tight. Shelly was safe for now. But Dexter Morrison was still out there, still wearing a badge, still thinking he could get away with it.

That's going to change.

"Keep me posted," Ben said. "If you need backup—"

"You'll be my first call," Kyle promised. "I'm sure you've had a long day. Why don't you head home?"

Ben glanced back into the office where Shelly and Charlie were talking. Shelly looked relieved. And Charlie looked, well, like a warrior princess.

"Do you mind if I stay close until Shelly is settled?"

Kyle shrugged. "Suit yourself."

"Thanks."

Kyle stepped back into the office. Ben stayed in the hall, watching Shelly, who was smiling at Charlie now. But he couldn't shake the image of her terrified face when she'd first seen him. How vulnerable she'd looked standing next to her sabotaged car. How hard she'd been shaking in his truck.

Men like Morrison counted on that fear. They weaponized it.

Ben's phone chimed with an alert. Anger seeped into his blood, heating it.

That was quick.

Ben unlocked his phone, opened an app, and checked his security camera feed. Sure enough, a Douglas County cruiser sat in front of his Victorian, lights off. He zoomed in on the license plate and his jaw clenched.

It matched the cruiser that had driven past Shelly's broken-down Civic.

I knew it wouldn't take them long to find me if they ran my plates.

Ben glanced in the conference room. Everyone was standing up, Charlie a head taller than Shelly. Ben looked back down at his phone as she looked his way. As everyone filed out, Ben pulled Kyle, Shane, and George aside.

"I've got company at my house." He showed them the live feed on his phone. "That's the same cruiser that drove past Shelly and me."

George's expression hardened. "Morrison's buddies."

Ben nodded. "Or Morrison himself. He probably thinks Shelly's with me, that I'm the guy she's supposedly cheating with."

"Got an office I can borrow?" George asked Kyle. "I know the Douglas County sheriff. He's a straight shooter. It would be interesting to see if Morrison has complaints in his file—and I'm betting he does." He turned his attention back to Ben. "You want backup?"

Ben shook his head. "We've got it under control."

George smiled grimly. "I'll bet you do. Give me twenty minutes to make some calls, then I'll head your way with Sylvie."

Ben looked at Shane, who nodded.

"Make it thirty, George."

George studied the two men. "Understood." He followed Kyle down the hall.

Ben pulled out his phone and sent a group text to Mountain Division.

6. Watchdog.

The number six was their code meaning they had business to take care of. The responses came fast.

Gabe**:**

Ready.

Bear:

Be there soon.

Elias:

Time to go to work.

Waylon:

Gotcha.

Ben smiled grimly. Dexter Morrison was about to learn what happened when you hurt someone under Mountain Division's protection.

And it wouldn't be pretty.

TWO

Sunday afternoon, Charlie King sat at her desk in the quiet Watchdog office, staring at the expense report from her last client protection detail. Watchdog charged their wealthy clients bank, which they could afford. That allowed for what Kyle referred to as 'the widows and orphans fund' which let them provide free services to people who couldn't afford protection otherwise. It wasn't called that because it was only offered to widows and orphans—but because widows and orphans are what Watchdog and Mountain Division would create if necessary.

Sundays weren't usually Charlie's shift, but the alternative—sitting alone in her apartment—held even less appeal.

The Long, Dark Teatime of the Soul, she thought, channeling the book by Douglas Adams. At least here she had paperwork to distract her from the silence. It was funny—she usually didn't have a problem being alone. It was her default mode. But lately, after a 24/7 protection detail, the idea of her empty apartment made her stomach feel hollow. Not that the office was a hotbed of activity on a Sunday. Kyle was in though, along with Alex the kennel master, out in the training yard. Everyone else was either out on their own assignments or home with their families.

Charlie logged another receipt. Hotel in Vail. Meals. Mileage. The work was mind-numbing, which was exactly what she needed. Anything to keep her brain from circling back to the same thought pattern.

You'll never have your own family. You're always going to be alone. Who'd want someone like you?

Stop it, she told herself firmly. *Just finish the damn receipts.*

Her desk phone mocked her. The message light had been blinking when she got it that morning—one new voicemail, received Friday evening when she'd already left for the day. The extension was internal—forwarded from the main Watchdog line. She'd listened to it, and now it kept sticking in her mind.

She lifted the phone receiver and made herself listen to it again.

Might as well.

"Hi. Um." A young man's voice, familiar but changed, spoke carefully like he was choosing every word.

"This is...my name is Joseph King. I'm trying to reach Charlene King. I think she might work there? I'm her brother." He paused. "Charlie, if you get this message, hi. I know it's been a long time. I wanted to talk about something. That's all." Another pause, longer this time. "I hope you're doing okay."

The message ended with his phone number.

Charlie sat very still.

Joey. Twenty-seven years old now. Practically a stranger, except she could still picture him at eight—scabbed knees, gap-toothed smile, dragging her sleeve so she'd read to him before bed because their father was at the bar and their mum was somewhere else and Charlie was the one who was always there. She'd been his whole world, once. Before he'd gotten older and fell in line with Patrick and James, their older brothers.

He wants to talk about something? Right. More like he wants something from me.

That was how it worked. Growing up, someone in her family always wanted her to do something—wash the clothes, clean the house, cook the food. And nothing was ever good enough for her older brothers or their father. Eventually, nothing was good enough for Joey, either.

Old news. She wasn't falling for it.

Still, she re-saved the message instead of deleting it, then went back to her receipts.

Her phone buzzed. Kyle's name flashed on the screen.

"Yeah, Boss?"

"You busy?" Kyle's voice was relaxed, friendly. "Need you outside at the kennels."

She straightened, grateful for the interruption. She put her hands on the small of her back and arched it. Her spine popped like gunshots. Too much time spent in boats hitting waves at sixty-five MPH like they were on a washboard road.

"On my way, Boss."

The late afternoon sun hit her face as she stepped into the training yard by the kennels. Kyle stood with Alex Hoff, Watchdog's lead dog trainer, near the obstacle course. Three dogs sat at attention —Camo, Kyle's gold-and-black mottled Lab; Mac, Alex's Malinois; and a younger Malinois Charlie had worked with a few times during training sessions.

Flo.

Seeing the dog, her heart did a stupid little skip, but she kept her expression neutral as she approached.

"Afternoon," she said, nodding to both men.

"King." Kyle gestured at the dogs. "Thought you could help us run them through their paces. We're working on some detection drills."

"Sure." She couldn't help but reach down and pet Flo, who was watching her with those intelligent amber eyes. *Don't get your hopes up. She's going to the Boulder police department. Just like the others.*

They spent the next twenty minutes running exercises. Kyle sent

Camo through a drug search. Mac practiced his protection routine with Alex. And when it came time for Flo's turn, Kyle nodded at Charlie.

"Take her through the obedience sequence. Let's see how she responds to you."

Charlie's pulse quickened, but she kept her voice level. "Flo, heel."

The Malinois moved to her left side instantly, head up, alert but not anxious. They moved through the course together—sit, stay, down, recall. Flo was flawless. Not just obedient, but *connected*. The dog anticipated Charlie's commands, reading her body language like they'd been working together for years instead of a few scattered training sessions.

When they finished, Charlie gave Flo a quick ear scratch and her very own Kong, then stepped back. Professional. Controlled. Even though her chest felt tight with something that felt a lot like hope.

Don't love what you can't keep.

She tamped down her expectations like a reflex.

Kyle and Alex exchanged a look that Charlie couldn't quite read. Kyle was fighting a smile. Alex was full-on grinning.

"What?" she asked, suspicious.

Don't get your hopes up.

"Well," Kyle said slowly, drawing it out. "Alex and I have been talking."

"Uh-huh." Charlie crossed her arms, bracing herself for disappointment. *They're sending Flo to Boulder PD. Or giving her to Badger since Valkyrie's having puppies. Or—*

"Flo's finished her basic certification," Alex said. "She needs a handler for the specialized protection work."

"Right." Charlie swallowed. "I heard Boulder PD was interested—"

"They were," Kyle interrupted. "But I told them that's a negative."

Charlie blinked. "You... what?"

"Flo's not going to Boulder PD." Kyle's ice-blue eyes were warm with something that looked like satisfaction. "She's yours, Charlie. If you want her."

The world tilted sideways for a second.

Mine.

Flo. Was. Hers.

Charlie felt her face want to split into a massive grin, felt excitement bubble up in her chest like champagne, felt her throat get tight with emotion—

Hide what you love or they'll take it away.

She locked it all down. Nodded once. "Yeah. I want her."

Kyle's eyebrow rose slightly. Alex's smile faltered just a little, like he'd expected more reaction.

"Great," Kyle said, studying her face. "She's all yours then. You two are officially a team."

"Thanks." Charlie's voice came out steady. Controlled. She reached down to pet Flo again, letting herself run her fingers through the Malinois's fur for just a moment. "This means a lot. I appreciate the trust."

"You've earned it," Alex said. "Flo's lucky to have you."

I'm the lucky one. But Charlie didn't say it out loud. Instead she straightened, professional mask firmly in place. "I'll get her set up in my apartment tonight. Start the integration routine."

The door to the training yard opened and Shane stepped out with his dog, Pete. Shane's dark eyes swept the area before landing on their little group. He'd been Charlie's crewmate back in their SWCC days, one of the few people who'd seen her in combat, who knew exactly what she was capable of.

His gaze dropped to Flo, then back to Charlie's carefully neutral expression. One corner of his mouth quirked up.

"Don't let her fool you," Shane said, walking over. "King's over-the-top excited right now."

"Shut up, Elk," Charlie muttered. He was one of the few people who could read her better than she liked.

"Can't hide it from me, King. I've seen you after a successful exfil. Same spark in your eyes."

"I have no idea what you're talking about." But she could feel heat creeping up her neck.

Shane just grinned at her, then looked at Kyle. "Charlie finally got her dog, huh?"

"Finally," Kyle agreed.

"About damn time." Shane crouched down and Flo immediately went to him, accepting the ear scratch he offered while Pete looked jealous. "She's been waiting for you, Charlie. Even a blind man could see that."

Charlie rolled her eyes, but warmth spread through her chest.

My dog. I have my own dog.

Growing up, she'd wanted a pet so badly. But her father had always said no. They were too expensive, too much work, and Charlie already had enough responsibilities. As a SWCC, she wasn't allowed to train with military dogs—they weren't exactly made for the tactical boats that came in guns blazing to rescue a SEAL team under fire. They belonged to the teams, to the mission. Charlie glanced at Camo, remembering the horrible circumstances under which she'd seen the dog for the first time, and her heart felt suddenly heavy.

She shook off the old sadness. Camo was good now, and hell, so was she. This was a good day. Now, for the first time in her life, she had someone who'd always be happy to see her, who wouldn't judge her or find her lacking.

Don't cry, for God's sake. Do not *let them see you cry.*

Kyle's phone buzzed. He pulled it out, read the screen, and his expression shifted from relaxed to all-business in an instant.

"We've got someone coming in," he said, already typing a response. "Woman escaping an abusive situation." He looked up at Charlie. "You available to stick around? Might need you on protection detail."

"Absolutely." Charlie's mind was already shifting gears, professional mode engaging even as her heart went out with empathy to the woman. "What's the situation?"

"Still getting details, but it sounds serious. Ben Massey's bringing her in."

Charlie's heart did that stupid skip thing at the mention of Ben's name.

Focus. Someone needs help.

Kyle glanced at Shane. "You good to provide backup if we need it?"

"Yeah." Shane pulled out his own phone, thumbs flying over the screen. "April and Kevin are at the movies and heading to dinner after. I've got time."

"I'll grab my go-bag," Charlie said. "In case we're setting up at a safehouse."

Kyle nodded. "Good thinking." Kyle turned his attention to Alex. "You know if George is available?"

Alex raised his eyebrows. "He and Sylvie are working on her Mustang before her shift tonight. Why are you calling my father-in-law in on this?"

"The abuser's a cop."

Charlie's jaw tightened. Cops who hurt people were the worst kind of abusers—they knew the system, knew how to manipulate it, knew their victims were terrified to report them. And if the ranks closed in to protect the bad cop...

"Then she definitely needs protection," Charlie said. "I've got her."

"I know you do." Kyle's voice held absolute confidence, and Charlie felt that warmth in her chest again. Kyle didn't give compliments lightly. When he said someone was good at their job, he meant it.

Shane was watching her again, that knowing look in his eyes. "You good, King?"

"Fine." She met his gaze steadily. "Why wouldn't I be?"

"No reason." But his slight smirk said he'd caught the way she'd reacted to Ben's name.

Damn him.

She turned to go inside.

"Hey, King Charlemagne," Shane called, using her full nickname. "Aren't you forgetting something?"

She stopped and turned. "Forgetting—Oh! Shit!"

Flo sat patiently beside Pete, hopeful gaze glued to Charlie.

Charlie let herself smile this time. "Come, girl. We've got work to do."

The Malinois sprang up and loped to Charlie's side, tongue hanging out, big doggy smile giving away exactly how she felt about her new human.

HIDE WHAT YOU LOVE.

The words echoed in her head as she headed to her locker to grab her go-bag. She kept a packed duffel for exactly this kind of situation —clothes, toiletries, tactical gear, everything she'd need for an unexpected protection detail.

As she checked the contents, making sure her backup weapon was loaded and her phone charger was packed, she let herself have one moment. Just one.

She was getting to see Ben Massey today. The man she'd been half in love with since the first time she'd seen him at Sean's memorial, standing with his brothers, looking both powerful and gentle at the same time. The man whose picture she'd seen in Sean's wallet for years before she'd ever met him, standing in the St. Vrain River with his friends, laughing.

She'd come to Lyons partly because of that picture. Because those guys looked like they were good men. Like they were the kind of people worth knowing.

And Ben... Ben looked like someone special.

Not that it mattered. He'd never see her that way. She was just Charlie King, Shane's old crewmate, one of the Boat Guys. Too tall, too masculine, too intense. Not the kind of woman men like Ben would want to ask out. They liked dainty women. Women who had no problem showing their affections. Princesses they could rescue and protect.

Just like Princess Evelaine.

Otherwise, why did he avoid talking to her whenever they were at the same party?

You're too masculine.

Stop it. Focus on the job.

Charlie zipped the duffel and slung it over her shoulder. She had a woman to protect. That was what mattered.

Not the fact that her heart was beating too fast at the thought of seeing Ben walk through those doors.

Not the fact that she'd finally gotten her own dog, something she'd wanted her whole life.

Not the fact that for just a moment, standing in that training yard with Flo at her side, she'd felt like maybe—just maybe—she deserved to have good things, too.

Hide what you love.

The mantra whispered through her mind as she headed for her desk to finish up her paperwork, Flo following her.

Because the only way to keep good things was to make sure no one knew they mattered.

KYLE BUZZED her an hour later and she headed for his office, Flo heeling beside her. Shane met her in the hall. Sergeant George Williams arrived a couple minutes later. The older cop had the kind of weathered face that came from decades of seeing humanity at its worst and still choosing to believe in the good, like his daughter, Officer Sylvie Hoff. He nodded at Charlie.

"Heard we might need your skills tonight."

"Whatever you need."

"Sounds like we're going to be working closely on this one." He pulled out a small notebook as Kyle filled everyone in.

"Woman's name is Shelly DuPaul. Boyfriend's a cop named Dexter Morrison. Works out of Douglas County. Ben found her broken down on the side of the road—car was sabotaged. Loose lug nuts, damaged serpentine belt."

Charlie's stomach twisted. "He tried to kill her."

"That's my read on it, too." George's expression was grim. "Morrison's going to claim it was mechanical failure if we can prove anything at all."

"But we're going to make sure Shelly's safe first," Kyle said. "Everything else comes after that."

"Understood," Charlie said. Flo sat at Charlie's left heel, alert but calm, like she knew something important was happening.

My dog, Charlie thought, and allowed herself one small moment of pride before locking it away again.

Kyle's phone buzzed. "They just went through the gates. Here's how we'll play it." He stood up and came around the desk. "I'll meet them up front with Camo. You all hang back until I get a read on her, get her calm. We don't need to overwhelm her."

"Sounds good," George said.

Kyle and Camo headed for the parking lot. Kyle's office was at the front of the building, so Charlie heard the truck before she saw it. The low rumble of a diesel engine, tires crunching on gravel. Her pulse kicked up and she told it firmly to calm down.

It's just Ben. Shane's friend. That's all. Nothing special.

Except he was special. She'd known it the moment she'd seen him. The way he carried himself—that combination of quiet strength and unexpected gentleness—and the way he made himself smaller around people who were scared, like he understood what it meant to be intimidating without wanting to be.

Charlie, Shane, and George watched as the truck pulled into the parking lot and stopped. In the low light, Charlie could see two silhouettes in the truck.

The driver's door opened and Ben climbed out.

Six-seven, easily. Broad shoulders, long hair tied back, moving with the kind of controlled grace that came from years of military training. He was wearing cargo pants and a black t-shirt that stretched across his chest, and Charlie's mouth went dry.

Get it together.

He walked around to the passenger side and opened the door, stepping back to give the woman inside plenty of space. Even from this distance, Charlie could see the way he made himself smaller, less threatening. The woman—Shelly—climbed out slowly, looking exhausted and scared.

Ben's hand hovered near her elbow, ready to steady her if she needed it but not touching without permission. The gesture was so gentle, so careful, that Charlie felt something twist in her chest.

He's one of the good ones.

Kyle stepped forward with Camo at his side. Shelly's attention immediately went to Camo. She knelt and smiled as she scratched his ears.

"Kyle has fantastic instincts," Charlie said.

George nodded beside her. "We'll give 'em a few minutes to settle into the conference room. Better leave the other pups here for now." He looked at Flo and Pete, curled up beside each other in the corner but alert to every word and movement.

Charlie and Shane agreed as they watched the three of them head inside, Charlie painfully aware of Shane studying her. He'd poked fun at her more than once, implying that she had a crush on Ben—which she vehemently denied. Charlie blanked her expression. Shane had even offered to set them up once, but she shut that down immediately. She didn't need her teammate to set her up on a pity date.

As they approached the conference room, Charlie heard Shelly talking.

"But Dex is a cop," Shelly said. "Won't they protect him?"

"Not if I have anything to say about it," George said as he walked in.

Ben's gaze landed on Charlie for just a second—long enough for her breath to catch—before moving to Shane, then George, then back to Shelly.

Professional. Focused.

Of course he is. What did you expect? That he'd see you and suddenly realize you're not just another bodyguard?

Idiot.

Charlie locked her expression into professional neutrality as George spoke to Shelly, reassuring her and making introductions. She studied Shelly, her heart breaking silently for the woman with fear in her eyes.

"This is Charlie King," George said. "She's the best bodyguard here at Watchdog and she's gonna keep an eye on you." He nodded at Shane. "Shane Foti here's not half bad, either," he added with a smile.

Charlie smiled warmly as she reached out to shake Shelly's hand. "You're safe with me, Shelly." The next words came out before she could stop them. "I swear it to you upon my honor."

It was a quote from *Sword of Embers*, one of her favorite books. The words the knight spoke to the princess when he swore to protect her.

She saw Ben's expression change—surprise flickering across his face for just a moment—and then Shane was smirking at her like he knew exactly what she'd just revealed.

Damn it.

But Shelly was smiling, looking less scared, and that was what mattered.

Still, that surprise on Ben's face and smirk on Shane's stayed on her mind for the rest of the night as she got Shelly settled into the safehouse.

It's nothing.

And another, familiar voice in her head added, *No man would ever want you.*

THREE

Ben drove his truck up his long driveway and slowed when the cruiser's rollers kicked on. He parked directly behind the vehicle and kept the headlights on. In the glare he watched two men step out of the cruiser. The driver's face was tight with rage.

"Police!" he shouted.

As if I couldn't tell.

"Turn off your headlights *now*!"

Ben killed the headlights, sighed, and climbed out slowly, keeping his hands visible. He watched the second officer hesitate the moment he got a good look at Ben's size. He looked at his partner but the other officer wasn't intimidated. Ben could see the driver's red face even in the cold glare of his yard light as his eyes searched the passenger side of Ben's truck, frowning when he realized Ben was alone. The nametag on his uniform said Morrison.

"Benjamin Massey?" Morrison said, voice dripping with acid as his hand rested on his service weapon.

"That's me. How can I help you?"

The other officer's nametag read Keller. Ben recognized him from the drive-by earlier. "We're here to search your vehicle and residence for controlled substances," he said.

Ben snorted. "Controlled substances? Is that how you're going to play this?"

"Where is she?" Morrison snarled.

There it was.

"I don't know what you're talking about," Ben said calmly.

"Bullshit!" Morrison's face flushed red. "You think you can fuck my woman and get away with it?"

"Morrison," his partner said in the same tone he might have used to calm an angry dog.

Ben kept his voice level and addressed Keller. "You aren't searching anything without a warrant."

Morrison stepped closer, his jaw clenched. "You got something to hide? Besides that ungrateful slut?"

"I've got rights. You have no proof of any misdeeds, you have no warrant, so we are done here." Ben crossed his arms and stood in front of the driver side door.

Keller moved to flank Ben on the right. "Don't make this difficult. Get out of the way and let us search your truck."

"Where is she?" Morrison's voice cracked with barely controlled fury. "Where's Shelly?"

"Fuck you."

Keller's hand moved toward his gun. "Turn around. Hands on the truck."

"I don't think so."

"That's resisting arrest," Keller said, grinning.

Ben's expression didn't change. "Your body cams off for a reason? Does that make it easier to plant false evidence?"

Morrison smirked. "Can't record you claiming police misconduct when we find the fentanyl. Or when we kick your ass."

There it was. The admission.

The tarp in the truck bed shifted. Shane sat up, phone held high, recording everything.

"Hey fellas," Shane drawled as he jumped down from the truck bed. "Smile for the camera."

Morrison spun, his hand at his holster—but he didn't draw. Not with Shane's phone capturing every move.

"That's entrapment," Morrison yelled.

Ben laughed. "Pot, meet kettle. And what his phone didn't capture, my security cam did."

"You son of a—" Morrison lunged at Ben, fist cocked back. Ben caught his wrist mid-swing, twisted, and slammed Morrison face-first against the truck with one smooth motion.

At the same time, Keller rushed Shane, but the former SWCC put him in an arm bar before the deputy could land a punch.

Behind them, tires crunched on gravel. Three trucks pulled up, followed by two more vehicles—George's police SUV and a Boulder PD cruiser.

Bear, Elias, Waylon, and Gabe climbed out and spread into a loose perimeter.

From the Boulder cruiser emerged Officer Sylvie Hoff, George's daughter, and her partner, Officer Carla DeVivo.

Morrison struggled against Ben's hold. "Officer! These assholes assaulted us—"

"Dexter Morrison," George said, his voice flat and official. "Wade Keller. You're both under arrest."

Morrison's face went white. "What?"

"Just got off the phone with the sheriff. Turns out there's fentanyl missing from evidence. And surveillance footage shows you in the evidence locker earlier today." George nodded to Sylvie. "Officer Hoff will take it from here."

Sylvie stepped forward, cuffs ready. "You have the right to remain silent."

Morrison's bravado crumbled. "This is bullshit. We didn't—"

"Save it for IA," George said. "And for the DA. You're done."

Ben released Morrison into Sylvie's custody. Keller didn't resist when Shane handed him over to Carla.

As Sylvie and Carla loaded the scumbags into their cruiser, George turned to Ben. "Your cameras get all that?"

"Every word."

"Good. I'll need a copy for evidence." George paused. "Morrison's landlord is meeting officers at his apartment right now. We'll make sure Shelly gets her belongings back safe."

Ben nodded, watching the cruiser pull away. Morrison stared out the window, his face a mask of impotent rage.

"Think that's the end of it?" Shane asked, brushing dust off his cargos.

"For Shelly? Let's hope so," Ben said.

"I'll make sure of it," George said. He looked around at the band of brothers. "You boys have a nice evening."

Ben turned to Shane. "I owe you lunch, brother."

Shane scoffed. "For this? I know you'd do the same for me."

I swear it to you upon my honor.

"Not just for this. And I think you know it."

BEN WALKED into the Watchdog reception area at noon the next day and found Jodie at the front desk.

"Hey, Ben! What brings you here?" she asked with a bright smile.

"Just here to take Shane out to lunch. I owe him."

"Oh, if you're going out for burgers, bring me back some fries?" She batted her eyes at him.

Ben felt himself start to blush. It didn't matter what woman it was. Didn't matter if she was serious or kidding. Didn't matter how long he'd known her. He lacked the confidence his brothers had around women.

"Sure," Ben said. "I'd be happy to."

"Great! I think Shane's in his office. If not, he's out with Alex and the dogs. Go on back." She made a gesture like she was sweeping him further into the building.

Ben nodded. "Thanks, Jodie."

Shane had offered to meet him at a restaurant in Lyons, but Ben wanted to check in on Shelly and make sure she was all right. At least, that's what he told himself as he started down the hall. The offices could be a bit of a warren, and he wasn't exactly sure where Shane's office was, but he'd find him. If not, he could ask. The place was full of people he knew. Most of them friends, some just acquaintances.

And one very special lady.

Charlie King.

Just thinking her name did something wonderful to his belly. And, he had to admit, a place just south of his belly.

Charlie wasn't only the most beautiful woman he'd ever seen—though she absolutely was that, with her intense eyes that could pin a man at fifty yards and that smile that made his knees weak on the rare occasions she aimed it his way. Just watching her put Shelly at ease the night before warmed his heart.

But it was more than that. Charlie was *talented.* Brilliant, really. Fierce when she needed to be. She could clear a room faster than most of his Ranger buddies and moved with a lethal grace that was somehow both terrifying and mesmerizing to watch. She was someone he'd want at his back in a gunfight without hesitation.

Hell, she'd *just* had his back in a gunfight at Echo Ridge Ski Lodge. When bullets were flying and the world had gone to hell, Charlie had been steady as a rock, professional and deadly and absolutely fearless. Watching her intelligent face as she took in the plan Gina laid out. Seeing her in action during the firefight—grace and power and bravery. She had to be the bravest woman he'd ever met—

A sudden, unexpected sound stopped him.

Wait—is that Charlie...screaming?

Ben took off at a run down the hall. Where was she? What was going on? Something had to be seriously wrong. He'd never heard her scream. Had Morrison somehow breached Watchdog?

He turned the corner.

And there she was, standing in the middle of a cubicle maze. For some reason, he could see all the way down to her waist over a cubicle wall.

Wait. Charlie's tall but not that *tall,* he thought. *What's going on?*

She was in profile, looking down at something below her, with an expression of absolute terror on her face.

"Charlie!"

Her head whipped around in his direction. "Ben! Oh—ah—um—"

He ran to her. Rounding the aisle and reaching her cubicle, Ben discovered why she was so tall. Charlie was standing on an office chair.

Well, that explains the extra height.

"What's going on?" he asked.

"It's—it's—" She pointed at her desk.

Ben followed her finger. On her desk was a day planner, a laptop, some sticky notes, and a pen caddy. She was pointing at the pen caddy full of pens and pencils.

"You're afraid of pens?"

"What, no! No, no. Look closer. Look on *that* one." Her hand shook as she leaned forward and pointed.

Ben bent down and looked closer. A tiny jumping spider—fuzzy and as adorable as a kitten—sat on top of a pencil eraser, staring at him.

He grinned. "Hey, little guy." He looked up at Charlie. "Congratulations, you've got yourself a pet jumping spider. Technically it's a *Phidippus audax*, better known as the Bold Jumping Spider. And wow, he's got yellow spots instead of the usual white—"

"Ben."

"Yeah?"

"Please?"

Ben was absolutely confused. Charlie looked terrified. Was she messing with him? This was the same woman he'd watched take down two Russian oligarch henchmen with brutal efficiency.

But judging by her expression and the fact that she was standing precariously on an office chair, he was pretty sure she was serious.

"You're telling me the warrior princess is afraid of an adorable, fuzzy little jumping spider?"

Charlie reared back. "What did you just call me?"

Oh God, I really overstepped. The words had just flowed out of him without thinking.

"Um. Warrior princess. Emphasis on warrior?" he added quickly.

Charlie blinked. Several times.

"I mean, you're a bodyguard. Former Swick. That makes you more warrior than princess, right?" He tried a smile.

Something flashed across her face, too quick for him to catch. Disappointment, maybe?

"Please don't tell anybody I was afraid of a spider," she said quietly.

"No, of course not."

"I'm just lucky everybody's off to lunch." She looked around. "I'd never live it down."

"Cross my heart, I won't tell anyone."

"Thank you." She smiled sheepishly. "And do you think maybe you could—take him with you? Or something?"

"Yeah, sure. I—" Ben looked back down at the pen caddy. "Hang on, where'd he go?"

Charlie had been stepping down from her chair. She immediately stopped and jumped back up. "What do you mean? You can't find him?" She looked around wildly. "Oh my God, he could be anywhere." She looked up at the ceiling above her head as if the spider would materialize there and drop into her hair.

"Charlie, he wouldn't have gotten that far that quick."

"But you said he's a *jumping* spider! Couldn't he have, I don't know, jumped up onto the ceiling?"

Ben chuckled. "Well, they do jump pretty far, but not *that* far." He peered into the pen caddy again. He didn't want to rummage around in it just in case the little guy had gone to the bottom. He'd feel terrible if he squished him by moving the wrong pen at the wrong time.

"Maybe you could take the whole caddy?" Charlie suggested. "I don't know."

"I could," Ben started, "except I'm a little afraid of crushing the guy if he's down at the bottom."

"Oh. Right. I mean, I don't want him *dead.* I just don't want him crawling on me." She shivered.

"Hmm. All right, I'll just be very careful with it then."

He picked the caddy up gingerly, carefully, so that not a single pen or pencil moved. There had to be at least twenty-five shoved in there, with pens of all different colors.

"Once I de-spider your caddy, I can bring it back to you."

"Oh, thank you! That would be great."

She stepped down from the chair. She stood so close to him. God, she was beautiful.

And they were standing so close.

And no one was shooting at them.

She took a step toward him.

But then her gaze fell back onto the caddy in his hand and she stepped back. Her cheeks turned pink.

Absolutely adorable.

"You promise?" she asked. "Promise you won't tell anybody I'm afraid of spiders?"

"I promise-promise. And don't worry—it's one of the most common phobias. You're hardly alone. My guess is that half the guys who work here have arachnophobia, they just aren't brave enough to admit it. Which puts you ahead of them."

Shit, should I have said that?

"Well, I need to get going," he added quickly. "Shane and I are going to lunch and—oh, I'm late—and, uh, caddy, and I'll clean it up for you and—okay, bye."

Ben took off back through the maze of cubicles toward the kennels.

Smooth. Real smooth, Moose.

But as he carefully carried the pen caddy away, searching for one tiny fuzzy spider among twenty-five colorful pens, he couldn't stop smiling.

Charlie King was afraid of spiders.

And just now, she'd let him be her knight in shining armor, even if it was just for a jumping spider no bigger than his thumbnail.

He'd take it.

Just before Ben reached the restrooms, the jumping spider crawled to the top of the same pencil where Charlie first spotted him. He waved his front legs in the air and Ben stopped walking.

"Good, at least I can see you now. I'll make sure you don't get squished." He started walking again, gaze planted firmly on the spider. He reached the doors to the outside training area and pushed one open with his broad shoulder. It was a beautiful summer's day, with the lightest breeze that played with a loose lock of his hair. He tossed his head back and headed for the nearest tree, singing under his breath a verse from a Loreena McKennitt song:

"She left the web, she left the loom
She made three paces through the room
She saw the water-flower bloom,
She saw the helmet and the plume,
She looked down to Camelot."

When he reached the tree, he slowly, gently reached for the pencil, hoping he wouldn't scare the spider back down into the caddy. It watched his fingers but thankfully stayed put as Ben pulled the pencil out like a magic wand and lifted the eraser end toward the lowest branch.

The spider leaped from the pencil to the branch and turned around to stare at Ben at eye level. Ben chuckled, then softly sang:

"Out flew the web and floated wide;
The mirror cracked from side to side;
'The curse is come upon me!' cried
The Lady of Shalott."

"Whatcha singing?" Shane asked behind him. Dammit, the man was silent when he wanted to be. Then again, talking to Charlie often had the effect of sending Ben into a daze.

"N-nothing," Ben said.

One of Shane's eyebrows rose—he wasn't fooling his friend one bit. Shane had known Ben since they were in grade school, knew that one of the techniques Ben had used when his stutter stopped him mid-sentence was to sing something quickly under his breath then continue where he'd left off talking. It usually worked—but also made the other kids think he wasn't all there, and so they teased him mercilessly, calling him 'dumb as a moose.' Ben's friends took on animal names of their own in response to the teasing, turning 'Moose' into a true nickname instead of a taunt. Ben would be forever grateful for the kindness of his friends—his brothers.

But right now, he would've given anything not to have Shane standing right there looking at him, knowing his secret. Shane's gaze went from Ben's face to the caddy clutched in his hands.

"That looks familiar," Shane said. He tapped his chin, pretending to ponder. "Now...where have I seen it before..."

"Just stop," Ben grumbled.

Shane's expression broke into a wide grin. "King Charlemagne doesn't let that thing out of her sight, man. She's damn near feral about anyone trying to steal one of her pens. And here you are with the whole enchilada. If you're trying to play a practical joke on her, I'd advise against it."

"I-I'd *never* do that," Ben said, defending himself. He turned and strode toward the door to go back inside and clean off every single pen, marker, and pencil and the caddy itself, as promised.

"Hey, wait up, Moose. Seriously, how'd you get ahold of that?"

"None of your business."

"Wait...did you actually ask her out?"

No, I made a complete fool of myself.

"I said, none of your business."

"Come on, don't be like that."

Ben paused as he opened the door. "I mean it, Elk. It's none of your damn business."

"Whoa, okay, man." Shane put his palms out facing Ben.

"P-please, just drop it, okay? I have to bring this back. I'll meet you after that for lunch."

"She didn't turn you down, did she?" Shane asked quietly, all seriousness as he closed the door behind them.

Ben sighed as he headed for the restroom. "I'd have to ask her out for her to turn me down."

"Well, swiping her pen caddy isn't going to endear you. Unless you're planning on holding it ransom?"

"Nope." Ben reached the restroom, checked the knob, and was relieved to find it unlocked. "Now if you'll excuse me."

He opened the door and the light flicked on automatically. He glanced at Shane's confused expression right before he shut the door in his face.

Ben looked at himself in the mirror over the sink. His face looked flushed, and he was hunching again, making himself smaller without realizing it. An old habit from school—he was the biggest kid in class always, and conscientious about it. His size scared the girls and made the boys dare each other to punch him.

"Thought I was past all that," he told his reflection, watching himself stand up straight and square his shoulders. The military had taught him to be proud of his strength and size, and now most days he was. Just every now and then, the young kid inside forgot.

Ben turned on the faucet and one by one washed each pen and pencil carefully. He realized there weren't just colored pens, but colored pencils meant for drawing. The corner of his mouth turned up as his heart sped up. A new piece of the puzzle that was Charlie King clicked into place.

A gob of webbing was stuck to a blue-green pen, and inside it, the shadow of a molted skin. *She wouldn't have liked to find that.* Ben's smile grew as he washed it off and watched it circle the drain. He checked the inside of the caddy for more webs and found the husk of a fly. He flicked it out into the sink and it joined the web down the drain. He carefully dried off each pen and pencil and placed them all back into the caddy. He chuckled again, remembering the sight of Charlie on the office chair. He wasn't laughing at her fear, but at his wonder at seeing her afraid of anything.

Warrior Princess.

He grimaced as he opened the bathroom door. He'd really flubbed it with that one. Imagine calling someone as strong as Charle a princess. No wonder she'd looked at him funny.

Shane was nowhere in sight. Ben's phone buzzed with a text. He checked it and found a message from Shane telling him to let him know when he was ready to go and he'd meet him out front.

Ben reached Charlie's cube. She was so engrossed in a book, she didn't notice him at first. The salad on her desk locked untouched. He cleared his throat and her head snapped up. Her desk drawer flew open and the book disappeared inside, but not before Ben noticed the multicolored highlighted lines on the pages and the telltale worn cover of a well-loved paperback.

The other thing he noticed was the title of the thick book. Shane had not lied when he told Ben the secret, and Ben had not been mistaken when he heard Charlie last night.

You're safe with me. I swear it to you upon my honor.

"Ben. I wasn't expecting you back until after lunch." Charlie stood and leaned her hip against the drawer as if to guard it.

Don't ask her what she's reading. Don't ask—

"What are you reading?" he asked, wanting to slap himself at the same time.

FOUR

Oh crap. Busted.

Charlie felt her stomach twist. Of all people, not only was Ben Massey the one to see her afraid of a tiny spider, but he had to be the one to catch her reading one of her favorite books in the entire world, a book that he'd probably think was stupid, and that she was nerdy for loving it.

Or soft.

She hated how her stomach now fluttered at the idea of Ben thinking of her as soft. Feminine. Of course he didn't though. He'd called her a warrior ten minutes ago.

No, a warrior *princess.*

And there went the flutters again.

"What am I reading?" she asked, dodging her answer. She looked around the office as if one of her co-workers would suddenly pop up like a Whac-a-Mole, laughing at her about her choice of books.

Ben nodded. His gorgeous eyes actually twinkled. Was he getting ready to make fun of her? No, that wasn't Ben's style. One of the many reasons she found him so attractive—Ben was quiet and thoughtful. Yes, he had a sense of humor, but it wasn't the mean kind.

It was never at the expense of a friend. Ben was considerate, kind. Sweet, even, from what little direct interaction they'd had. She relaxed just a teensy bit.

"Oh, you mean *that* book?" She glanced down at the desk drawer she was blocking like it was a client under fire. "Just some, uh, research. For a client." Just to make sure he wouldn't follow up with another question, she added, "I can't really say who."

"Client confidentiality. I understand," Ben said, nodding. "S-so... are you...enjoying it?"

Hide what you love.

The old words flashed through her mind like a reflex. Charlie's cheeks felt hot with embarrassment as she bit her bottom lip. Her gaze darted to the caddy filled with her colored pens and pencils in Ben's hand. "Thank you so much for taking care of that for me," she said quietly, dodging the question.

"You're welcome. It's clean now. I washed everything, even the pens."

"Did you find it? The spider?" She shivered at the mere thought of the eight-legged horror.

He nodded again. "He's spending the rest of his days in a tree outside."

"Good. I didn't want him hurt, just not jumping on me." Charlie smiled as she wrapped her hand around the caddy. As she took it from Ben, her fingers brushed his, which sent her heart racing. He had big, warm hands, and she imagined they were rough with calluses. Ben was a metalsmith; she knew that from the exquisite engagement and wedding rings he'd made for all his friends. Surely, working with metal would rough them up, right? Her skin tingled at the thought of how they'd feel touching her, distracting her enough to miss what he'd said.

"Sorry, what?" She shook the tempting thought out of her head, hoping she didn't seem daft.

"N-n-nothing," he said. His eyes darkened and for a moment and she thought he was mad at her for not paying attention. But she realized just as quickly that he wasn't mad, just frustrated. He sang a few words just under his breath, something she'd seen him do before. The tune was familiar, and then he came to the song title, singing softly, "*The Lady of Shallot*."

"Oh," Charlie. "That's a good song." *Shit. I shouldn't have pointed it out.*

Ben startled. "You...know it?"

"Loreena McKennitt singing a poem by Tennyson? Heck yeah, I know it. I love her music."

Stop! Hide what you love. The words whipped through her mind like a condemnation.

But...I don't feel like I have to do that with Ben.

Still, her stomach knotted at exposing a personal secret.

"It goes well with that book." Ben pointed at the drawer. His eyes widened. "I mean..."

"You saw what it was," Charlie confirmed. Then she felt herself grin. "You've read *Sword of Embers*?"

"It's one of my favorites." He grinned. "In a realm where kings are crowned with fire and ancient oaths bind men's souls..."

Charlie couldn't stop her smile as Ben started reciting the blurb from the back of the book. "A lost heir to a Fae kingdom must rise," she continued.

"Aldric Thorne, raised as a human commoner and fated to marry a Fae Princess, is thrust into a battle against forces both mortal and monstrous. Beside him stand Caidan Bramble, a humble Shield-bearer whose courage will alter the fate of kingdoms..."

"And Sir Mariel of the Ashensworn, a woman disguised as a warrior sworn to avenge her father," Charlie answered.

"But when an ancient evil stirs in the Ashen Mountains, even the Ashensworn—knights bound by fire and blood—may not be enough to hold back Lord Felldark."

They finished the last part together. "Loyalty will be tested. Legends will fall. And a kingdom will be forged anew... or lost forever."

Charlie laughed. "Oh my God, you *have* read it."

"Many, many times. I was just a kid the first time I stayed up all night every night for a week reading the whole series."

Charlie touched her chest. "Me, too. The summer I was twelve years old, I would only speak Fae."

Ben chuckled. "You learned the Fae language? At *twelve*? Wow. I am impressed."

"Thank you. I spent hours translating the poems and memorizing words."

"Must have driven your parents crazy."

Charlie felt her smile falter. "You could say that." She glanced away, staring at her sad little salad like it held the secrets of the universe.

"Have you seen the TV series yet? I think they did a good job with it, even though it doesn't always follow the books."

She looked back at him and tried not to give anything away. "I have, and I agree; it's good."

"Charlie?" Ben's voice quieted, deepened. "Are you b-busy..."

Her heart stopped. *Busy tonight? This weekend? Is he asking me on a date?* His gaze was fixed on her, intent.

"...watching Shelly?"

And, her hopes evaporated. Of course he wasn't asking her out. He was concerned about the woman he rescued, that's all.

"No. I drove her to her friend's place this morning. That's why I'm back in the office instead of the safehouse."

"Ah." Ben said. "Yeah, I sh-should have realized that." He shook his head.

Sure, castrate a guy, Charlene. Men don't like women who make them feel stupid. No wonder you're alone, the hated voice in her head said.

"Thank you for helping her," Ben said quietly, his voice low enough that only she could hear.

Charlie glanced up at him—*up*, because even at six feet she still had to look up to meet his eyes—and found him watching her with an expression she couldn't quite read.

"It's my job," she said, keeping her voice steady.

"It's more than that." He held her gaze for a moment longer, and Charlie felt her heart do something complicated and inconvenient in her chest.

Then he looked away, and the moment was broken.

Just a job, Charlie reminded herself. *He's just being polite.*

But what if it was more than being polite?

"I'll let you finish lunch." He started to turn away, humming *The Lady of Shalott.*

Before she could think better of it, Charlie said, "Maybe we—"

And men like pushy women even less. Damsels in distress, not women who act like men. Jesus, Charlene.

"—will see each other around sometime," she finished lamely.

We'll see each other around? Did I really just say that?

Ben stopped without turning back around. "Take care, Charlie."

Charlie watched Ben Massey's broad back disappear around a corner as his soft singing drifted back to her, making her shiver. He had a lovely, deep singing voice.

And I blew it.

She set her pen caddy down on her desk and opened the drawer. Her paperback copy of *Sword of Embers* wasn't a first edition, but she'd had it for years and it showed, the binding cracked in a dozen places where she'd read certain pages over and over, committing them to memory. She'd made a habit of reading the entire series start to finish at least once a year, and her favorite parts whenever she felt blue. Charlie ran her hand over the cover. She hadn't lied when she told Ben she was reading it for research on her next client.

I can't believe I told him it's my favorite book, let alone that I know Fae. She cringed. Charlie hadn't told anyone that, ever.

Just like Sir Mariel of the Ashensworn, Charlie couldn't afford to take off her armor and show anyone who she really was.

Though she had, just a little last night with Shelly.

Shelly had spent the night at one of the Watchdog safehouses even after Charlie had gotten word from Shane that Morrison was in custody. It was like a dam broke for her, and she spent most of the night pouring out her pent-up grief and fear to Charlie. How Morrison had seemed so protective of her in the beginning. How he promised that since he was a cop, he knew how to keep her safe. How his protection started to feel smothering. His expectations that she be home when he wanted her to be regardless of her plans. To agree with everything he said and believed because 'the world was dangerous, she was weak, he knew best, and it was for her own good.' Until finally she realized his 'protection' was how he controlled her.

"I told him yesterday that I didn't need his so-called protection," she said between sobs. "And do you know what he said? He said I didn't know what I was talking about and that I was getting it whether I wanted it or not." She shuddered so hard, Charlie did what she almost never did with a client and put her arm around her. "Then he went back to accusing me of cheating on him." She gave Charlie a bitter laugh. "Because why else would I possibly want to make my own decisions and live my own life?" she added, her voice dripping with sarcasm. "God, I'm so stupid."

"No, you aren't. It creeps up on us, sometimes," Charlie said. "The people who you think you can trust the most, who are supposed to be our protectors, can use that protection, twist it, until they have us caught, blaming ourselves, telling ourselves we're stupid, or weak, or naïve."

Shelly sniffled. "Voice of experience?"

Charlie smiled softly. "Something like that."

And that was as much as she was willing to share.

"I can't believe it. You seem like such a badass."

Right.

"Why don't you try to get some sleep? You've got to be exhausted. Tomorrow, you can think about your next move. I'll be right in the front room. If you need anything, just call out." Charlie gave her what she thought of as her 'professional smile' and stood to leave.

"Thanks, Charlie," Shelly called after her. "You're very honorable."

That did put a genuine smile on Charlie's face.

Shelly decided that morning to take up her friend's offer to stay with her, and George and Kyle's offer to collect the last of her things from Morrison's house. Charlie dropped Shelly off at her friend's place and refused any money from Shelly.

Her phone buzzed and she picked it up, irrationally hoping that Ben was somehow texting her. But it was just Kyle, letting her know that her client would be there in half an hour. She texted back a thumbs up, and returned to her favorite book.

My favorite...and Ben's.

FIVE

Charlie sat with Kyle in the conference room after lunch, waiting for her new client to arrive. Flo lay at her feet, the Malinois's calm presence grounding her even as her mind raced.

Don't get excited. It's just another protection detail.

But it wasn't just another detail. This was the job of a lifetime.

The fact that Kyle had chosen her—over all the other bodyguards at Watchdog—meant something. Kyle didn't do favorites. He matched people based on skillset and temperament.

He trusts you with this.

Watchdog was no stranger to protecting celebrities, especially the home office in Los Angeles, and Charlie had guarded plenty. She'd had the honor of protecting Annalie Givens on the Colorado leg of her book tour. Annalie was being stalked by a serial killer who had used her terrifying books as a blueprint. Charlie had worked with Kyle to keep her safe from a mob of fans and paparazzi.

This assignment was similar, but it was also extremely personal for Charlie.

The front door chimed. Jodie's cheerful voice carried down the hall, followed by deeper voices responding. Charlie stood up, her hand instinctively checking that her sidearm was secure.

"That's them," Kyle said. "You ready?"

"Always, Boss."

He opened the door and stepped into the hallway. Charlie followed, Flo heeling perfectly at her left side.

Three people walked toward them and Charlie had to push her excitement down deep. The man leading the way was Rowan McCrae, the actor currently playing Aldric Thorne in the *Legends of BattleLore* streaming series. He absolutely fit the role—he was tall, broad-shouldered, and moved with the easy confidence of someone comfortable in his own skin. His eyes were sharp, scanning the hallway the way operators did.

Beside him walked a woman in her mid-thirties with short, platinum hair and bright red lipstick, wearing jeans and a punk band t-shirt that read Fish Tank Doxy under a black blazer. She had a sparkling energy about her—creative, intense, like she was constantly thinking three steps ahead. Charlie liked her immediately.

Vivienne Cross. The director.

And trailing slightly behind her was a young woman who couldn't be more than twenty-three, clutching a tablet and a leather portfolio bag. She had that eager, slightly overwhelmed look of someone fresh out of school and desperate to prove herself.

That must be her assistant.

Vivienne smiled warmly at Charlie as Kyle made introductions. Rowan's face broke into a genuine smile as he extended his hand. "Good to meet you."

Kyle shook his hand, then gestured to Charlie. "This is Charlie King, one of our best."

"Charlie." Rowan's handshake was firm but not aggressive. "Heard good things about you."

"Likewise." She'd heard plenty about Rowan McCrae over the past year and had studied everything she could about both him and Vivianne the moment Kyle told her she'd be guarding them. Rowan was famously a lifelong fan of the books and had done some actual jousting with a Renaissance Faire in college.

Absolutely perfect choice to play Aldric.

Rowan stepped aside slightly so that Vivienne could shake hands. His posture remained tense and all his attention immediately went to the director. His protective body language wasn't lost on Charlie.

Interesting.

Vivienne stepped forward, her smile warm but tired. "Call me Viv. Everyone does." She shook Kyle's hand, then Charlie's. "Thank you for taking this on. I know it's probably not the most exciting assignment—babysitting a director who pissed off some keyboard warriors."

"Not boring at all. Anyone making credible threats is worth taking seriously." Charlie kept her voice professional despite the fact she wanted to fan girl all over the place right now. "We'll make sure you're safe while you're here."

"Thank you. Oh, and this is my assistant, Madison Pierce." Viv gestured to the young woman.

Madison shook hands eagerly, smiling brightly. "Hi. Maddie's fine. I handle Viv's schedule, social media, correspondence—basically anything she needs." The words tumbled out quickly, full of nervous energy.

"I couldn't get a thing done without her," Viv said. Maddie's cheeks turned bright pink and her eyes brightened. She looked like she'd just been launched into the stratosphere.

Viv looked down at Flo. "And who's this gorgeous puppy?"

Charlie grinned. "This is my new partner, Flo."

"Sure, Watchdog, of course. Our bodyguard with your outfit in LA has one, too. May I pet her?"

Charlie let Flo know Viv was a friend, then nodded. Viv carefully presented her hand to Flo before scratching her ears.

"Good to meet you all." Kyle gestured toward the conference room. "Let's sit down and go over the situation."

They filed into the room. Rowan pulled out a chair for Viv before taking the seat beside her. Maddie sat on Viv's other side, and immediately pulled something up on her tablet. Kyle and Charlie took seats across from them. Flo remained alert, studying the three clients.

"As I briefed you earlier, Charlie," Kyle started, "Viv's been getting harassed for months, but the threat level's escalated."

Charlie's jaw tightened. "Do the police know?"

"They do," Viv said quietly. "But they're treating it like fan mail gone wrong. Not taking it seriously."

"We are," Kyle said. "Which is why you're here."

"Can you walk me through what's been happening?" Charlie asked Viv.

Viv took a breath. "When I was hired on as the director for *BattleLore* three years ago, I knew I had a huge challenge. The books had a cult following—passionate fans who've loved these stories for decades. I should know because I'm one of them."

"Me, too," Rowan added.

Charlie nodded. "I'm familiar with the series," Charlie said carefully. *Understatement of the year*. "The books are excellent."

Viv's eyes lit up. "You've read them?"

"Multiple times." Charlie felt her cheeks warm slightly. "I was six when I first read *Sword of Embers*."

"Really?" Rowan asked, skepticism in his eyes.

"*Alante tokentare*," Charlie said, bowing her head.

Rowan grinned as he looked back and forth between Charlie and Viv, who had a delighted smile on her face. Maddie giggled.

"*Alante fendraken*," Rowan answered the traditional greeting, much to Charlie's delight.

Kyle looked confused.

"That's the Fae language from the books," Rowan told him. "A true fan. That's perfect. I take it you're not a BattleLorrior?"

"A...who what now?"

"That's what the fans call themselves," Rowan told him. "Battle-Lore-Warrior. BattleLorrior."

Viv turned to Charlie. "Since you're a superfan of the books, I have to ask—do you like the show?" she asked. "And don't lie on my account," she added with a laugh.

Charlie chuckled. "I do, and I can say that without lying. Even with the changes you've made to the story."

Viv nodded, looking pleased. "Thank you. It's been tricky. The stories you tell on film are structurally different from the ones you tell on paper. As big of a fan as I am, if I recreated the books scene by scene, the pacing would be totally off, especially for a mainstream audience. We would've been canceled after the first season, and we were still afraid that would happen."

"But it's been a runaway hit," Charlie said.

"It has, and I think that's part of the problem," Viv continued. "To keep that mainstream audience so that we can keep the show going, I have to make some major changes for season two. Combining characters, changing timelines, and..." She hesitated, glancing at Rowan who nodded. "Killing off Caidan Bramble in the avalanche at the end of season two."

Charlie blinked. "Killing off... You mean for good?"

"Yes," Viv said, her voice growing more passionate. "Killing off Caidan raises the stakes and shines a brighter light on some of the other characters who then step up to take his place. With the changes I've made to the plot, the series arc works better if Caidan's death is permanent. It's a creative decision as well as a financial one. Like I said, film is different from books. We have budget constraints, pacing issues, narrative compression."

Charlie was shocked.

Caidan Bramble was Sir Aldric's squire and one of the most beloved characters in all of *BattleLore.* At the end of book two, Lord Darkfell created a magical avalanche that buried the small band of heroes. Caiden was lost and presumed dead, but he came back midway through book three—one of the most emotional moments in the entire series.

The actor playing him, Duke Holloway, was as good a choice for Caidan as Rowan was for Aldric. He'd always played loveable, easygoing, salt-of-the-earth guys, which was Caidan Bramble in nutshell.

"I'd heard speculation on different fan sites that Caidan was going to be killed off," Charlie said. "I guess it's not just speculation anymore."

"It's not. The script was leaked."

"So, I take it you're getting threats over it," Charlie said.

Viv nodded. "Boy, am I. First it was just angry comments on social media—no big surprise. Then emails to the studio. Again, not surprised." She rolled her eyes.

Viv may not have been taking it seriously, but Charlie noted how Rowan watched her with worry in his eyes.

"You feel differently?" she asked him.

"I do. It's more than just online trolls and hate mail. There's a group calling themselves The Caidansworn," he said, a grim look in his eyes, as if he were actually Sir Aldric describing the Legions of Darkfell. "They've shown up at the studio twice now. Chanting. Holding signs. One said, 'Lady Darkfell the Betrayer must be destroyed.'"

Her stomach tightened. "When did things begin to escalate?"

Viv looked at Maddie. "How long has it been?"

"It started three weeks ago," Maddie said, scrolling through her tablet. "I have the exact dates and incidences here in a spreadsheet." She looked up at Charlie. "Someone doxed Viv and that's when the hate mail started showing up at her home." Her eyes darkened, the chipper assistant attitude gone. "Then the package."

"Tell us about the package," Kyle said. Charlie and Kyle exchanged looks. The package had triggered Viv's call to Watchdog in Los Angeles and they'd been briefed on its contents, but Kyle wanted to gauge Viv and Rowan's response to it.

Now Viv looked serious. "Inside was a partially-burned copy of the script for season two, episode twelve, the finale. The word 'heretic' was written on it."

"In what we were relieved to discover was red paint and not blood," Rowan added.

"The studio insisted on security," Viv said. "Me, I'm more pissed over the fact that the script leaked."

"Sounds like an inside job. Any suspects?"

Again, Viv rolled her eyes. "If only. A month ago, my computer was hacked and then bricked as the kids say." She winked at Maddie, who grinned and hunched her shoulders. "Maddie did her best to try and un-brick it, but it wouldn't even turn back on."

"I'm not really that great at computers," Maddie said.

"She's lying." Viv chuckled. "But even your team at Watchdog couldn't fix it. Anyway, whoever did it must have grabbed the script and leaked it because the threats started a week later. They waited another week before sending their little gift."

"That's when we...I mean Viv, called Watchdog," Rowan added.

"Bette Collins told me they were the best in the industry." Viv grinned. "Though she might be a little biased since her son works there."

Charlie had met Bette briefly when she first started at Watchdog. The Multi-Oscar-winning actress had thrown one of her famous Bashes when Charlie was orienting at the home office in Los Angeles and she'd been invited. The guest list was a who's who of Hollywood. And Bette turned out to be absolutely gracious and kind—in sharp contrast to the psychopathic character she played that made her career.

Kyle chuckled. "I consider Jake a brother, but I can tell you honestly he's excellent at what he does."

"I've been impressed so far," Viv said. "So of course we're continuing with Watchdog while we're here. The location scouts found a few places to film the winter scenes and the avalanche for the finale, so I'm out here to pick the ones I like best. We'll need a primary plus a couple backups in case of weather, of course.

"You aren't using CGI for it?" Charlie asked.

Viv shook her head. "I want realism. This is one of the biggest moments in the entire series and I don't want people distracted by CGI. I want them *feeling it* as it happens. I grew up on the Western slope, so I always pictured Colorado when I read that part. And, since Colorado also happens to be the avalanche capital of the US, it only makes sense to film one here."

"How are you going to do that? Aren't they unpredictable?" Charlie asked.

"You aren't a native, are you?" Viv said, not unkindly.

"Neither of us is," Kyle said. "I'm from Los Angeles and Charlie's from Ohio."

"Not many avalanches in Ohio," Charlie added.

Viv laughed softly. "We won't be caught in a natural avalanche—fingers crossed," she joked. "We've been talking to CDOT—the folks who trigger smaller, controlled avalanches before the snowpack builds up and threatens a big one. They're giving us permission to film some scenes on location ahead of time and then film the avalanche once it's triggered—from a safe distance. We just have to hope that at least one of the three locations will have enough snowpack early in the season."

"Otherwise, we'll need a real Lord Darkfell," Maddie said, and Charlie, Viv, and Rowan laughed.

Kyle looked lost.

Rowan leaned forward. "Kyle, you really need to read the books or at least watch the show. Charlie will have to catch you up on the story."

"With pleasure," Charlie said. "I'll have him speaking Fae in no time."

Then Rowan looked at Charlie, tipped his chin up, and used his Aldric-voice. "I command it, Sir Mariel."

Charlie's breath caught.

"Sir Mariel?" Kyle asked.

"Aldric's bravest warrior," Rowan told him. "A woman disguised as a knight."

Sir Mariel. The character who hid her true self behind armor. Who sacrificed everything to protect those she loved.

Charlie managed a laugh. "I'm flattered. Mariel's everything a knight should be—noble, brave, honorable."

"Wow. Sounds like you," Kyle said.

Charlie was caught so off-guard, she couldn't say anything beyond a muttered thank you.

"So we'll be in your hair for..." Viv looked at Maddie, "How long again?"

"For this trip, two weeks," Maddie answered, glancing down at her tablet again. "Then we're headed back to L.A. for pre-production and to start studio filming. But while we're here, we'll be doing a lot of mountain traveling. But first, Rowan has his PR appearance at the Renaissance Faire this Sunday."

"We'll be there on Saturday, too," Viv added, her eyes sparkling as she looked at Rowan. "Or else I'll never hear the end of it."

"You've jousted at Ren Faires, didn't you?" Charlie asked.

Viv answered for him. "That's how he got the role, actually. We wanted someone who could move like a real knight, not just fake it for the camera."

Rowan shrugged modestly. "I loved the books growing up and I wanted to live in that world, so I ran off and joined a Ren Faire." He chuckled. "I started as an extra, then a page, then finally, a knight. I'm lucky. Only a few Rennie entertainers end up successful. Penn and Teller are probably the biggest names."

"Until now," Viv said, smiling at him.

Rowan's smile back turned serious. "So, do you think we can sneak in ahead of my performance? Rowan asked Kyle. "Is it safe for Viv?"

"I think the bigger problem is if people recognize Rowan, we'll spend the whole day signing autographs instead of actually experiencing the Faire," Viv said.

Charlie's mind clicked into gear. "What about Nettie?" she asked

Kyle. Nettie was a makeup artist who worked for the CIA before going private. Watchdog had used her in the past. "She can disguise the two of you so thoroughly your own mothers wouldn't recognize you."

Viv's eyes widened. "Seriously?"

Kyle nodded. "She disguised a friend of mine recently for an undercover operation. Made her look completely different. It'll be easy at a Ren Faire—everyone's in costume anyway."

"That's brilliant," Maddie said, typing notes. "If she's willing, I'll add it to the schedule."

"All right," Kyle said. "I'll get Nettie's info from Gina to set up the disguises. We'll treat the Faire like any other public appearance—advance sweep, multiple exit routes, constant communication."

"Yes, Boss."

Everyone stood. Viv extended her hand to Charlie again. "Thank you. Really. It probably seems ridiculous to be upset over a few people throwing a temper tantrum, but these threats feel real."

"They *are* real," Charlie said firmly. "But we'll make sure nothing happens to you while you're here. And that you have a chance to enjoy yourselves at the Faire."

Rowan brightened. "Fantastic. There's someone I want Viv to meet one on one. An old Rennie friend of mine who's still there."

"And you still won't tell me why, will you?" Viv teased.

"I want to keep it a surprise," Rowan told her.

As they got ready to leave, Rowan turned to Charlie with a grin. "If we're all going in costume, you should go as Sir Mariel. It'd be perfect. You've got the height, the presence. You'd look incredible."

"Maybe next time," Charlie said, keeping her tone light. "I'm afraid I don't have any chainmail hanging in my closet."

"Considering what a huge fan you are, I'm surprised you don't," Rowan said. "She's gotta be your favorite character, am I right?"

No. That would be Princess Evelaine. Evelaine was beautiful. Graceful. The kind of woman heroes fell in love with and fought for.

Ben's words came back to her. *Warrior Princess...Emphasis on warrior.*

I'm proud of my strength, but just once, I wish someone would see me as Princess Evelaine instead of Sir Mariel.

SIX

It was early morning but the Renaissance Faire was already alive around Ben. The weather was perfect—not too hot yet, blue skies, and a light breeze that picked up the scent of pine sap, sawdust, and turkey drumsticks roasting over an open fire. Lute music drifted through the trees, along with laughter and the banter of merchants tempting visitors to buy their goods. Ben was right along with them, talking to the crowd as he worked a railroad spike into a knife. Because of the forge, his booth was one of the permanent structures at the faire—open at the front with two half-walls on either side, and the forge at the back. It was along the main path, across from the building housing the costume shop and tended to draw a curious crowd.

Ben wiped his sweaty hands on his leather apron and started in with his practiced stage patter.

"Lords and ladies, lend me thine ears! Come closer, brave souls and wandering knaves," he called, raising an iron railroad spike like a holy relic. "What you see here is not a magic sword, nor a rare treasure, nor a cursed talisman from the tomb of some forgotten mage of yore."

He waited half a beat before pointing at a boy at the front of the crowd. "You there, young squire. Can thou tell me what it is?"

"It's a giant's nail?" the kid answered. Several people in the crowd chuckled.

"Indeed, indeed." Ben placed it in the forge to heat up while he talked. "Once upon a time, this giant's nail was one of many used to build a steel and wooden road for fire-breathing iron dragons. This one comes from the far away, mystical kingdom of...Nebraska." Ben spotted a man in a University of Nebraska hat and added, "Home of the Knights of the Cornhuskers."

That earned him a few more laughs.

"There's one of them now. Sir Big Red, I believe." He pointed at the guy then mock-bowed as people glanced back smiling and laughing. The guy tipped his hat to Ben.

"Today, this humble spike will undergo a magical transformation right before your eyes." Ben waited until the spiked glowed orange before picking up his tongs and removing it from the fire.

"Through trial by fire, trial by hammer, and trial by my bad jokes, it will rise through the ranks and become a mighty weapon! One that's powerful enough to cut through yon turkey legs."

The crowd laughed good-naturedly.

Except for a woman in the front who called out, "How long is this gonna this take? I wanna catch the jousting tournament in half an hour."

"Well, my lady," Ben said with an exaggerated bow that made his leather apron creak, "if I'm working fast and the forge gods smile upon me? About twenty minutes. If I'm showing off for a crowd?" He grinned. "However long it takes to make thee laugh."

Even she cracked a smile as everyone else laughed.

Ben quenched only the pointed end of the spike, then stuck it vertically in a large shoe vise, the rest of the glowing orange spike pointing up. He took two adjustable spanners—giant wrenches—one in each hand, and clamped them opposite each other onto the spike just below the head to make a T-shape. Then he rotated the spanners, twisting the metal until it spiraled.

"The secret to getting it to do what you want is in the heat. Too hot, and the metal gets angry and twisted up the wrong way. Too cold and it won't move at all." He twisted the spanners again, slow and deliberate. "Kind of like my Aunt Gertrude at Thanksgiving."

More laughter.

He took the spike out of the vise and thrust it back into the coals to heat the other end.

"Now comes the fun part," he announced. "Turning this thick bit into something sharp enough to make those turkey legs nervous."

He pulled it out again, the metal now returned to orange, set it on his anvil, and began hammering the opposite end in earnest. Sparks flew upward like tiny stars. Each strike flattened and spread the spike, gradually transforming it from square stock into the recognizable shape of a blade.

Clang. Clang. Clang.

"You know what the best part about being a blacksmith is?" Ben asked between strikes, not breaking rhythm. "I get to hit things with a hammer all day." *Clang.* "You have therapists, I have percussive therapy."

The laughter made him glow inside as brightly as the metal he worked.

A woman in tight-fitting corset and peasant blouse piped up. "Aren't you hot in all that leather?" She looked him up and down appreciatively.

Ben paused, wiping his brow with his forearm. Out in the real world, her comment and gaze would have had him stuttering—if he could say anything at all. But not in here, where he wasn't Ben "Moose" Massey, but Sir Benjamin of the Forge, Royal Blacksmith to the King.

He shot her a grin. "My lady." He gestured at his kilt. "This isn't just for showing off me pretty legs."

The woman covered her heart and pretended to faint while the crowd roared, and Ben went back to work, shaping the curve of the blade with confident, precise strikes.

"Almost there now," he murmured, more to himself than the audience, though they leaned in to listen anyway. "See how she's starting to curve? That's what you want in a good blade—a belly to the edge. Makes for better cutting."

He quenched the blade in water, and it hissed and smoked dramatically. The crowd gasped, a few people stepping back.

"Don't worry, gentle folk," Ben said, deadpan. "That's supposed to happen. Probably."

The crowd laughed again as he lifted the knife back out of the water.

"And there you have it—fancy!" Ben held the finished knife up for everyone to see. "Because even a tough railroad spike deserves to feel pretty."

The crowd laughed and clapped.

"No need for applause, just buy one for yourself and for ten of thy closest friends." He gestured at the display cases of jewelry, the tables covered with knives, swords, leaf-shaped belt buckles, and real chain mail.

Behind him, one corner of the shop gleamed like a dragon's hoard: torsos mounted on wooden busts wearing hand-linked hauberks, the morning light glinting off steel rings. A coif hung from a carved post, draped like a hood over a leather helm. Nearby, gauntlets rested on a curved wooden rack, their fingers flexed into a loose grip, ready to knock on trouble's door.

A smaller mail shirt dangled from a nail near the front edge—right at kid height. He'd made that one out of light but sturdy aluminum for the little ones, so they could wear it without getting weighted down.

Across from the forge, and not for sale, hung his most impressive piece to date. Shoulder to mid-back chain mail shirt with the finest rings he could make, shined up until it looked like it was made of silver. He let it hang there deliberately, a quiet flex. The shirt looked like it'd been made with elven magic, but of course it wasn't. It took precision, patience, and weeks of his labor.

Ben admired it briefly as the crowd looked over his wares, deciding what to buy, before turning to answer questions and collect money. The crowd was thinning out, slowly making its way to the first jousting tournament of the day. He had just finished placing a necklace in a drawstring bag for a woman, when a man standing behind him beside the chain mail cleared his throat to get his attention.

"This chain mail shirt isn't half-bad, friend." He had the fakest British accent Ben had ever heard.

Ben stiffened. "Not *half* bad? Your average chain mail takes between two and three thousand links, depending on the size, while this one is made of six thousand, eighth-inch rings. It took me the better part of a year to make. And before you ask, it's not for sale today." He turned to look at the guy. "It was a...commissioned... piece..."

Ben squinted. He tilted his head as he looked the guy over.

"Rowan? Is that you?"

The guy was wearing a peasant costume. He had Rowan's eyes and build but his nose was way too big and his hair under a ridiculous leather hat was the wrong color. Then there was the weird accent.

Rowan McCrae—old friend, current television hero—burst into laughter as he clapped Ben on the back. Ben and Rowan went back years, to a time when they were both a couple of nerds busking their way up the Ren Fair food chain until Ben became a blacksmith and Rowan became a jousting knight.

"Well met, friend, well met," Ben said as he pulled Rowan into a one-armed hug. "I wasn't expecting you today. I didn't recognize you with this." He tapped Rowan's fake nose.

"That's the whole idea. I wanted to have a chance to bum around without being spotted," Rowan said, dropping the fake accent. "And I want to introduce someone to you while the crowd's thinned out." He looked over at a couple of women admiring a rack of blouses outside the costume shop.

Ben followed his gaze and froze.

One of the women was Charlie.

She was striking even in the plain clothes that contrasted with the brightly-colored skirts and peasant blouses. Charlie wasn't looking at him—her attention was focused on the woman beside her.

"I know her," Ben said, only half-paying attention to Rowan now. Why was Charlie here, and how did Rowan know her?

"Really? Even in disguise?" Rowan looked troubled.

"What? She's not in a ...*Oh.*" Ben realized Rowan wasn't talking about Charlie, but the other woman.

"Charlie," Rowan called, confusing Ben even more. So he *did* know her?

Both women looked up and across the path.

Charlie caught sight of Ben and blinked—clearly just as surprised to see him. Her gaze flicked between him and Rowan. The other woman smiled at Rowan, and they both started walking across the way.

She looked vaguely familiar. If Rowan hadn't mentioned she was in disguise too, Ben might not have taken a second look. But as she came closer, he recognized her.

The interviews. The red-carpet photos. The stills from *Legends of BattleLore* that had lit up every fan forum.

Vivienne Cross was standing ten feet from his forge.

His brain scrambled, trying to assemble the pieces.

Charlie... with Vivienne Cross... here?

He remembered his last conversation with Charlie when he'd caught her reading *Sword of Embers.*

Just some, uh, research. For a client. I can't really say who.

Of course. Vivienne Cross had come to Colorado with Rowan, and she needed a bodyguard.

Ben straightened instinctively, then immediately hunched again, annoyed with himself. Charlie didn't acknowledge knowing him and for a moment he felt crushed. Charlie dealt with celebrities for a living. She didn't need some blacksmith trying to impress her by association.

Stop it. This isn't her day off. She's working.

God, she probably thought he'd kept quiet about knowing Rowan because he didn't want to look like a name-dropping jerk.

He swallowed, wiped his hands on his leather apron, and focused on Vivienne Cross. She paused in front of the armor stand, her head tilting as she took in the pieces before returning her attention to Rowan. Charlie hung back half a step, scanning the crowd with practiced ease.

Rowan grinned like a kid about to light a fuse.

"This is him," Rowan said. "Viv, this is Ben Massey. Best metalworker on the Front Range. Possibly the continent." Rowan ran his hand over the chain mail. "I commissioned this chain mail shirt. Amazing, isn't it? Better than what the prop department's done."

Ben winced. "Rowan—"

Vivienne's gaze was sharp and curious. "You made all of this?"

"Yes, Ms. Cross," Ben said. He ran his hand over his hair, realizing just how sweaty and sooty he must look.

"Please, it's Viv." Her mouth twitched. "You must be the surprise Rowan told me about."

"I-I..."

She reached for the chain mail and tested its weight. "This looks historically accurate."

"It is," Ben said, falling into familiar rhythm. "As much as possible without sacrificing safety or function. Some compromises for wearability and weight. But the same techniques."

Charlie's gaze flicked to him, measuring. He felt it like a hand brushing his cheek.

"Try it on," Ben told Rowan. "Let's see if it needs any adjustments."

Rowan slipped the chain mail over his costume. It was a perfect fit.

"This is excellent," Viv said, circling Rowan. "What?" she added, smiling at his grin.

"You know what I'm going to say," Rowan replied. "It hasn't been made yet."

Viv's grin widened. "No. It hasn't."

Ben blinked, confused. *What hasn't?*

She turned her attention to the knives and swords, then to Charlie. "You know weapons, right?" She looked back at Ben. "By the way, This is Charlie King, my very own Sir Mariel."

Charlie winced. It was subtle, but Ben caught it.

"We know each other already," she said, glancing away from Ben.

"Oh," Viv said, studying Charlie. "Small world, or are you a Ren Faire regular?"

"Small world," Charlie said. "This is my first Faire."

"But you do know weapons?"

Charlie nodded. She stepped closer to the table, her interest clearly piqued. She examined a sword then picked it up carefully, respectfully. Not the way some tourists who'd never touched a sword in their life handled one. The way someone who understood them did.

"This is very well-balanced," she said, testing it.

"Th-thank you."

"Light, too." She stepped back to a safe distance and swung the sword. Ben's heart flipped in his chest.

Rowan looked back and forth between the two, grinning like a cat with a canary. Ben wanted to sock him.

"So you give it your stamp of approval?" Viv asked Charlie.

"Approval? For?"

Rowan shook his head. "Come on, Charlie, you've read the books. What's Sir Aldric's first quest all about?"

"Finding the lost Ember Sword, of course." She looked at the sword in her hand. Her eyes widened at the same time Ben realized what Rowan was getting at.

"And you've read the books, too?" Viv asked him.

"Yes, ma'am...Viv."

Her smile widened. "Then you know what the Ember Sword is supposed to look like."

His heart thudded once, hard.

"I do."

Rowan snorted. "He made one once. Years ago. Wouldn't let anyone touch it."

Ben shot him a look. "It was a prototype."

Viv's eyes lit up. "You *made* the Ember Sword."

"An early version," Ben said carefully. "I've learned a lot since then."

She held his gaze. "I want you to make it again. For the show this season. If that would interest you, of course."

Ben barely registered Rowan's laugh as the world narrowed to a pinpoint.

"Yes," Ben said, without hesitation. "I-I'd be honored."

"As if he'd say no." Rowan clapped him on the shoulder, beaming. "Congratulations."

Charlie watched Ben, her eyes gleaming.

Wait. Did I just impress her?

Viv launched into logistics—timelines, materials, historical versus cinematic needs. Ben answered confidently, the way he always did when he talked about his work.

When Viv told him how much she'd pay him for the sword, he had to brace himself against the table.

"It's a deal."

"Great! I'll get a contract written up for you." Viv nodded toward the costume shop across the path. "Now, I want to take a look in there before the jousting's over. Ben, it was a pleasure meeting you. We'll see you again at Rowan's jousting match?"

"Of course."

"Maybe we could go to dinner as well," she added, glancing at Rowan. "You could regale with me stories I can't get out of him otherwise."

Rowan laughed and Ben realized his old friend was head over heels for Viv.

"I'll pay you double what's she's giving you for the sword to keep your mouth shut," Rowan said.

Ben laughed. "Pay me triple, and you have a deal."

"A bargain!" Rowan slapped him on the back again and they started across the path. Charlie walked beside Viv, her head on a swivel. Rowan followed the women.

Ben watched them go, barely believing what just happened.

He was going to forge *the* Ember Sword.

Even better, Charlie looked at him like he was...someone special.

No. It's just your imagination.

But he couldn't take his eyes off of her.

Charlie slowed just slightly as she reached the shop. She lifted her hand and brushed the edge of a gown hanging beside the entrance. Pale gossamer fabric. Intricately embroidered bodice. A gown fit for a princess out of a story.

No, not just any story.

Her touch lingered no more than a second, but even from here, Ben could see the longing on her face.

Then she disappeared inside.

The way she winced only a few minutes ago. Maybe it wasn't because she was embarrassed to know Ben. Maybe it was because Viv called her Sir Mariel.

Could it be...?

Every warrior wanted the best armor.

But maybe Charlie longed for silk and starlight, too.

Warrior Princess.

"Here's the forge but I don't see them," Ben heard someone say, the voice sharp with anger.

"They've got to be here somewhere," someone answered. "This is the only place selling chain mail."

Were they talking about Vivienne and Rowan?

Ben turned toward the voices and saw a knot of people—five of them—clustered together, all wearing Caiden Bramble's Embersworn capes. They were scanning. Hunting.

Shit. How did they know Rowan and Viv were coming here?

Had they been recognized earlier? No—the prosthetics had changed their faces completely, and the costumes did the rest. There was no way they could have picked them out.

"Maybe they're checking out the other shops first," one of them said. "Let's split up and keep looking. Text when you see them."

"Bitch thinks she can just walk around like nothing's happening," one of the men said.

Shit. These weren't just fans hoping for autographs. This was an angry mob.

One of them was headed straight toward the costume shop.

And Charlie.

I've got to get them the hell out of here.

Not caring about his forge, Ben moved.

SEVEN

When Charlie stepped off the elevator into the hotel lobby that morning, still damp from her shower, she stopped.

Viv and Rowan were already in their Ren Faire costumes, and she barely recognized them, even though she'd been there while Gina's friend, Nettie, measured and later fitted them with prosthetic noses and cheeks the day before.

If I can't recognize them, there's no chance anyone else will, either.

That loosened the tight knot in her belly that worried they'd be spotted and harassed. And gave her brain just enough room to think about something else entirely. Like seeing Ben at his forge today.

Stop it. Focus.

So far, the week had been uneventful---no sign of any Caidansworn, no protests, no threatening messages waiting at the hotel desk, not even a lot of chatter on the fan sites.

Do not think easy day, she told herself. *Don't jinx this.*

They were waiting for her at a table on the outside edge of the lobby bar, in full Ren Faire costumes—which also helped draw attention away from their faces, especially the goofy hat on Rowan's head.

The two of them were leaning in, staring intently at each other with soft smiles, not saying anything.

If I didn't suspect it before, I sure do now. Those two are having an affair.

Which was perfectly fine—neither was currently married—and it was none of her business unless it interfered with her ability to protect Viv.

"Hey," she said to gain their attention. Neither one looked away. Charlie cleared her throat and tried again. "Hello?"

"Oh!" Viv's head snapped to the side to look at Charlie. Her cheeks turned bright pink as she leaned back.

Charlie clocked the brief disappointment on Rowan's face as he took in her outfit—no armor or even a wool cloak, just casual street clothes. She'd decided it was more important to have comfortable, familiar clothing than to try and blend in. The last thing she needed was to trip over her own costume if Viv were in danger.

"Sir Mariel." Rowan stood and bowed. "I was hoping you'd conjured some armor to wear."

Charlie hoped her smile wasn't too awkward. "I'm afraid Princess Evelaine's court magician lost his way to my house, so no conjured armor."

"And you don't have your father's battle armor either? How will you avenge him without it?"

Now she was really struggling to keep the disgust off her face.

He's only teasing. He has no idea my father is nothing like Sir Mariel's.

Viv saved her. She stood and said, "Rowan, please stop tormenting my bodyguard, would you?"

Charlie forced a laugh. "Are you ready? Or are we waiting for Maddie?"

"I gave her the day off, poor thing. Shopping in Cherry Creek is much more her speed than hanging around us olds at a Ren Faire. She looked relieved when I handed her a company card and told her to go have fun."

"She's a *BattleLore* fan though, right? I'm surprised she didn't want to come along." They started walking toward the hotel entrance.

"I think she exaggerates her love for the books." Rowan held the glass door open for Viv and Charlie. "She's not fluent in Elven like we are." He winked at Charlie.

"So where's your pooch?" Viv asked.

Charlie's heart squeezed. "I wish I could have brought Flo, but dogs aren't allowed in. I was told they upset the elephants." It just figured she couldn't bring Flo with her on her first detail after getting her. Instead, Flo was spending the day back at the Watchdog kennels. Charlie hoped she didn't think she'd been rejected and sent back. Even if she hadn't worked out—and she had because Flo was the best dog ever—Charlie would have begged to adopt Flo. Her apartment finally felt like a home now that she had someone to share it with.

"This way." Charlie led them to one of the unmarked white SUVs Watchdog used when their clients needed to stay incognito. It was parked with its hazard lights on under the porte-cochère.

Rowan opened the passenger side door for Viv before Charlie could, then let himself into the back. Charlie got in and pulled into downtown Denver traffic. The Ren Faire was a forty-five minute drive away.

Viv pestered Rowan the entire time.

"You won't even give me a hint who this surprise person is?" She pretended to pout.

"Then it wouldn't be a surprise, would it?" He sat back in his seat looking totally smug.

"I'm not happy about it, either," Charlie added. "I don't like surprises on my watch."

"Trust me, ladies. you won't be in any danger."

It turned out Charlie was in far more danger than Viv when she saw who the surprise was.

I'm going to throttle Shane the next time I see him.

Why the hell hadn't he mentioned that Ben was a blacksmith at the fucking Renaissance Faire?

For that matter, why didn't *Ben* tell her he knew Rowan McCrae? Or that he and Rowan were buddies? They'd been talking about the *BattleLore* books like two nerds in a pub, and she'd sat there in her office nodding like a fool.

He didn't tell you for the very same reason you didn't tell him you were about to guard Viv and Rowan, she thought grimly. *Because you wear thicker armor than Sir Mariel's.*

She hated that it was true almost as much as she hated that lately she was starting to notice how heavy the armor had become. Maybe she was tired of hiding inside it, tired of being the one who never let anyone see the soft spots.

No, stop. She needed to be sharp. To stay aware of any danger that might threaten Viv. This was why she didn't take off her armor. She needed to focus on her job, not on the absurd possibility that some man—no, not *some* man, a *good* man—was actually interested in her.

And yet...

As she walked away from his forge, she could feel Ben watching her. She didn't have to look back to confirm it; the air changed when he focused on her. Heat, weight, tension—like the moment before a storm breaks.

You're imagining it. Wish-fulfillment, anyone?

The possibility that some drop-dead handsome blacksmith with kind eyes might actually see her? Not on the list of possibilities in this lifetime. She was Sir Mariel whether she liked it or not. Everyone knew it. It was how everyone saw her. If she was being honest, it was how she saw herself, too—just one of the guys. Competent and cool.

Untouchable. *Undesirable.*

Still, when they passed the gown hanging outside the costume shop, she hesitated. Silver and blue silk shimmered in the sunlight, the royal colors of Lady Evelaine's court. The dressmaker had probably put it there on purpose—made it in honor of Rowan's appearance next weekend, hoping to cash in on the popularity of *BattleLore*. Smart merchandising.

It was also... breathtaking.

Exquisite embroidery stitched in shimmering silver thread glittered like dew on morning grass. The fabric looked like moonlight had been coaxed into silk.

Charlie's fingers brushed the fabric before she could stop herself. It was cool and impossibly smooth, the kind of material that didn't belong to her world of Kevlar and cargo pants. She imagined what it would feel like against her skin—how it would feel to wear it for someone who thought she was beautiful.

And that little voice inside her whispered again—quiet, persistent, irritatingly tender.

If just for one day... One night... I could take off the armor and be soft. Let someone else protect me for a change.

The thought startled her as much as it tempted her. She snatched her hand back, squared her shoulders, and shoved the softness down where it belonged. The moment passed quickly, and Charlie was back on her guard.

She hadn't sensed any threats so far, but the day was still young. Luckily, the disguises were holding. Nettie had been a miracle worker; even Charlie had done a double take that morning. No one recognized Viv or Rowan. If anything, the curious looks were landing on her—as usual.

That happened a lot on protection details. People noticed the tall, broad-shouldered woman scanning every corner. Sometimes she used that to her advantage, dressing in a way that pulled eyes away from her principal. Heels, a skirt, and an up-do could accomplish what a sidearm couldn't—take attention away without threatening violence. She'd been called statuesque more times than she could count, as if that were a compliment. Maybe it just meant she filled the space like a warning sign.

The shop was a riot of color and fabric. Corsets, skirts, vests, fancy hats stacked on every shelf. Laughter spilled out of three dressing booths in the back as women tried to wrestle themselves into stiff corsets with miles of laces. Charlie kept a sharp eye out for anybody who might have noticed Vivienne and Rowan. But so far everyone was just having a fun day out, helping each other into and out of corsets, trying on different hats, taking photos of themselves dressed up in their finest medieval attire.

"Look at this," Viv said, tugging a gown from a rack. "The detail work—unbelievable. I think I'll send the costumers out here to talk to the owner." She looked around. "I wonder where she is. They could take some pointers from her."

"I think she's over there." Rowan pointed to a woman speaking in a Cockney accent to a couple of girls holding up fairy princess wings. Her cleavage looked like the Grand Canyon, barely contained by a peasant's blouse and corset.

Viv started that way, but Charlie's instincts snapped. "Hold up," she murmured, stepping close enough that her voice didn't carry. "I don't think it's a good idea to talk to her here and now." She lowered her voice. "Too many people. If you start talking about sending out costumers from Hollywood, your cover is blown before she finishes her next sale."

Viv closed her eyes. "Right. Of course. I'm not used to this." She opened her eyes and gave Charlie a guilty smile. "I'm sorry. I'm probably making your job a lot harder than it needs to be."

"No, no, don't apologize. I understand. You wouldn't be the first person who isn't used to this." Charlie's expression softened. "It's a shame you have to be guarded at all."

"It's stupid, is what it is," Viv said, exasperated. She turned and looked back toward the forge. "Maybe your friend Ben could make introductions later?" she asked Rowan. "Or approach her on the down low?"

"I'm sure he could," Rowan said. He looked at Charlie. "Am I right?"

Charlie blinked hard as she was taken off-guard by Rowan

assuming she was close with Ben. "Yes. Absolutely. I'm sure Ben would love to."

"Perfect." Viv clapped her hands, her mood already bouncing back. "Now, I want to see that dress outside again."

Charlie led the way to the front of the shop, to the dream of a dress.

Viv sighed as she touched the skirt. "It would be perfect for Lady Evelaine, don't you think?"

"Yes, I do," Charlie agreed, wistfully. Then the hairs on the back of her neck stood up.

She froze. Something in the air had shifted. There was a tenseness that Viv and Rowan hadn't picked up on. Charlie glanced across the way and realized Ben was coming toward the costume shop, jaw tight, looking both confused and worried. The second their eyes met, he flicked his gaze left.

Charlie put her arm out to block Viv and Rowan from sight and looked in that direction. She scanned the crowd, eyes sweeping over tents, vendors, wandering knights. And there—five people in matching capes, hoods up despite the warm afternoon, walking in a tight knot straight for the costume shop.

She recognized those capes—the same kind worn by Caiden Bramble once he became one of the Embersworn.

Only they weren't Embersworn. They were Caidansworn.

"Hang on," she murmured. "We've got trouble."

Viv's voice was barely a whisper. "What kind?"

"Put your hood up. Don't stare. Stay close."

Ben reached them. "Charlie—?"

"I see them," she cut in. Her mind was already running the map of the fair: security, exits, blind spots, crowd density.

"Let me help you," Ben murmured. "We'll take the back door out of the shop. Security is to the left, opposite the jousting ring, away from the crowd."

"Perfect. I was thinking that, too." She turned to Viv and Rowan.

"To the back of the shop. Don't move quickly. I want you to laugh and talk, but quietly. We don't want to draw attention to ourselves, but we do want to get out of here quickly. We blend, we move, we don't panic."

They obeyed without question. The four of them headed back in. The shop owner glanced up and gave Ben a puzzled smile. Ben made some sort of sign as he passed her and her eyes widened as she nodded. They found the exit, headed out of the costume shop, and turned left toward the security tent, walking casually but quickly.

Then a hand brushed the small of her back—steady, guiding, possessive without being invasive.

Ben.

"'Tis a fine thing you could be here today, milady," he said, back in his Ren Faire blacksmith persona. His accent hit somewhere inconvenient in her chest, and if she was being honest, elsewhere. He was playing the role, pretending they were a couple.

Which was very dangerous for her focus.

She glanced over and realized that Rowan had taken Viv's hand. She smiled to herself. She didn't think it was much of an act—more like an excuse.

They slipped into the tide of fairgoers, dodging mead mugs and flower crowns. But the prickling at the back of her neck wouldn't settle down.

They passed a shop selling cloaks and Charlie made for it. She grabbed a dark cloak from a rack at the front, calculating whether she had time to pay for it. Ben read her mind.

"Just to borrow," he called to the vendor and made the same sign. The woman's eyes widened, then she nodded and waved them on.

Charlie threw the cloak over Viv's shoulders. "Keep your head down."

Then out of nowhere, to their right, the shouts started.

"There she is!"

"Lady Darkfell the Betrayer!" they shouted as they approached the shop.

Murderer!"

The words knifed through the air, freezing half the crowd. Charlie's stomach clenched. *Two groups*, Charlie thought, her heart sinking. *How many of them are here?* Luckily, there were only three people in this group.

"How did they recognize us?" Viv asked.

Great question.

The disguises were perfect. Then she remembered Ben heading for them before they'd even stepped out of the costume shop, alerted to danger, even if he didn't know what it was.

The Caidansworn were already looking for Viv before they stepped out of the costume shop.

They were tipped off.

"We'll figure it out later," she told Viv. "First, we need to get you to safety."

Ben's eyes met hers. "Go. I'll distract them."

He peeled away before she could argue. She immediately missed his hand on her back. Ben moved toward a juggler in motley. A quick word, a nod, and the man launched himself into a wild tumble right into the path of the cloaked intruders, wooden knives scattering like hail.

"Oh, what a fool I am!" he bellowed, earning laughter from the crowd and blocking pursuit.

Beside her, Charlie heard Ben's low chuckle as he rejoined them. "Magpie still has good timing."

Two fairies spun into the space behind them, glittering wings flaring wide to obscure sight lines.

"Oh, let us sprinkle you with fairy dust!" they told the Caidansworn, who tried to push past them and failed.

Charlie grinned. All of Ben's Renaissance friends were helping them escape.

She moved Viv and Rowan through the confusion, pulling off Rowan's hat, tightening Viv's cloak. Drummers appeared, followed by dancers in colorful skirts flaring out as they spun. A mock sword fight erupted behind them, drawing every eye.

"Almost there," Ben said under his breath. "Between those two shops."

A final shout cut through the noise. "Vivianne Cross!"

Charlie swore softly.

Ben turned, expression hard as iron. "What's this about Vivianne Cross?" he demanded.

"You can't silence us!" one of the protesters yelled.

"I can't," Ben said evenly. "But security can."

As if on cue, three Faire security guards in period costume pushed through the crowd toward the shouting Caidansworn, hands up, voices calm but firm. Not a request.

Charlie didn't wait to watch. She moved Viv and Rowan between the two shops, where Faire management waited — two men and a woman, one holding a radio that very clearly did not belong in the fifteenth century.

"I'm head of security," the woman said briskly. "We're escorting eight people out right now. They've been told they're banned permanently."

"Good," Charlie said. "Is there any chance they'll test the perimeter later? Try to sneak back in?"

"We're ready if they try," one of the men said grimly. "And God help them if they do."

A warm hand settled against her back again. She turned to find Ben smiling, relief softening the angles of his face.

"They're gone," he said quietly. "No one's spotted any others." He looked at Viv and Rowan. "It should be safe to go back in—if you still want to spend the day here after that."

"We absolutely do," Viv said immediately. Her eyes flashed. "I refuse to be intimidated by anyone." She looked at Rowan. "What do you think?"

Rowan gave an exaggerated sigh. "As if I have any say in the matter when it comes to you making up your mind."

Ben laughed, the sound rolling low in his chest. He looked at Viv. "Now, what's this about Lady Darkfell?"

Viv sighed. "I don't want to talk about it right now, if you don't mind."

"Understood."

"However, I don't know what your week looks like, but I would love it if you would join us at our scouting sites. That is, if you're not busy doing anything else."

Charlie caught Ben glancing at her. Was that warmth in his eyes? The hint of a smile?

"I'd be honored," he said.

"Awesome," Rowan said. "This is gonna be fun."

Charlie stayed silent, scanning the crowd. She was outwardly calm, inwardly coiled, searching for more Caidansworn capes, waiting for more shouting.

Someone had tipped off the Caidansworn, and until she found out who, she wasn't taking her armor off for anyone.

No matter how reassuring Ben's hand felt.

EIGHT

Monday morning light slanted through the kitchen window, bright and warm, turning the dust motes into tiny sparks. Ben rubbed the heel of his hand over his jaw, listening to the faint rasp of stubble. The kitchen smelled like coffee and his fingers smelled like silver from his latest jewelry project, still lying on black velvet spread across his kitchen table. It had to be perfect. It was the only thing that could take his attention away from sketching out more designs for the Ember Sword. Truth be told, he already knew exactly how he wanted it to look.

This is the chance of a lifetime.

Only one person could distract Ben from his task.

He'd been back at the Faire yesterday, pretending he wasn't thinking about a tall blonde with eyes like hazel fire. Even though she was working full-time as long as Viv and Rowan were in town, part of him hoped he'd see Charlie in the crowd, watching him like she had Saturday afternoon after the damn Caidansworn incident.

Ben sipped his coffee and chuckled, remembering Magpie and the others. He loved the way his Ren Faire family watched out for each other.

When those five assholes had started toward the costume shop, he hadn't understood what the hell they were on about. He'd hoped for a moment that he was overreacting and this was just some weird Ren Faire improv gone wrong. Turned out it was fandom rage. Ben had spent an hour that night reading the comment threads on *BattleLore* fan sites like they were evidence from a crime scene. Viv was apparently killing off Duke Holloway's character, Caiden, and half the fandom had lost its collective mind.

He poured himself another cup of coffee and leaned on the counter as the mug warmed his hand. He thought about the day ahead. He'd almost backed out of Viv's invitation to join them but Rowan talked him up some more, telling Viv that Ben was a former Ranger, knew the Front Range like no one's business, and he'd be helpful navigating the wilderness—as if they were going off on a quest to slay a dragon. Now, the kitchen felt too quiet. It was too early to start for Viv and Rowan's hotel in Denver, but he didn't have enough time to get back to his jewelry project.

Images of Charlie started haunting him again.

During their getaway, he'd watched her move through that crowd like she owned the entire Faire. Calm, precise, eyes tracking threats before anyone else even noticed there was a problem.

Warrior Princess, through and through.

After the Caidansworn were banned, they'd all walked back from security to his forge. Luckily, his friend Della, who ran the costume shop and had a sixth sense for trouble, had sent her son over to his stall to handle sales while he was helping to get Viv to safety. Ben tipped the kid from the cash box and sent him back across the way as people gathered for his next sword-making demonstration. He'd expected Viv and Rowan to want to wander the Faire, but they stayed for his show.

Ben had started in on his usual bad jokes as he forged another knife from a rail spike. The crowd laughed, but he only cared about Charlie's reaction. She was still on her guard, watching the crowd and braced for another attack, but he'd gotten her to smile, *and* cover a laugh twice.

It made him feel like he'd found his way through a tiny crack in her armor for the second time that day.

The first was that moment before the trouble started—that moment with the dress.

Ben hadn't meant to stare. But he'd watched her touch the silver-blue silk like it was holy. Like it was something she'd never allow herself to want.

That image had been looping in his head for two days.

Sunday before the gates opened, he'd gone to Della's shop under the pretense of thanking her for sending her son across the way.

Della had seen right through him, of course.

"I can see you screwing up your courage. You're here for something else, Benjamin Blacksmith."

"W-what are you talking about?"

"Come on, out with it. It's the amazon," she said, chin lifted, eyes bright with gossip. "The tall one who looks like she could stop lightning from striking with a stern look at the clouds."

Ben shook his head. "That'd be her," he'd admitted.

"I saw her admiring the dress at my door." She held up a finger calloused from countless needle pricks. "Among other things."

"She's got good taste," Ben said.

"Yes, she does. And good taste in *dresses*, too."

Ben's eyes went wide. "N-no, that's...there's nothing..."

Cackling, Della had already turned on her heel and was weaving her way through the maze of crowded clothing racks. "Come along, come along. You've got good taste as well."

He'd almost laughed. Instead, Ben followed Della, stopping every few feet to pick up a dress or blouse he'd knocked off a rack. He'd squeezed through wider hidden tunnels than this.

"Can it be adjusted?"

"You mean *tailored* to fit her?" Della grinned as she took the dress off its hook and held it up. "Of course, I do it all the time." She studied the dress. "She's built long and strong. I can take out the hem in the skirt, make the sleeves three-quart length, and add a couple panels to the lace-up bodice. That'll make it hers." She slipped into the Cockney she usually saved for the fair-goers. Give me 'til the end of the day, Benjamin Blacksmith, and you'll have a fine gown for your lady fair, won't you?"

He'd left with a receipt and a smile.

Now the gown was in a garment bag hanging behind his workshop door, and he couldn't decide if he'd done something brilliant or utterly stupid.

Probably both.

He drained the coffee, grabbed his phone, and hit Shane's number before he could talk himself out of it.

Shane picked up on the second ring. "Moose. What's up?"

" When we went to lunch the other day, why didn't you tell me that Vivienne Cross and Rowan McCrae were Charlie's principals?" Ben asked without preamble.

Silence. Then Shane's laugh came warmly through the phone. "You two bumped into each other at the Ren Faire."

"You could say that. Rowan's an old friend of mine. I met him the summer of my senior year when I was apprenticing for the blacksmith while the rest of you were off punishing your livers."

Shane chuckled. "Good times."

"So why didn't you tell me?"

"Client confidentiality, brother. You know how it works."

"Bullshit," Ben growled. "You could have given me a heads-up."

"And spoil the surprise? Where's the fun in that?" Shane was clearly enjoying this. "Besides, I've gone above and beyond already, trying to give you every possible in with Charlie and you haven't taken any of them. I'm done trying to set you two up. You're both adults. You'll figure it out yourselves."

Ben scrubbed a hand over his face. "Shane—"

"Okay, okay." Shane's tone softened, turned serious. "What's really going on? Something happen at the Faire?"

Ben took a breath. "I bought her a dress."

A beat of silence. "You...what now?"

Ben ran his hand over his stubble. "It looks like the one Princess Evelaine wore the first time Aldric professed his love in the Forest Between the Worlds in book two."

"I'm not a nerd so you just lost me."

"Asshole. Then you're the only person on the planet who hasn't watched *Legends of BattleLore* yet."

"Yeah, don't I know? April can't stop talking about it. I haven't told her Rowan McCrae's in town because I'm afraid she'll trample me on her way to meet Sir...Aldric Dude or whatever."

"I shouldn't have called you."

"I'm exactly who you needed to call, brother. So why'd you buy this dress for King?"

Ben paused. "I saw Charlie touch it right before she went into the costume shop across from my forge. Just for a second, but..." He trailed off.

"But you saw something," Shane said evenly.

"Yeah. Like..."

Like she wanted to be a princess. Ben didn't dare betray Charlie and tell Shane that. He remembered Charlie swearing him to secrecy over her arachnophobia. How much worse would this be?

"...like she wanted it or something."

"You sure about that? King's not much into dresses."

Are you *sure she's not?* he wanted to ask. But maybe Shane was right. He knew Charlie much better than Ben did.

"Rowan keeps calling her Sir Mariel," he said half to himself.

"Again, Moose, I'm not the nerd you are and you've lost me."

"She's another character in the book." Ben blew out a breath. "Never mind. It was a stupid idea. Maybe Della will take it back—"

"Dammit, Ben. You're the smartest dumbass I know. Shane's voice held equal parts pride and frustration. "You're really doing this, you're finally making a move and now you're doubting yourself? Did you call me for advice or to talk you out of it?"

"I don't know. It's weird, right? Men are supposed to start with candy and flowers, not dresses—"

"Dude, stop." Shane's voice went firm. "First off, Charlie's not going to think it's weird. She's going to think it's thoughtful. Which it is."

"But—"

"Moose. *Listen* to me. Ever since we were all kids, how many times have you saved our asses?"

Ben barked out a laugh. "More times than I can count. What does that have to do with anything?"

"Everything, brother. Back in high school, you kept Elias and Waylon from a life of crime, or at least dumb-assery."

Ben laughed. Yeah, maybe he did.

Shane went on. "You pulled Gabe out of his funk when he came back to Lyons. He'd probably still be sitting at home alone feeling sorry for himself if you hadn't reached out to him."

"He would've sorted himself out without me."

"That's bullshit. And if you wanna go way back, I remember you beating the shit out of those little assholes who picked on Bear in middle school."

Ben smirked. It was hard to believe Bear had once been a scrawny little kid who couldn't defend himself. "He saved me as much as I saved him back then. You all did. You were the only ones who didn't think I was a d-damned idiot." Bitterness had crept into his voice, remembering how cruel the other kids had been, making fun of his stutter and calling him stupid.

Shane ignored him. "And brother, you helped me out the most. If it weren't for you...that day April left..."

"You couldn't help that, Shane."

"Look, what I'm trying to say is, you've always been our voice of reason. You're the smartest out of all of us. You see things the rest of us miss. So with King, you saw something real when she touched that dress. You paid attention to what she wanted—something that in a million years would've never crossed *my* mind, and I've known her a lot longer than you have. So, you not only recognizing that, but giving it to her? That's you seeing her. Really seeing her."

Ben was quiet, turning Shane's words over.

Not just the warrior—the princess too.

"And she's going to appreciate it," Shane continued. "I don't have to tell you she doesn't give anything away about herself. She doesn't let a lot of people in. But she'll let you in, Ben. You do this, and she'll have no choice."

"I don't want her to feel obligated—"

Shane laughed. "Shit, Moose. Sometimes you're too smart for your own good. You remember what you told me? Back when I was dancing around April? You told me to stop overthinking it. Right now, you are overthinking the hell out of this. You told me to just show up. So show up, brother. Give her the dress. See what happens."

"And if she hates it?"

Shane sighed, exasperated. "Then at least you tried." Shane's tone softened. "But I've seen the way she looks at you, Ben. When you're not watching. She's interested. She's just waiting for you to make a move."

"You think so?"

"I know so. King's one of the toughest people I've ever met. But around you? She softens. She smiles." Shane paused. "Now all you have to do is loosen up around *her*."

Ben scoffed. "Easier said than done."

"That's the other thing I've never understood about you, Moose. You've got all the confidence in the world except when it comes to women. Even when you scored at the bar and took someone home, you always talked yourself out of thinking it could turn into more."

"Keep telling yourself you don't notice things, Elk."

Shane laughed, then grew serious again. "Look. You two would be good together. You both love those fantasy books, you're both uber-nerds, and you are about to give her something that will make her little nerd heart go pitter-patter. She's going to love it."

Ben couldn't help but grin. "Maybe."

"Maybe nothing. Stop second-guessing yourself, dumbass."

As Ben laughed, he felt something in his chest unclench. "Thanks, brother."

"Anytime. Now go give her that dress."

"Hang on. How do you know I'm seeing her today?"

"I know because I already talked to King about you, among other things."

Ben almost dropped his phone. "You what? So you already knew everything when I called."

"I did. Ain't I a stinker?"

"You suck. So why'd you talk to her?"

Shane laughed. "We do work together, remember? I was at her debriefing about what went down on Saturday. She spoke highly of how you helped with getting her principal to safety. *Highly*. You hear what I'm saying?"

Ben's heart sped up. "Yeah."

"You better. Like I said, Moose—you two are adults and it's up to you to work your shit out."

"I hate it when you're right, Elk."

"It's for the record books, I know. And Moose?"

"Yeah?"

"When she says yes to going out with you—and she will—don't make me regret giving you this pep talk by chickening out again."

Ben grinned despite himself. "Deal."

He looked toward the dress bag. The morning light spilled through the doorway, catching the faint glint of the zipper. He should leave it alone. Let it hang there, like a secret he'd keep forever.

But the thought of Charlie's face when she saw it—surprise first, then that reluctant, wary smile she tried to hide—that was worth every risk.

He rinsed the mug, set it in the sink, and reached for his jacket.

"Warrior Princess," he muttered under his breath. "You're gonna be the death of me."

NINE

Monday morning, Charlie caught Flo's big, doggie smile in the hotel's bathroom mirror and smiled back. She wasn't sure which one of them was happier that Flo was coming along today instead of getting sidelined again. They were going up into the mountains today, to check out potential filming sites with Viv, Rowan, and Maddie.

And Ben.

Charlie closed her eyes and felt her cheeks heat up. How was she supposed to face him after the debriefing at Watchdog on Saturday night?

THE CONFERENCE ROOM at Watchdog felt small with six people crammed around the table. Charlie sat with Flo at her feet, the Malinois picking up on the tension thrumming through the room. Viv and Rowan sat side by side, still in their Ren Faire costumes minus the prosthetics. Maddie clutched her tablet like a life preserver. Viv hadn't wanted to disturb her on her day off, but she insisted on coming in the moment she heard what happened. Shane sat beside Maddie. Kyle stood at the head of the table, arms crossed, his expression grim.

"Let's go over what happened," Kyle said. "Charlie?"

She kept her voice professional, clinical. "At approximately 13:45, I observed five individuals in Caidansworn capes converging on the costume shop. Ben Massey alerted me to their presence before they reached our position. We evacuated through the back exit with his assistance. Faire security escorted eight individuals off the premises total—the original five plus three more who attempted to intercept us."

"The disguises held?" Kyle asked.

"Completely. Nettie's work was flawless." Charlie glanced at Viv.

Kyle's jaw tightened. "Which means someone tipped them off to your location."

Charlie nodded. "Ben said as much. He heard them discuss how they expected us at the forge, right before we were spotted at the costume shop."

The room went quiet for a beat.

"We need to identify the leak," Kyle said as he looked at Viv. "Walk me through who knew you'd be at the Faire."

"Everyone at this table," Viv said quietly. "Plus Gina and Nettie. And of course Ben."

Charlie's chest tightened just thinking about it. *Not Ben. He wouldn't.*

"Maddie?" Kyle asked. "Did you mention it to anyone?"

Maddie's face went pale. "No! I swear, I didn't tell anyone. I know better than that." Her voice cracked slightly. She set her tablet down with trembling hands and pushed it toward Kyle. "You can check my phone, my emails, everything. I wouldn't—"

"Easy," Kyle said, his tone gentler. "We're just covering all bases."

Maddie nodded but she looked like she might cry. Charlie wanted to reach across the table and squeeze her shoulder, but stayed still. This was procedure. Everyone got looked at after a security breach. Everyone.

Viv looked at Rowan. "How...well do you know Ben?"

Charlie's stomach twisted at the implied accusation.

Ben, who'd moved without hesitation to help them. Who'd rallied his Ren Faire family to create cover. Who'd stood beside her with his hand warm against her back while they navigated the crowd. Who was ready to defend them all, even her.

"He was the one who helped us," Charlie said in his defense. "When he heard them talking he was just as surprised as any of us."

Kyle shot her a look and she knew she'd spoken out of turn. Even Viv was looking at her curiously. But dammit, Ben didn't deserve this accusation.

"He wouldn't tell anyone," Rowan said. "The guy is steady as a rock." He scrubbed a hand over his face. "It's probably my fault." He sighed heavily. "I told a few people on set that I was getting chain mail armor made. That I was picking it up in Colorado at the Ren Faire." He looked at Viv. "I'm sorry. I wasn't thinking."

Viv reached over and squeezed his hand. "You couldn't have known they'd come looking for us ahead of next week's joust."

"But I should have been more careful," Rowan said bitterly. "After everything that's happened, I should've kept my damn mouth shut."

Kyle nodded slowly. "That could explain it. Someone on set passed it along, either deliberately or accidentally. The Caidansworn have been monitoring social media, fan forums, anywhere they might catch wind of Viv's location."

Ben was off the hook. Charlie felt relief flood through her, followed immediately by guilt.

"I'll inform the home office that we might have a mole on set and Elissa can investigate on that end," Kyle continued.

"I don't think you'll have to look far." Rowan grimaced. "Duke was on set at the time."

Viv sighed and closed her eyes. "I think we have our answer."

Kyle frowned. "Something you want to tell me that didn't come up the other day?"

Viv opened her eyes and shook her head.

"No—"

"I'm sorry," Rowan said softly. He took Viv's hand, raised it to his lips, and kissed her palm. "We don't have to go public, but they need to know. I don't want you in danger, especially if it's my fault."

Kyle crossed his arms and waited.

"Sorry. I lied," Viv said. "Rowan and I have been seeing each other since March. We aren't telling anyone because..."

"Because of my divorce last December," Rowan finished. "I don't think I have to tell anyone here how messy it was." He smiled softly and stroked Viv's cheek with the back of his hand. "I don't want any speculation that Viv's the reason. It's the last thing she needs right now."

"So what does this have to do with Duke Holloway?" Kyle asked.

"It's...well, it's ridiculous," Viv said. "Ever since Duke won the Emmy for Outstanding Supporting Actor, he's let it go to his head. He thinks Rowan is jealous because he didn't win an Emmy—"

"Absolutely ridiculous," Rowan reiterated.

"—and that's why I'm killing off Caiden. Because Rowan and I are seeing each other and I'm getting revenge for him." She shook her head sadly. "That decision was made long before Rowan and me, and I'd never be so petty as to do that to anyone."

Both Rowan and Maddie looked upset.

Kyle nodded. "So you think he's leaking intel about you. All right. Going forward, we're switching hotels, tonight. I have one in mind in Boulder. I'm friendly with their security team. Charlie, you're on twenty-four-seven until HQ verifies Holloway's the leak or identifies who if anyone on set is feeding information. No more public appearances without advance security sweeps. And Rowan—no more talking about logistics with *anyone* outside this room."

"Understood," Rowan said. "Boy, do I."

Kyle looked at Charlie. "You good with twenty-four-seven?"

She nodded. "Yes, Boss. So long as I can have my girl here." She leaned down to pet Flo.

Kyle smiled. "Of course you'll be working with your partner." He turned to Shane. "You good as back-up?"

"Yup."

"Good. Let's pack up and move locations tonight. I want everyone in the new hotel before midnight."

As they filed out, Shane caught Charlie's eye and gave her a small nod.

"What?" she asked.

"Thanks for speaking up for Ben."

Charlie shrugged. "You would have done the same."

"Yeah. That's why I'm saying thanks." He slugged her upper arm the way he used to when they were Swicks. "Sounds like you guys made a great team out there."

Yeah. Team. I'm just one of the guys.

WHAT WOULD Ben think if he knew he'd been on a list of suspects, even for a short time? Did he deserve to know?

She could tell him. But once she did, she'd be asking him to carry a doubt that didn't belong to him. Charlie wasn't willing to do that.

So long as Shane said nothing, neither would she.

Why does it bother me so much?

Because Ben Massey was one of the most upstanding men she'd ever met. And if he thought *she'd* suspected him—of carelessness, of betrayal, of *anything*—she wasn't sure he'd look at her the same way. And that might just break her heart.

Stop with the romance. This isn't BattleLore and you are no princess. Wanting to be one is a liability you can't afford.

Charlie met Flo's eyes again. "All right, girl, let's go check on Viv."

Charlie clipped Flo's leash to her collar and they left the room.

She knocked on Viv's door—two quick raps, pause, then three more, which was their code—and then let herself in with the spare keycard.

Viv gave her a distracted wave. She was pacing angrily back and forth as she argued with someone on the phone.

"No. Absolutely not. We are *not* doing CGI for this. No, you're not going to change my mind. I want it to look real. CGI is just not going to cut it. Look, I don't care what showed up at the..."

She paused, glancing at Charlie. "I need to go. My bodyguard just walked in. Doesn't that make you happy? I have a *bodyguard.* Nope. We're done. Goodbye."

She disconnected and tossed the phone on the bed. She glared at it like it was a snake about to strike. "Do I *have* to take that thing with me?" she asked Charlie.

"I take it somebody's upset with you."

"Yeah. That's one of the producers. Apparently, someone sent another 'warning' to the studio." Vivienne pinched the bridge of her nose. "A photo of me at the Ren Faire, with red crosshairs painted across my head and a demand that they fire me."

Dammit. There were so many people in the crowd, anyone could have taken that photo. *It was probably the second group before they approached.*

"So, what does that have to do with CGI?"

"They want me to come straight home. They see the Caidansworn incident as more of an attack than I do. Honestly, it's just a few entitled fans with their noses bent out of shape. They'll get over it once they see how it all plays out in season three. They don't have my vision. Not even the writers do..."

She stopped and shook her head. "I know how that sounds. Probably like I'm some spoiled director throwing a tantrum. But I know where I want the story to go. It's not the same as what happened in the books, but it's going to work better for the series overall. I don't want to compromise. I don't want to do CGI just because of a few idiots who think they know how to direct the show better than I do.

I'm a Colorado native, and when I read the chapters about the avalanche I pictured it *here*."

Charlie tilted her head. "No, I actually understand about letting your artistic vision come through." She felt a little surprised at herself. "I'm not a director or anything. I'm not even really an artist, but—"

Viv had perked up and was smiling. "What do you do, my dear? You're full of surprises. Come on, tell me." She held up a hand when Charlie started to deflect. "No. Tell me. You've sparked my interest. What do you do on your days off? I know you don't have a suit of armor to polish."

Charlie grinned at that. "I like drawing things."

Viv tilted her head. "Like what?"

"Landscapes, mostly. Sometimes people."

Viv's eyes brightened. "You have to show me sometime, okay?"

Charlie looked at the floor. "Like I said, it's just a little hobby."

"I imagine it's more than that," Vivienne said quietly. "There's some serious depth to you." She grinned and pointed at Charlie. "Does Ben have any idea you—"

Mayday! Mayday!

"Let's get Rowan from his room," Charlie interrupted, already moving toward the door.

"Oh." Viv laughed self-consciously. "No need for that. He's, um—"

"Here!" Rowan called from behind the closed bedroom door. "Give me a sec."

So they're sharing rooms now. Not her business unless it became a security concern, but it was good to know.

"Take your time," Viv called back, then met Charlie's eyes with a sheepish smile.

"Your secret's safe with me," Charlie said. And meant it. She understood wanting to keep something precious hidden from the world.

Hide what you love.

The bedroom door opened and Rowan strode out, wearing a beat-up ball cap with a nondescript t-shirt, jeans, and work boots.

"Morning, Sir Mariel." His eyes went straight to Viv and stayed there. "And how are you, Madam Director?" he asked.

Viv rolled her eyes. "Oh, cut it out," she said.

"Are we ready for today's adventure?" Rowan asked, already crouching to pet Flo. The dog wagged her tail at the attention. Charlie was pretty sure Flo had developed a crush on the handsome actor.

"If all goes well, we *won't* have an adventure," Charlie said.

Rowan chuckled. "Right. Just a boring old day up in the mountains. Got it."

"Have you heard from Ben?" Viv asked. She grabbed a broad-brimmed straw sunhat and a pair of cheap sunglasses off the credenza. She was dressed in yoga pants and a t-shirt that read *Colorado* she'd picked up at a souvenir shop. She didn't look like a high-powered director, just another tourist on vacation.

"I haven't," Charlie admitted.

"He texted me earlier. He's meeting us down in the lobby," Rowan said, straightening. "I'm sure he's there by now."

They gathered Maddie from her room next. She answered the door almost immediately, hair still damp, tablet already in hand like a shield.

"Sorry," she said quickly. "I just needed five minutes to finish syncing the schedule."

"You're fine," Viv said warmly. "We've got plenty of time."

Maddie smiled, looking relieved, and fell into step beside Viv as they walked to the elevators.

Charlie brought up the rear with Flo, scanning the hallway, professional mode engaged. Which was good, because in a few minutes she'd be seeing Ben, and she needed all the professionalism she could muster.

The elevator ride down felt like it took forever and no time at all. Charlie watched the numbers descend, hyper-aware of her reflection in the polished doors. She'd dressed practically—tactical pants, boots, a light jacket that concealed her sidearm. Her dark-blond hair was pulled back in its usual no-nonsense ponytail.

Nothing special. Just Charlie King, bodyguard. One of the guys.

The doors opened.

Charlie spotted Ben immediately. He was standing near the entrance, holding a to-go carrier with five coffees from Riversong and a bag of what Charlie hoped were their breakfast burritos. He was dressed in practical hiking gear—cargo pants, boots, a flannel shirt over a black t-shirt that somehow made him look even broader. She felt sudden, sharp disappointment that he wasn't wearing his Ren Faire kilt. Just the thought of his muscular legs...and the question of whether or not he wore anything underneath made her knees weak.

Stop it.

When Ben saw her, something flickered across his face—warmth, maybe nervousness? His eyes held hers for a beat too long, a faint flush creeping up his neck. right before his gaze moved to Rowan.

Her stomach did an inconvenient flip.

Professional. Stay professional.

"Hey, bud!" Rowan said, clapping his friend on the arm. "Thanks for picking up coffee." He turned to Charlie. "Hey, sorry, when I texted Ben earlier, I didn't know how you take your coffee—"

"I got you a dark roast with a splash of cream," Ben rushed out.

"That's my exact order," Charlie said, keeping her voice steady.

Oh, stop. That mean voice spoke in her head. *You think you're special enough, he knows your coffee order off the top of his head? Pathetic.*

Ben looked relieved. "Th-that's what I'd hoped when I ordered it."

Her heart did a little flip.

April probably told him how you take it now. That mean little voice just wouldn't shut up. And it was probably right. April had teased her after the hundredth time she'd ordered just plain black coffee. 'You know you're allowed to live a little, right?' she'd said as she splashed cream—not half and half—into her coffee. Charlie had to admit it was fantastic. Pretty soon she'd have Charlie putting in sugar or cold foam or something girly like that.

"Thank you. Here let me..." She took the to-go holder and her fingers brushed his, sending the room sideways for a moment. Viv, Rowan, and Maddie eagerly grabbed their coffees.

"I brought some breakfast, too." Ben held up the white paper bag. "I hope breakfast burritos are acceptable. I got several kinds."

"Oh, more than acceptable," Maddie said, looking relaxed for the first time since Charlie had seen her on Saturday night. "Any chorizo ones?"

Ben flicked a glance at Charlie. Chorizo burritos were her favorite.

And oh my God, he knows it.

"I mean," Maddie went on, catching his look, "if no one else wants that kind. Actually, I'll just take whatever." She laughed self-consciously.

Before Charlie could tell her it was fine, Ben spoke.

"I made sure to get several of those, actually." He reached into the bag and pulled out two. "Here you go." He handed one to Maddie, and the other to Charlie without a word.

This will be the best burrito I've ever eaten.

"Dibs on bacon," Rowan said. He winked at Viv. "Because I know you're going to want any of them that are blow-your-head-off spicy."

"Damn straight." Viv took the burrito Ben offered her and thanked him.

Flo looked up at Ben with all the hope she could muster in her eyes.

"Don't worry, girl," Ben told her as he knelt. He reached into the bag and pulled out a clear plastic bag tied with a pink bow. "It's not a burrito, but it's a bag of Riversong's Doggie Snax."

And...I think my ovaries just exploded.

He looked up at Charlie. "But only if it's okay with you?"

Ka-boom. Ka-boom.

"I think Flo would never speak to me again if I said no." She couldn't hold back her smile.

Especially when Ben beamed back at her.

And...there goes every last lady bit I had left. Ka-blooey.

"Are we ready?" Charlie was amazed her voice didn't shake.

"Do we need to wait for Shane? Is he coming, too?" Viv asked Charlie.

"He'll be by tonight. Right now, he's coordinating with Elissa at HQ in LA. They're tracking down our leak." She switched Flo's leash to her hand holding the burrito. "So it's just us today."

Ben cleared his throat. "Rowan told me where you all are headed. If you don't mind, I could show you around up there. I know these mountains like the back of my hand. I grew up in them. Hiking, camping, war games with my friends, the whole nine yards."

"War games? And fought dragons too, I imagine?" She was grinning, clearly teasing him.

Ben's ears went slightly red. "Nope. Just soldiers. I was the only one into fantasy back then."

"Hard to believe," Rowan said. "You make the best medieval weapons and armor I've ever seen."

"And jewelry," Viv added. "Don't think for a minute I missed your display case the other day."

Ben, who played war games in these mountains, knows them like the back of his hand. Charlie filed that information away alongside Ben the skilled metalworker, Ben the fantasy nerd.

Ben the Ranger.

She'd picked up bits and pieces about Ben's service from parties and their mutual friends. Honorable discharge. Exemplary service record. Tactical training that rivaled her own. And of course they'd fought side by side at the old ski resort, each having the other's back.

Warrior recognizes warrior, she thought, then immediately shoved the thought down where it belonged.

Charlie pulled her keys out of her pocket. "The SUV's this way."

They crossed the lobby to a door leading to the parking garage. She hadn't used the valet service—she didn't want anyone in the vehicle. She couldn't be too careful.

The parking garage was dim and cool, their footsteps echoing off concrete. Charlie led them to her SUV parked in the corner. She'd chosen the spot for its clear sightlines to the entrance and exit.

"All right," Charlie said, unlocking the vehicle. "Viv, Rowan, Maddie—you're in the back seat. Ben, you're up front. I might need you to navigate."

"Yeah. Of course." He climbed in, and the SUV dipped slightly under his weight. Charlie walked Flo to the rear and opened the hatch. Flo hopped in obediently, settling into her travel crate with a contented huff.

Charlie did a final walk around the vehicle—tires, undercarriage, no signs of tampering. The whole time, she couldn't help but think about Morrison sabotaging Shelly's car. She sent up a silent prayer that Shelly was doing well.

She slid into the driver's seat and immediately became hyper-aware of Ben beside her. The SUV suddenly felt smaller. Charlie caught a faint scent of cedar and woodsmoke, probably from his forge. They set their coffees in the cup holders at the same time and their hands brushed.

Focus.

Charlie started the engine and pulled out of the garage, checking her mirrors.

"So which one are we going to first?" Maddie asked from the back, tablet already open. "We have Eisenhower Tunnel, Berthoud Pass, and Loveland Pass."

Charlie turned to Ben. "Navigator?"

"Berthoud first. That should take us just over an hour and put us there around nine. Then Eisenhower's about half an hour from there. After Eisenhower, we'll head for Loveland Pass. That's a quick drive, maybe twenty minutes. Then it's an hour and a half back to the hotel. I imagine we'll get back here around seven tonight."

"Long day," Viv said.

Ben turned in his seat. "Are you sure about Eisenhower Tunnel?"

Viv nodded. "I know what you're saying. Aldric and his knights are supposed to be cut off, isolated when Felldark triggers the avalanche. I grew up on the Western Slope and the last place in Colorado that says Felldark's Mountain Keep is the Tunnel. But, CDOT's guaranteed to set off at least one avalanche there that we can film. With the right angle, it *might* work." She was sounding less hopeful.

"Which one do you think best matches the scenery in your head?"

Charlie glanced at Ben. He was smiling. "Not the Eisenhower Tunnel, that's for sure. Berthoud and Loveland have potential. There are old mines up there too, for when Aldric and Caiden are in the secret tunnels. And the Seven Sisters almost guarantee you'll have your avalanche."

"Seven Sisters?" Viv asked.

Maddie nodded as she looked over her tablet. "At Loveland, right? There are seven avalanche paths that converge."

"Perfect name, at least," Viv said.

Charlie glanced at Ben again. "You know the area well?"

"I do." He half-turned to look at Viv. "Shane and I used to camp up there with our friends. Waylon, nearly broke his ankle jumping across a creek one time. Bear had to carry him three miles back to the trailhead."

Rowan laughed. "I remember you telling me that story. Didn't Waylon claim he could've walked if you'd just let him?"

"Oh yeah. Until Bear told him to prove it and he turned green." Ben's smile was warm, easy. This was his element—talking about the mountains, his brothers, the place he knew better than anywhere. Charlie watched his hands as he gestured, describing the terrain. Big hands, scarred from forge work, but gentle when he'd helped Shelly into the truck. When he'd steadied Charlie at the Faire with his hand warm against her back.

Stop it.

"Charlie?" Viv's voice pulled her back.

"Yeah?"

"Sorry, don't mean to distract you when you're driving. I was just wondering since you're a huge fan of the books, what did you think of my changes for the show last season?"

Charlie navigated around a slow-moving truck before answering. "I think combining Sir Godwin with Sir Mariel into one character made sense for screen time. And honestly?" She glanced at Viv in the rearview. "Caiden dying in season two is going to wreck people, but it's the right call."

"Thank you!" Viv threw her hands up. "See, Rowan? Someone gets it."

"*I* get it," Rowan said. "I just also get that Duke is going to make my life hell until we wrap."

"Why do you think it's the right call?" Ben asked Charlie, genuine curiosity in his voice.

Charlie's fingers tightened on the wheel. "Because in the books, Caiden disappearing for a whole novel weakens Aldric's arc. He spends *Throne of Ash* grieving, and it's powerful, but then Caiden comes back and it undercuts everything. On screen, if you actually kill him? Aldric has to become the king without his chronicler. He has to *be* a legend that lasts instead of having someone who worships the ground he walks on exaggerate or embellish his story."

Silence from the back seat.

Ben was staring at her.

"What?" Charlie asked, defensive.

"Nothing. That's just—" Ben cleared his throat. "That's exactly what I thought when I read book three. Caiden coming back felt like a cheat."

"Right?" Charlie felt herself relaxing despite the confined space. "Don't get me wrong, I cried when he showed up at the Battle of Ashenmoor. But story-wise—"

"It weakened the stakes," Ben finished.

They looked at each other for a beat too long, and Charlie forced her eyes back to the road.

"You two are adorable," Viv said, not even trying to hide her smile.

"When we get up to the Eisenhower Tunnel, we should talk about camera angles," Maddie said quickly, bless her. "For the avalanche scene."

Charlie tuned out the conversation as Viv, Rowan, and Maddie discussed technical details. She focused on driving the road winding up into the foothills to distract her from the fact that Ben was sitting eighteen inches away and they'd just had an entire conversation about character arcs and narrative structure.

He reads the same books I do. He thinks about story the same way I do.

Hide what you love.

But he already knew what a *BattleLore* nerd she was. And Ben hadn't looked at her like she was ridiculous for caring about fantasy novels. He'd looked at her like—

Like he understood. Because that was him, too.

TEN

The road climbed steadily as they approached Berthoud Pass, and Ben watched the landscape transform through the windshield. Ponderosa pine gave way to spruce and fir, the trees growing shorter and more gnarled until they surrendered entirely to the alpine zone. The morning sun hit the mountains at an angle that made the distant peaks glow, and Ben felt the familiar pull of this place—the quiet, the vastness, the sense of being close to something ancient and indifferent and beautiful. He loved these mountains. Always had.

Memories filled his head—like the summer he was sixteen and Shane piled everyone into his pickup with all their camping gear. One minute the sky had been blue; the next, freezing rain had hammered Gabe, Waylon, and Elias in the truck bed while Ben, Shane, and Bear laughed like idiots. Waylon's face plastered to the back window still made him grin. He didn't have a care in the world back then.

The mountains had been his playground as a kid, his classroom as a soldier, his refuge when he needed to think. Shane used to joke that

Ben was part mountain goat, the way he could navigate terrain that made other people nervous. He'd driven this route hundreds of times.

Today, Charlie sat eighteen inches to his left, her hands steady on the wheel, her attention focused on the winding road ahead. She handled the wheel like she handled everything else—precise, economical, no wasted motion. The SUV hummed steadily as she navigated the grade.

He was much too aware of her beside him. The faint scent of her shampoo. The way her shoulders squared when she checked the mirrors. Ben stole a glance at Charlie every time she picked up the coffee. The way her expression softened just slightly each time she took a sip. How she'd looked at him when he'd handed it to her—*that's my exact order*—like he'd done something more significant than remembering she took it with a splash of cream, no sugar after April had teased her about it.

Same thing with the chorizo burritos. He'd heard her mention them once at a Watchdog party months ago, talking to Shane about their SWCC days and the breakfast burritos at some dive near Coronado. Ben had filed it away automatically. But the way that she'd looked so grateful when he'd said he'd gotten extras, you would have thought he'd just bought her a house.

It told him she wasn't used to having someone pay basic attention to her. That sat heavy in his chest. He felt lonely on her behalf.

Then there was the way she occupied space. On duty, she moved like she owned every inch of it—confident, capable, unshakeable. Off-hours, she folded inward just slightly, like someone who'd learned early not to ask for too much.

Only girl in a house full of brothers, she'd mentioned once. Judging by the way she acted sometimes, he doubted they'd been the protective kind.

Maybe that was why she was always on her guard.

Well, not always. He thought about the way she smiled when she thought no one was watching. Not the professional bodyguard smile she gave clients or the easy camaraderie she shared with Shane and the other guys. But the real one, rare and unguarded, that made something in Ben's chest pull tight.

He'd seen that smile Saturday at the Faire, after they'd gotten Viv and Rowan to safety. On their way back to the forge, she'd caught sight of the ring with the elephant rides and her smile was a mix of surprise and pure delight. He wished she'd had a reason to smile like that all the time—unguarded.

"Ben?"

He blinked, realizing Charlie had said his name twice.

"Sorry, what?"

"The turnoff. Is it coming up?"

"Yeah, just ahead." He pointed. "The summit parking lot. You'll see the warming hut."

She nodded, already adjusting her approach, scanning the road ahead with the same tactical precision she brought to everything.

Behind them, Viv and Maddie were talking about sight lines and camera placement, Rowan chiming in occasionally. Ben let their voices fade. He was thinking about how excited he was to share his mountains with Charlie. He wanted her to see what he saw. The way snow moved across the tundra, how wind shaped the landscape.

Charlie eased the SUV into the Berthoud Pass Summit parking lot, gravel crunching under the tires. From here, the switchbacks below were clearly visible, etched into the mountainside like a sidewinder.

Ben stepped out as soon as the vehicle had fully stopped, his body already adjusting to the elevation, the thinner air, the relentless wind at eleven thousand feet. He stuffed down the urge to go around the SUV and open Charlie's door for her. It wasn't his place right now, but he was determined that as long as she wasn't working, he'd make sure she felt taken care of in all the tiny ways she deserved. Instead, he opened the back door for Viv and Maddie, while Rowan got out on Charlie's side. The wind tugged at their jackets and carried the faint scent of stone and sun-warmed trees.

Ben scanned the slopes automatically—old habits from Range

training, from too many missions where terrain meant the difference between success and catastrophe.

Charlie opened the back and Flo jumped down, immediately at her side. After she snapped Flo's leash into place, Ben watched as she took in the landscape. Her posture shifted—still alert, still professional, but something in her expression opened. Appreciation, he hoped.

"This is a good example of readable terrain," he said, loud enough for everyone to hear. "You can see where snow would move. Where it would stop. Nothing's hidden."

"It has potential," Viv said, already moving toward the edge of the parking area. "Maddie, can you bring up some winter photos?"

"One sec." Maddie handed her tablet to Viv, who was all-director now, quiet and serious as she looked from the screen to the landscape in front of her, and back again. Rowan went to Viv's other side and studied the photos.

Flo sniffed the wind, her tail wagging slowly, and Ben crouched to scratch behind her ears.

"She likes you," Charlie said.

Ben looked up. Charlie was watching him, something soft in her expression that made his heart speed up inconveniently.

"I like her too," he said. Then, because he couldn't quite help himself, he added, "Good judge of character, dogs."

Charlie's mouth quirked. Almost a smile. "Is that so?"

"Absolutely." He stood, brushing gravel off his knees. "They know who's safe. Who's steady."

"And who brings them treats tied with pink bows?"

There it was. The real smile. The one that made his pulse kick.

"That too," Ben admitted, grinning back at her.

For a moment, they just stood there, the wind pulling at their hair, the mountains spread out before them like an invitation. Ben wanted to tell her things he had no business saying—that she looked beautiful with her hair whipping around her face, that he'd been thinking about her since Saturday, that he'd bring her a hundred cups of coffee the way she liked it made if it meant she'd look at him like this again.

Instead, he cleared his throat and pointed toward the slope in front of them.

"See those paths?" he said. "The ones that look like wide chutes running down? Those are called the Eighties and Nineties. Old ski runs from when this was still a resort. Now they're just avalanche terrain. CDOT monitors them pretty closely."

Charlie followed his gesture, her tactical mind already working. "How often do they slide?"

Viv had wandered over, Rowan and Maddie trailing behind. Ben had everyone's attention now.

"Depends on the winter. Heavy snow year? Multiple times. They've got Gazex systems on some of the paths—remote-controlled explosives that trigger slides before they get dangerous."

"Gazex," Charlie repeated, filing it away.

"That's where we'd film the controlled avalanche," Viv said.

"Exactly." He pointed further south. "Path Five—Stanley—has five Gazex units. That's probably your best bet for filming. Safe, predictable, still dramatic."

"Which one would look best on camera?" Rowan asked Viv.

She considered. "Stanley's got good sight lines. We could set up on the road below, get the full path in frame."

"If you want something more exposed, more dangerous-looking?" Ben gestured toward the eastern peaks. "The Mines paths are bigger. Steeper. More... consequential."

"Consequential," Viv echoed, her eyes lighting up. "I like that word."

Ben felt Charlie's gaze on him again. When he glanced over, she was studying him with an expression he couldn't quite read. Curious, maybe. Or impressed.

He'd take either one.

"Can we get closer?" Viv asked, already moving toward the edge of the parking area where a viewing platform overlooked the western slopes.

Ben led the way, Charlie and Flo falling in beside him. The group spread out along the platform, and Ben pointed out the features of the terrain—the natural chutes carved by decades of avalanches, the rocky outcroppings that would catch and hold snow, the wind-loaded cornices that would form along the ridgelines come winter.

Maddie took notes on her tablet while Viv asked practical questions about access roads and talked about filming permits. She was already framing shots with her hands, muttering about camera placement and lighting angles.

"The Continental Divide Trail runs right through here," Ben said, gesturing to the trail marker near the warming hut. "In winter, this whole area becomes backcountry skiing terrain. You'd have people hiking up and skiing down all day. Might complicate your filming schedule."

"We're coordinating with CDOT and the Forest Service anyway," Viv said. "They close the road for a few hours, control the avalanche, we'll get our shots."

Charlie had wandered a few steps away, Flo at her side, looking out over the tundra stretching toward the distant peaks. The wind whipped her ponytail sideways, and she tilted her face up to the sun like she was drinking in the altitude and the light.

Ben wanted to go stand beside her. Wanted to point out the landmarks he knew by heart—Stanley Mountain to the southwest, Vasquez Peak to the west, Colorado Mines Peak to the east. Wanted to tell her about the time he and the guys had camped up here at the end of August and woken to four inches of fresh snow, or the afternoon Bear had spotted a moose at fifty yards and they'd all frozen like they were on patrol.

But she looked peaceful standing there alone, and Ben didn't want to intrude.

"All right," Viv said, grabbing her hat just as the wind tried to whip it away. "I've seen enough here. Let's check out the Eisenhower Tunnel area."

"We can hit Georgetown for lunch, if you're getting hungry," Ben said.

"Sounds good," Rowan said.

"Everyone ready?" Charlie asked, turning back toward the SUV. "Make sure you're drinking water. I brought plenty of bottles."

They piled back in, Ben taking his navigator seat up front. Charlie pulled out of the parking lot and started the winding descent toward Georgetown. The road dropped through switchbacks, trees gradually thickening again as they lost elevation. Charlie handled the curves with the same steady competence she brought to everything, and Ben found himself relaxing into the rhythm of it—the hum of the engine, the shifting light through the windshield, the easy conversation from the back seat.

"Georgetown's an old silver mining town," Ben said as they approached the final curves before town. "Lot of history. Good sandwiches, too."

"Where are we stopping?" Maddie asked.

"There's a little mom and pop place called Mountain Buzz Cafe," Ben said. "Best sandwiches in town, and we can grab them to go. There's a good spot near the Eisenhower Tunnel where we can eat with a view."

Charlie glanced at him. "You've got this whole day planned out, don't you?"

"Maybe." Ben grinned. "Is that okay?"

"It's perfect," Viv said from the back seat before Charlie could answer. "I love a man with a plan."

Rowan laughed. "She really does."

Georgetown appeared below them—a cluster of Victorian buildings tucked into the valley, the old Georgetown Loop Railroad visible as a thin line cutting through the canyon. Charlie followed Ben's directions down the main street, past historic storefronts and restaurants, until they reached Mountain Buzz Cafe.

"I'll run in," Ben said. "What does everyone want?"

They called out orders—turkey and Swiss for Viv, Italian sub for Rowan, veggie wrap for Maddie. Charlie hesitated.

"The roast beef's good," Ben offered. "Or they've got a killer chicken salad."

"Roast beef," Charlie said. "Thanks."

Ben mentally added *roast beef sandwiches* to the growing list of things Charlie liked, right below chorizo burritos and coffee with a splash of cream.

Small victories.

He jogged into the cafe, placed the order, and waited by the counter while they assembled the sandwiches. Through the window, he could see Charlie leaning against the SUV, Flo sitting at her feet, both of them watching the street. Always scanning. Always aware. Always ready.

The guy behind the counter called his number, and Ben grabbed the bag of sandwiches and a carrier with five drinks—black coffee with cream for Charlie, because he'd noticed her cup from this morning was empty.

When he climbed back into the SUV, he handed Charlie her coffee first.

"You didn't have to do that," she said, but she was smiling.

"I know," Ben said. And he did know. He just wanted to anyway.

The Eisenhower Tunnel sat like a concrete bunker carved into the mountain, swallowing westbound traffic in steady pulses. Charlie pulled into a designated overlook area just east of the tunnel entrance, and they climbed out into air that smelled of trees and diesel exhaust.

"Well," Viv said, hands on her hips as she surveyed the scene. "This is... brutalist."

She wasn't wrong. The tunnel portal dominated the view—massive, utilitarian, designed for function over form. Above it, Interstate 70 cut a wide swath through the landscape, guardrails and concrete barriers marching up the slope. It was impressive from an engineering standpoint. From a cinematic one? Not so much.

"The avalanche paths are up there," Ben said, pointing to the steep slopes above the highway. "Loop Road, Batch Plant, Whistler. CDOT's got eight Gazex systems on Loop Road alone."

Maddie was taking notes, but even she looked dubious. "It's very... visible. All the infrastructure, I mean."

"That's the problem," Viv said, rubbing her temples. She asked Maddie to pull up a conceptual rendering showing Lord Felldark's Mountain Keep perched on an isolated peak, surrounded by nothing but snow and stone.

Rowan unwrapped his sandwich as he leaned against the SUV. "This doesn't read as remote. It reads as 'busy highway with avalanche danger.'"

"Could we shoot it from a different angle? Make the tunnel disappear?" Maddie asked.

"Maybe," Viv said, but she didn't sound convinced. "Ben, do you know any secret spots?"

Ben had been quiet, chewing thoughtfully on his roast beef sandwich while he studied the terrain. Now he gestured up the slope with his free hand.

"If you hiked up about half a mile," he said, "got above the infrastructure—say, near the Loop Road path—you could frame the shot to avoid the highway entirely. Get nothing but mountain and sky. The avalanche chute would still be dramatic, you'd just need permission to position your cameras up there."

"That could work," Viv said. "If we're shooting from above, we wouldn't see any of the road, but I'm still not sure about the angle." She rubbed her temples again.

"Do you want to see it from there?" Ben asked.

Viv shook her head. "No. Honestly, I think the altitude is getting to me. I've been too long at sea level."

"Hang on," Charlie said. She jogged back to the SUV and opened the back. She returned a minute later with three canisters.

"O_2," she said as she passed them out to Viv, Rowan, and Maddie. "You just flip the top up, point the nozzle at your mouth, and press down on the top."

"Oh, I'd forgotten these existed," Viv said as she studied the canister and flipped the top open. She closed her eyes and took a couple of breaths. "That's better."

Viv studied the slope, then looked back at the photo. She sighed. "It's not... right." She turned to Ben. "What about Loveland Pass? The Seven Sisters, right?"

"Different animal entirely," Ben said. "More exposed. More dangerous. But also more isolated. No guardrails, no tunnel, nothing that screams 'modern highway.' Just switchbacks cutting through avalanche terrain."

Viv's eyes lit up. "That's what I want. That's Felldark's Mountain."

Charlie had been eating her sandwich quietly, Flo lying at her feet with her head on her paws. Now she looked at Ben. "How much more dangerous are we talking?"

"The Seven Sisters are seven separate avalanche paths that all converge on the same stretch of road," Ben said. "The pass sits at almost twelve thousand feet. No guardrails on a lot of it. In winter, avalanches have pushed cars right off the road. The Gazex systems up there fail pretty regularly—self-destruct, freeze up, you name it."

"So it's the real deal," Viv said.

"It's the real deal," Ben confirmed.

Viv looked at Rowan, who shrugged. "If that's where you want to film, that's where we'll film. I trust you."

"Then let's not waste any more time here," Viv said, already wrapping up the rest of her sandwich. "How far is Loveland Pass?"

"Twenty minutes," Ben said. "Maybe less."

"Perfect." Viv climbed back into the SUV. "Let's go see the Seven Sisters."

Charlie met Ben's eyes as she opened the driver's door. "You good with that?"

"Yeah," Ben said. "I want you to see it. It's worth seeing."

And he did want her to see it. Not just because Viv needed a filming location, but because Loveland Pass was the kind of place that demanded respect. The kind of place where you felt small and mortal and alive all at once. The kind of place that separated people who understood the mountains from people who just looked at them.

Charlie King, Ben was willing to bet, would understand.

They piled back into the SUV, and Charlie pulled out of the overlook, merging smoothly onto I-70 westbound. The tunnel swallowed them for a moment—bright sunlight to sudden darkness to bright sunlight again—and then they were climbing toward Exit 216.

In the back seat, Viv was already talking strategy with Maddie and Rowan. But up front, Charlie was quiet, focused on the road, one hand on the wheel and the other resting on the center console.

Ben finished his sandwich, balled up the wrapper, and stuffed it in the bag at his feet. Through the windshield, the mountains rose higher, sharper, the peaks ahead dusted with early snow that hadn't melted even in August.

Twenty minutes to Loveland Pass.

Twenty minutes until Charlie saw the Seven Sisters.

Ben found himself hoping she'd look at the mountains the same way she'd looked at the elephant rides at the Faire—with that unguarded smile that made his chest go tight.

He wanted to see that smile again.

ELEVEN

The road to Loveland Pass climbed higher than Charlie had expected. Higher than Berthoud, higher than the Eisenhower Tunnel. The SUV's engine worked harder as they switchbacked up US-6, the pavement narrowing, the shoulders disappearing.

Charlie's hands stayed light on the wheel, but her attention sharpened. This wasn't the tourist-friendly summit they'd just left. This was serious terrain.

Beside her, Ben sat forward slightly, his gaze tracking the landscape. Not nervous—just aware. The same way she was aware when entering a room for the first time, cataloging exits and sight lines and potential threats.

Except Ben was reading the mountain itself.

"Almost there," he said quietly. "The summit's just ahead."

The road crested, and suddenly the world opened up.

Charlie eased into a wide pullout near the summit marker—11,990 feet, the sign proclaimed—and killed the engine. For a moment, nobody spoke.

The view stole everyone's breath.

Mountains stretched in every direction, ridge after ridge folding into the distance like frozen waves. The sky was so blue it hurt to look at, and the wind—God, the wind never stopped up here. It poured over the pass like an invisible river, cold and clean and relentless.

But it was the terrain directly below them that held Charlie's attention.

Seven massive chutes carved down the mountainside, converging on the road like fingers reaching for prey. The switchbacks cut directly through them—no guardrails, no barriers, just asphalt and air and a long drop to the rocks below.

Charlie's artist brain kicked in automatically, the way it always did when confronted with something worth capturing. She could see the drawing already—the brutal geometry of the switchbacks against the organic chaos of the avalanche paths. The way light and shadow played across the slopes. The sense of scale, of exposure, of consequence.

She'd need charcoal for this, maybe conte crayon. Something that could capture the rawness, the weight of all that stone and sky. Pencil would be too delicate. Watercolor too soft. This landscape demanded something bolder.

"Holy shit," Viv breathed from the back seat.

"Yeah," Rowan said.

Maddie was already out of the vehicle, tablet forgotten, just staring.

Charlie climbed out more slowly, Flo at her heels. The wind hit her immediately, strong enough to make her stagger. She leaned into it, letting it anchor her to this moment, this place.

Ben appeared at her side, close enough that she could hear him over the wind. "What do you think?"

What did she think? She thought this was the kind of landscape that painters spent their whole lives trying to capture and never quite got right. The kind of place that made you want to sit down with a sketchbook and not leave until you'd committed every line, every shadow, every impossible angle to paper.

"It's perfect," she said, and meant it in ways that had nothing to do with filming.

Ben's expression shifted—pleased, maybe a little surprised. Like he'd hoped she'd understand but hadn't been sure.

"Come on," he said. "I'll show you the Sisters."

He led them to the edge of the pullout where the slope dropped away in a dizzying sweep. One by one, he pointed out the avalanche paths, naming them like they were old friends.

"First Sister, closest to the summit. Second Sister just below that. See how they funnel together? By the time you get to the Seventh Sister down there—" he gestured to where the road made its final hairpin turn "—you've got all seven paths converging on the same hundred yards of asphalt."

Charlie studied the terrain with a protector's eye first—sight lines, escape routes, places where things could go catastrophically wrong. But underneath that professional assessment, her artist's mind was already sketching. The sweeping curves of the chutes. The sharp angles where rock met sky. The way the road looked so fragile, so temporary, cutting through all that permanence.

She wanted to draw this. Needed to, the way she sometimes needed to capture a face or a landscape before it slipped away from memory.

"In winter," Ben continued, "when these paths load up with snow, they become terrain traps. Vehicles get caught in slides, pushed off the road. People die up here."

"But CDOT monitors them?" Viv asked.

"Yeah, but the Gazex systems fail all the time. They self-destruct, freeze, malfunction. It's harsh up here. Equipment doesn't last." Ben's voice carried the weight of someone who'd seen what happened when systems failed. "If you're going to film here, you need to be smart about it. Controlled avalanche, staged carefully, everyone in safe positions."

"That's exactly what we want, of course," Viv said. "Are there old mines here, too?"

"Yes. They're everywhere, if you know how to look."

Viv was glowing now, energized in a way she hadn't been at the tunnel. "This is it. This is Lord Felldark's Mountain."

Maddie was taking photos, Rowan was walking the length of the pullout, and Viv pulled out her phone to call someone—probably the studio, Charlie guessed.

Ben stayed beside Charlie, both of them looking out over the Seven Sisters.

"You're quiet," he said.

Charlie glanced at him. "Just thinking."

"About?"

She hesitated. This was the part where she usually deflected, kept people at arm's length. But Ben had shared his mountains with her today. He'd explained terrain the way some people talked about their friends.

He'd trusted her with something he loved.

Maybe she could trust him with something small.

"I'm thinking about how I'd draw this," she admitted. "What materials I'd use. How to capture the scale of it without losing the detail."

Ben turned to look at her fully, and something in his expression made her chest go tight.

"The colored pens and markers on your desk." He grinned. "They aren't just for color-coding spreadsheets."

Charlie felt herself smile. "No, they aren't."

"You'd want to draw this?" he asked.

"Yeah." She felt herself flush slightly, unsure why she was embarrassed. "I mean, if I had time. If I came back up here when I wasn't working."

"Plein air," Ben said.

Charlie blinked. "You know that term?"

"Sure." His mouth quirked. "I'm a metalworker. I know artists. And I've seen enough landscape painters set up at the Faire to know what plein air means."

Of course he did. Because Ben wasn't just a blacksmith who happened to read fantasy novels. He was someone who paid attention. Who noticed things.

Who remembered her coffee order and her favorite burrito and apparently the colored pens on her desk.

"I'd bring you back," Ben said quietly. "If you w-wanted. To d-draw it, I mean."

Charlie listened to him hum "The Lady of Shalott" under his breath. Her chest tightened.

"You would?"

"Yeah." He held her gaze. "Whenever you wanted. I know this area well. I could show you good spots. Places with the right light, the right angles."

I should say no. I should keep this professional.

But she didn't want to say no.

"I'd like that," Charlie said.

Ben's smile was slow, genuine, reaching all the way to his eyes. "Yeah?"

"Yeah."

The wind pulled at their hair, cold and sharp and carrying the scent of snow from the peaks above. Flo pressed against Charlie's leg, her warmth grounding.

Viv's voice carried over from where she stood with Rowan and Maddie, something about camera permits and weather windows. The professional part of Charlie's brain noted that they'd probably be here another thirty minutes, maybe forty-five, going over logistics.

But right now, standing at the edge of the Seven Sisters with Ben beside her, Charlie let herself just be here. Just be present in this moment, in this place, with this man who wanted to bring her back so she could draw mountains.

"Thank you," she said. "For today. For showing us all this."

"My pleasure," Ben said. And from the way he looked at her, she believed him.

CHARLIE ESCORTED VIV, Rowan, and Maddie through the hotel lobby to the elevators, Flo padding quietly at her side. Her shoulders ached from the drive and her brain was still processing the day—Ben explaining geological formations, avalanches, Colorado history. Ben catching her eye as she imagined capturing the landscape and smiling like she was the view he'd come to see.

Hide what you love.

But it was getting harder.

"I'm exhausted," Viv said, stretching. "Maddie, can you send me those location photos before you crash?"

"Already queued up," Maddie said, tapping her tablet. "Should hit your inbox momentarily."

"You're a miracle worker."

Maddie beamed back at her. "I work for the best."

The elevator doors opened and everyone got in.

Viv looked at Charlie. "Are we good for the night?"

"Shane's coming to debrief about the investigation."

"Oh." That one syllable said volumes.

"Don't worry. You don't need to be there for it. I can check in before you go to sleep and let you know what he's found, or it can wait until tomorrow."

"Let's go with option two." Viv squeezed her arm. "Thank you. For everything today."

Charlie nodded, throat tight. Many clients treated you like you were furniture. Some even got belligerent when all you were trying to do was protect them. Viv had treated her like she mattered beyond just the security she provided.

The elevator doors opened on their floor. After saying their good nights, Viv, Rowan, and Maddie headed for their rooms. Charlie turned and found Ben standing beside the elevator, hands in his pockets, looking uncertain.

"I should probably—" he started.

"Yeah, I need to—" Charlie said at the same time.

They both stopped. Ben's ears went red.

"You first," Charlie said.

"I was just going to say I should head out. Let you get back to work." He shifted his weight. "Unless you need me to... I don't know. Stick around?"

Yes. Stay. Please.

"Shane's coming to brief me on what he and Elissa found," Charlie heard herself say. "But thanks for today. You were really helpful."

Helpful. God, could she sound more like she was thanking a coworker?

Ben nodded, that uncertain look still on his face. "Right. Yeah. No problem."

He was leaving. He was going to head down to the lobby and she'd eat room service alone until Shane arrived, and the next time she saw Ben they'd do this awkward dance again and—

The elevator doors opened and Shane stepped out, Pete at his side. His eyes went from Charlie to Ben and back again, and that knowing smirk appeared.

"King. Moose." He nodded at both of them. "Perfect timing. Let's debrief." He looked at Charlie. "Your room?"

"Yeah. There's a decent-sized table we can use." Charlie's professional mask slammed back into place. "This way." Charlie led them down the hall, hyper-aware of Ben behind her. She unlocked the door and they filed in. The room was nice but generic—table, chairs, queen-sized bed, small fridge, and a credenza.

Shane pulled out one of the chairs and sat down. Charlie started to take the one beside him when Ben reached past her and grabbed it. It took her a second to realize he wasn't claiming the chair for himself, but pulling it out for her. When was the last time anyone had done that for her?

Shane took his laptop out and set it up on the table. "Okay, so

Elissa and I have been digging into the online chatter. Found something interesting."

He pulled up screenshots and turned the laptop around. "There's a figure coordinating the Caidansworn. Calls himself 'The Chronicler.'"

Charlie and Ben exchanged looks. "It ties back to Caiden Bramble's role in the books," Charlie said. "He's supposed to be the one who chronicles Aldric's legend. The loyal companion who records everything."

Ben nodded slowly. "In the books, Caiden keeps a journal. It becomes a holy text for the Embersworn after he's believed dead."

Shane smirked. "Yeah, Elissa already explained it to me. Y'all are nerds."

"Asshole," Charlie and Ben said at the same time. The surprised expression on Ben's face when he looked at her made Charlie bark out a laugh.

Totally worth it to see him laugh, too.

"Takes two to know one," Shane told them.

"The Chronicler is the perfect handle for someone leaking information," Charlie said. "Any luck finding him?"

"Nope. Problem is, we can't find The Chronicler's actual account. He doesn't post himself. Other fans reference him instead. 'The Chronicler says,' 'The Chronicler knows,' that kind of thing. He's feeding them information somehow, but we can't trace the source."

"Duke Holloway?" Charlie asked.

Shane's expression darkened. "Can't prove it's him. But can't prove it's *not* him either. The timing lines up—whenever Duke's on set, new 'Chronicler intel' appears within hours. But if it's him, he's careful. He's got someone else doing the posting, and it always seems to be someone new breaking the news."

"Maybe he's using different accounts?"

Shane shook his head. "Not according to Elissa. They all check out as legit people with longstanding accounts."

"So we're stuck," Charlie said.

"For now. Elissa's still digging." Shane studied Charlie. "How was today? Any incidents?"

"Easy day. No one followed us, no unusual activity at the locations. Viv's happy with the sites."

"Good. I'll email you the posts we found."

"I'll start reading them and see if there's anything—"

Just then, Charlie's stomach decided it would be a great time to embarrass her with a growl.

"First, you're going to go eat something that isn't a protein bar." Shane closed his laptop and stood.

Charlie blinked. "Actually, Ben's fed me well today. I'm fine—"

"King." Shane's voice went firm. "You've been on since Saturday. You need a break. I've got this tonight."

"I can just order room service, or better yet, we could all get a pizza."

"Pizza sounds great—" Shane started.

"Or," Ben spoke up, "I can continue feeding you well, Charlie. There's a nice restaurant downstairs." He looked pointedly at Shane.

Charlie's heart started hammering.

"Even better idea, Moose," Shane said. "I'll get outta your hair. I've got the room across from Rowan's. You've got your phone. Anything happens, I'll call and you're back in thirty seconds." He moved toward the door, then paused. "That's an order, King. Good night, Moose."

He couldn't close the door fast enough behind him.

The sudden silence in the hotel room was deafening.

"I, uh." Ben's voice was quiet. "It wasn't—I mean, I shouldn't assume—"

Charlie's head snapped toward him.

"It's fine," Charlie said quickly. "You don't have to feed me; you should go enjoy your dinner."

"No."

"No?"

"I'd really like it if you'd have dinner with me, Charlie."

Her mouth went dry. Ben Massey was asking her to dinner. Right now. This was happening.

Not out of pity. Not because Shane set it up.

Because he wanted to.

Say yes, her heart screamed. *Say yes say yes say yes—*

"I'm not exactly dressed for a nice restaurant," she heard herself say as she ran a hand through her wind-tangled ponytail, and wanted to punch herself.

Ben's mouth quirked. "I'm not dressed for it either. But I don't think they'll kick us out for tactical pants and flannel."

Charlie felt a smile pulling at her lips despite herself. "You sure about that?"

"Pretty sure." He took a step closer. "So? Will you have dinner with me?"

Hide what you love.

But maybe—just maybe—she didn't have to anymore.

"Yeah," Charlie said. "Yeah, I'd like that. Just give me a sec to do something with my hair so I don't walk in looking like I have a rat's nest on my head."

"You look like a woman who's spent a happy day in the mountains." He lowered his voice. "You look gr-great."

Her cheeks heated. "Thank you."

The smile that broke across Ben's face was worth the risk.

TWELVE

The restaurant was even nicer than Charlie expected—white tablecloths, candlelight, soft music playing in the background. She felt suddenly, acutely aware of her tactical pants and the ponytail she'd hastily redone in the bathroom mirror. She wished she'd at least brought along some mascara and made a mental note to add it to her go-bag.

And yet, Ben looked at her like she was...well, a princess.

Butterflies fluttered in her stomach as Ben held the restaurant door for her, and again when he pulled out her chair before she could even think to sit down. The gesture made her chest go warm.

"Thank you," she said, settling into the seat.

"Of course." Ben took the chair across from her, looking equally out of place in his flannel and cargo pants. But that quiet confidence he showed the maître d' made it work.

Their server appeared with menus and water glasses. Charlie opened hers and tried to focus on the words instead of the fact that she was on a date—an *actual* date—with Ben Massey.

"The ribeye's good here," Ben offered. "If you like steak."

"Are you kidding? I love steak. Who doesn't?" Charlie looked up from the menu. "You've been here before?"

"A few times. Shane's dragged us all out here a couple of times for special occasions." Ben's mouth quirked. "It beats Cocktails and Chicken Strips."

"Oh, yeah, I actually love Cocks and Strippers," she said without thinking, just as their server passed their table of course. He nearly dropped his water pitcher. Charlie slapped her hand over her mouth as her eyes bugged out.

Ben laughed, deep and low. He picked up his water glass.

"I would crawl under the table right now but the server might get the wrong idea," Charlie practically squeaked.

Ben's face turned bright red as he nearly spit his water out.

"Oh, God, I'm making a mess of this. You're never going to want to be seen in public with me again."

"Oh, quite the contrary. I haven't had this much fun in a while."

Charlie laughed, and some of the tension eased from her shoulders.

They ordered—ribeye for both of them, medium-rare—from a different server. Suddenly it was just the two of them, candlelight flickering between them, and Charlie's brain went blank.

Say something. Anything. Well, maybe not anything because see how that turned out?

"So," Ben said at the same time she started, "How—"

They both stopped. Ben chuckled again.

"You first," Charlie said.

"I was just going to ask how you ended up in Colorado. I mean, I know Shane recruited you, but that's a big move from the coast."

Charlie nodded, grateful for a normal question. "I'm actually from central Ohio. Nowhere near the ocean, or even Erie."

"Really? Where?"

Charlie hesitated. She never talked about herself like this. But Ben put her at ease. His questions didn't feel like an interrogation.

"Believe it or not, I grew up near a place called Dead Man Crossing, just outside of Chillicothe."

His eyebrows rose, but not in judgement. More like curiosity. "Wow. Sounds like a haunted place."

It is, but not for the reasons you think.

"A man named James Caldwell was killed in the eighteen-eighties in a railway accident. That's about all I know, except for the ghost stories of course. Weird lights, a man who calls for help then disappears. Typical urban legends." She grinned, trying to turn the subject back around. "I'm sure you know plenty of ghost stories about lost miners and pioneers in the mountains."

"Yeah, one or two." Ben grinned. "Arden ever tell you about Nancy Silks?"

"You mean her great-great-great grandmother who haunts the ranch? No, she hasn't." Charlie gave Ben a soft smile. "But Sean did."

Ben's expression shifted—pain and understanding. They both missed their friend. He reached across the table and placed his hand over hers. Charlie marveled at how small her hand looked compared to his. Almost...dainty.

"On the boat, he talked about Lyons and the St. Vrain. He loved that river. I guess I wanted to see it for myself."

And you. I wanted to see you for myself.

Ben's thumb traced small circles on the back of her hand. Charlie took a breath and looked at Ben through her lashes. She turned her hand over so their palms pressed together.

Their food arrived then, breaking the moment. Without meaning to, Charlie pulled her hand away quickly, but Ben didn't seem to take offense. The server set down two enormous steaks with loaded baked potatoes and grilled asparagus. Charlie's stomach growled again.

She caught Ben's eyes on her as she cut into her steak, and for half a second she wondered if he'd prefer a woman who ordered salad and picked at it delicately. But then she thought, *screw it, I'm hungry*, and took a proper bite.

The steak was perfect—seared on the outside, pink and juicy in the middle. Charlie let out an involuntary sound of appreciation.

When she looked up, Ben was grinning at her.

"What?" she asked.

"Nothing." But his eyes were warm, pleased. "Just good to see you enjoying it."

"Are you kidding? This is amazing." Charlie cut another piece. "On assignment like this I usually live on protein bars."

"Then I'm glad we're fixing that."

They ate in comfortable silence for a few minutes. Charlie found herself relaxing into it—the easy rhythm of the meal, the way Ben didn't seem to need to fill every silence with conversation. He just... was. Present. Comfortable in his own skin in a way that made her want to be comfortable in hers.

"Can I ask you something?" Ben said eventually.

"Sure."

"The drawing thing. How long have you been doing that?"

Charlie swallowed her bite of potato. "Since I was a kid, I guess. But I got serious about it in the military. You know how it is. I needed something to do with my hands during down time. Considering we were in different parts of the world I'd probably never see again—some of them I'm glad I'll never see again." She added that last part ruefully. "I wanted to capture them. I took photos for a while, but that sort of thing can get you in trouble, right?"

Ben nodded knowingly.

"So I picked up a sketchbook and some pencils instead." She paused. "Why?"

"Just curious. You mentioned it earlier—about wanting to draw Loveland Pass. I liked seeing that side of you."

Charlie shrugged. "I think it's kind of silly. A bodyguard who sketches."

"I don't think it's silly at all." Ben's gaze was steady. "I'm a former Ranger and a blacksmith who reads fantasy novels and makes medieval armor. I don't get to judge anyone's hobbies."

Charlie felt herself smiling. "Fair point."

"Besides," Ben continued, "I meant what I said earlier. About bringing you back up there to draw. Whenever you want."

"You really mean that?"

"Yeah." He held her eyes. "I know all the best spots. Good light, good angles. And I promise I won't hover. I'll just... keep you company. If you want."

Charlie's heart did something inconvenient in her chest. "I'd like that. A lot."

Ben's answering smile made her forget about her steak entirely.

They talked through the rest of dinner—about the mountains, about the Ren Faire, about books they'd both read. Charlie found herself laughing more than she had in months, found herself leaning forward across the table, found herself not wanting the meal to end.

When the server brought the check, Ben reached for it immediately.

"I'll get it," Charlie offered. "I have an expense account."

"Not a chance." Ben's voice was firm but gentle. "I asked you to dinner. I'm paying."

"Ben—"

"Charlie." He looked up at her. "Let me do this. Please."

She could have argued. Probably should have, just on principle. But the way he was looking at her—like this mattered, like *she* mattered—made her relent.

"Okay," she said softly. "Thank you."

"Walk you home?" Ben said with a grin.

"I don't know. It's pretty far." Charlie grinned back.

"I think I can manage it."

They walked back through the lobby toward the elevators, not quite touching but close enough that Charlie could feel the warmth radiating off Ben's shoulder. When the elevator doors opened, they both stepped inside.

Ben pressed the button, then stepped back beside her. The doors slid shut, leaving them alone in the small space.

Charlie could feel her pulse in her throat. Ben was close enough that she could smell the faint scent of cedar and woodsmoke that seemed to cling to him. Close enough that if she turned slightly, they'd be face to face.

The elevator dinged and opened onto her floor.

The doors opened and Charlie stepped out, Ben following. They walked down the hallway toward her room in silence. The air felt charged. Every last cell in her body screamed for her to drag Ben into her hotel room and spend the rest of the night working off dinner.

Remember you're on the job? This isn't a hook-up.

"I should probably let Shane know I'm back." She looked across the hall at his door. "I'll text him when I get inside."

Just then, her back spasmed and she hissed through her teeth.

"Charlie?" Ben was immediately on alert. "What's wrong?"

"Nothing, nothing." She rolled her shoulders, feeling the familiar ache settle between her shoulder blades. The drive had been long, and sitting in one position for hours always made her back stiffen up. "I'm just stiff. Spending years speeding across waves like speedbumps in a little boat out on the ocean takes a toll on your body." She twisted at the waist and her spine popped like gunfire.

"Do you have anything for it?"

"I have some muscle relaxants, but I don't take them on the job. A couple ibuprofen and I'll be fine."

Ben shook his head. "That's not good enough."

Charlie tilted her head. "No?"

"No." He lifted his chin at the door. "Let me help you."

Charlie's eyes widened.

"N-nothing like that, I p-promise."

Charlie felt her breath speed up. "No, of course not." She smiled and tapped her key card on the pad, then opened the door.

"Have a seat on the bed," Ben told her. His voice wasn't stern, but it was a firm enough command that she felt it land in her belly and travel lower.

Charlie sat on the edge of the bed. Ben knelt beside her and she stopped breathing.

Then he bent and untied her boots. He slipped them off her feet one by one, cradling her heels each time.

"You can breathe, Charlie."

She inhaled quickly. "Right." She laughed nervously.

"Lie down on your stomach." That firm voice was going to absolutely ruin her panties.

Oh God, which pair of underwear am I wearing? How crappy are they?

No, no, no, you're not taking off your pants. Even if he tells you to.

Uh-uh. If he tells me to in that voice, I'm totally *taking off my pants.*

Charlie scooted onto the bed and laid down on her stomach. She felt Ben pull her t-shirt up to just below her athletic bra. The hotel room air felt cool on her skin. She heard him rub his palms together briskly—a rough, sandpaper sound.

"I'm going to touch you now, Charlie."

I've wanted to know how this feels for so long she thought just before he placed his hands on her lower back. His hands felt rough but warm.

And then he started to knead her lower back.

Heaven. It feels like heaven.

Ben's hands moved with surprising gentleness for their size, working methodically up her spine. He found every knot, every tight spot, and eased them loose with steady pressure. She tried not to groan and failed.

"How bad's the pain?" he asked quietly.

"It's at zero now."

She heard him chuckle. "Good. I can imagine you took a beating or two."

"Or two, yeah, you could say that." Charlie's voice came out muffled. "There was one time we were on the edge of a cyclone. Pitch black, swells at thirty feet. Our boat took a nosedive off a wave and hitting the water was like slamming into concrete. I cracked three ribs, broke a fourth."

Ben's hands paused for just a moment, then continued their work. "Jesus, Charlie."

"But there was a team waiting for extraction," she continued, her words coming slower now as his thumbs worked along her shoulder blades. "On time, on target, never quit. We got them out." She took a shaky breath. "That's what always mattered. In all those years serving as a Swick, I never lost a SEAL." Her voice dropped. "Just Sean."

"I know." Ben's voice was soft, understanding. His hands moved to her shoulders, kneading the tension there. Charlie felt herself sinking into the mattress, her body finally releasing the tension it had been holding.

"Sean came ashore to help with casualties. One of the wounded was a dog handler. Sean took control of the dog while his teammate got the handler to safety."

"Camo," Ben said quietly.

"Yeah. Camo." She couldn't finish the sentence. Didn't need to. Ben knew.

Ben's hands stilled for a moment on her shoulders, then resumed their gentle work. "I'm sorry you had to go through that."

Charlie wanted to say something else, wanted to tell him how much it meant that he understood, that he didn't try to fix it or make it better. But his hands were working magic on her upper back now, and her eyelids were getting heavy.

"That feels amazing," she murmured.

"Good." There was warmth in his voice. "Just relax."

His thumbs worked along either side of her spine, firm but careful. Charlie felt her breathing slow, felt the last of the day's tension draining away. The mattress was soft beneath her, Ben's hands warm and steady on her back.

"You're really good at this," she said, her words slurring slightly.

"Blacksmithing teaches you about muscle tension. And how to

work it out." His voice seemed to come from farther away. "Just breathe, Charlie. Let it go."

She tried to stay awake, tried to enjoy every second of his hands on her skin, but her body had other ideas. The combination of the long day, the emotional evening, and Ben's skilled touch was too much.

"Don't want to fall asleep," she protested weakly.

"It's okay." Ben's voice was gentle. "I've got you."

The last thing Charlie registered was Ben pulling her shirt back down, his hand lingering for just a moment at the small of her back.

Then nothing.

CHARLIE'S PHONE alarm blared into the quiet room. She jolted awake, disoriented, still fully dressed on top of the covers except—

Her boots were off. Lined up neatly beside the bed.

Memory flooded back. The restaurant. The elevator. Ben untying her boots, his hands on her back, his voice telling her to breathe.

Oh God. She'd fallen asleep while he was giving her a massage.

Charlie grabbed her phone to silence the alarm and saw a folded piece of hotel stationery propped against the lamp on the bedside table. Her name was written on the outside in neat, careful handwriting.

She unfolded it with trembling fingers.

> Charlie,
>
> You fell asleep around 10:30. I didn't want to wake you—you needed the rest. I let Shane know you were back safe.
>
> Thank you for tonight. For trusting me with your story. For letting me get to know the real you.
>
> I meant what I said about Loveland Pass. Whenever you want to go back and draw, just say the word.

Sleep well. You deserve it.

—Ben

P.S. I left your boots where you could reach them. Didn't want you to have to hunt for them in the morning.

Charlie read the note three times, her chest going tight.

He'd stayed until she fell asleep. Made sure she was comfortable. Told Shane she was safe.

The thoughtfulness of it all—the care—made her throat ache.

She pressed the note to her chest and closed her eyes.

Hide what you love.

But maybe not this time.

THIRTEEN

The Faire wouldn't open to the public for another hour, but the grounds were already buzzing with vendors setting up, performers running through routines, and security doing their rounds. Ben ran the polishing cloth over the chainmail one more time, even though it didn't need it. The steel rings gleamed in the Saturday morning sunlight. Perfect. Just like it had been perfect fifteen minutes ago when he'd checked it the first time.

Ben's phone sat on the workbench, screen dark, but he kept glancing at it anyway. Charlie's last text had come through at six-thirty that morning.

On our way. See you soon

It was now seven-twenty-five. She'd be here any minute.

Ben set down the cloth and picked up his phone, scrolling back through the week's worth of messages. Brief exchanges, mostly. Charlie texting between shifts, during Viv and Rowan's interviews, late at night when she finally had a moment to herself.

Tuesday, 11:47 PM:

Long day. Radio interview ran over, then two podcasts back to back. Viv's a trooper but I can tell she's exhausted.

You holding up okay?

Yeah. Just miss having someone to talk to about normal things. Like which dipping sauce goes best on Strippers.

Definitely Jerk Sauce.

YOU DID NOT JUST SAY THAT!!

I'm dying right now. Literally cannot breathe.

Wednesday, 9:23 PM:

Denver Post interview went well. Rowan's good at this stuff. Very smooth.

And you? How are you doing?

Fine. Keeping Viv safe. Easy days.

That's not what I asked.

I miss being up in the mountains. Does that sound weird?

Sounds perfectly reasonable to me.

Can't wait for Saturday.

Me neither.

Friday, 10:47 PM:

One more day. You ready for tomorrow?

Chain mail's polished. Embersword sketches are done. Rowan's going to look like a proper king.

She'd paused a long time before texting again after that response. Then:

That's not what I was asking.

To see you again? Yeah. That goes without saying.

I'm glad you said it anyway. Because I can't wait.

Ben smiled at his phone, reading that last message again.

I can't wait.

Three simple words that had kept him up half the night, wondering what it meant that Charlie King—careful, guarded Charlie—had said them so plainly.

His phone buzzed with another text.

In the VIP lot. See you in ten.

Ben stepped out of the forge to meet them, wiping his palms on his apron like a nervous teenager.

When he caught sight of Charlie, Ben forgot how to breathe.

She was in her usual tactical gear—dark pants, boots, fitted jacket over a t-shirt—but seeing her again after spending the week remembering how good she felt under his hands and fantasying about everywhere else he wanted to touch her made everything sharper. The way she moved, scanning the area with professional efficiency. The way the morning light caught her hair as she turned. The way her eyes found his immediately.

Shane walked beside her, grinning like he knew exactly what Ben was thinking. Viv and Rowan were on her other side, Maddie trailing slightly behind them, everyone stretching and talking after the drive from Boulder.

Charlie walked toward him, professional mask firmly in place, but there was something in her expression—a softness around her eyes, the hint of a smile peaking through her professional armor—that made his chest go tight.

"Morning," she said when she reached him.

"Morning." His voice came out rougher than he intended. "Good week?"

"Long week." Charlie glanced back at the group, then at him. "But we're here now."

"Yeah." Ben couldn't stop the smile spreading across his face. "You are."

Shane smirked. "Moose. You gonna stand there grinning at her all day, or are we getting this show on the road?"

Charlie's cheeks flushed pink, and Ben wanted to punch Shane in the shoulder. Instead, he cleared his throat and stepped back, gesturing toward the forge.

"Chain mail's ready. Come on in."

The group filed into the forge—Viv immediately gravitating toward the display cases, Rowan heading straight for the armor stand where his mail waited, Maddie pulling out her ever-present tablet. Shane stayed near the door, eyes scanning the area like the operator he'd always be.

And Charlie stayed close to Ben, close enough that he could smell her shampoo—rich and warm, a familiar forest scent.

Sun on ponderosa bark.

When she looked up at him, he could see the gold flecks in her hazel eyes.

"Missed you," she said quietly, just for him.

Ben's heart did something dangerous in his chest. "Missed you too."

Shane cleared his throat. "I'm gonna go coordinate with security. Make sure we've got eyes on all the entry points." He looked at Charlie. "You good here?"

"Yeah. I've got Viv." Charlie's professional mask slid back into place.

"Text me if anything feels off." Shane nodded at Ben, then headed out toward the Security tent.

Viv was examining the display cases with the intensity of someone who understood craftsmanship. She traced a finger along the glass near a perfectly balanced longsword. "These are incredible, Ben. The detail work is..." She shook her head. "I can't believe you make all of this by hand."

"Thank you." Ben moved to stand beside her. "Actually, I wanted to show you something. The preliminary sketches for the Embersword."

Viv's eyes lit up. "Lead the way."

Ben crossed to his workbench and retrieved a leather portfolio. He laid it open on the counter, revealing detailed sketches—multiple angles of a sword that managed to look both elegant and deadly.

The blade was straight and true, medieval in style, but the pommel and crossguard carried subtle flame motifs. Not cartoonish. Just enough to catch the light, to suggest fire without screaming it.

"Oh," Viv breathed. She leaned closer, studying every line. "Oh, Ben. This is perfect."

"I was hoping you'd say that, because the prototype's about sixty percent done." Ben pulled back a canvas drop cloth on the far end of the bench, revealing the sword in progress. The blade was forged and ground but not yet polished to its final finish. The hilt waited for its leather wrapping and final assembly and the Wyvern Fire Jewel hadn't been attached yet.

Viv actually gasped.

"It's going to be functional," Ben explained, feeling his pride swell at her reaction. "Not just a prop. When Rowan holds this, it'll have real weight, real balance. It'll feel like what it's supposed to be—a weapon worthy of a king."

"Aldric's sword." Viv picked up one of the sketches, her fingers trembling slightly. "This is exactly what I saw in my head when I read the books. Exactly." She looked up at him, eyes shining. "How did you do it?"

"I read the descriptions pretty carefully." Ben shrugged, trying to downplay how many times he'd reread those passages through the years, how many sketches he'd thrown away before getting it right. "And I figured if you were going to all this trouble to film an actual avalanche to make it look authentic, the sword should be authentic, too."

"Can I touch it?" Viv was already reaching for the prototype.

"Carefully. The edge isn't sharpened yet, but—"

Viv lifted the blade, testing its weight. Her whole face transformed—pure joy. "Rowan needs to see this. Rowan!" She turned, still holding the sword. "Get over here!"

Rowan looked up from where he'd been examining his chainmail. When he saw what Viv was holding, his expression shifted to something like awe. "Is that—?"

"The Embersword," Viv said. "Well, the beginning of it."

Rowan crossed to them in three strides. Viv handed him the blade carefully, and he held it like it was precious, which filled Ben with pride.

"This is extraordinary work," Rowan said quietly. He moved through a slow practice form—testing balance, weight distribution, the way the hilt sat in his palm. "This is a real weapon."

"That's the idea." Ben watched the actor move, pleased to see that his calculations had been right. The sword fit Rowan's build, his reach, the way he carried himself.

"When will it be finished?" Viv asked.

"Two weeks, maybe three. I want to get the engraving perfect on the blade. And the Wyvern Fire Jewel pommel stone—I'm still sourcing the right amber for it."

Viv was beaming now, the stress of the week melting away. "This is going to be the centerpiece of our production photos. The marketing team is going to lose their minds."

Ben felt Charlie's presence before he heard her. She'd moved closer, watching the exchange with that quiet attention she brought to everything.

"It's beautiful," Charlie said softly. "The craftsmanship is incredible."

Their eyes met, and Ben saw real appreciation there. Not just politeness. She understood what this meant—the hours at the forge, the precision required, the care in every detail.

"Thank you," he said.

The moment stretched between them, warm and private even with Viv and Rowan right there.

Then Maddie's voice cut through. "Viv? The gates will be opening in twenty minutes and we need to be at the main stage for the sound check."

Reality crashed back in.

"Right," Viv said reluctantly. "We should get Rowan into his armor."

Ben carefully returned the Embersword prototype to its place on the workbench and covered it again. Then he turned to the armor stand where Rowan's chainmail waited, gleaming in the morning light.

"Come here," Ben said to Rowan. "I'm no Caiden Bramble, but I can help you into the armor."

Rowan scoffed. "Don't remind me that Duke's going to be here today."

"Playing nice is part of the job, love," Viv said, but there was tension in her voice.

"I know." Rowan sighed. "Doesn't mean I have to like it."

Charlie and Viv stepped back to give them room. Maddie was already tapping notes into her tablet, and Ben could hear her muttering about scheduling and camera angles. She sounded vaguely annoyed.

Rowan put on a gambeson—a thickly-padded shirt—as Ben lifted the mail shirt—a full hauberk that would hang to mid-thigh when worn. The steel was heavy, substantial. Real protection, not just a costume.

Bend down a little," Ben said. Rowan complied, and Ben guided the chainmail over his head. The rings whispered and clinked as they settled into place, the weight distributing across Rowan's shoulders.

"How's that feel?" Ben asked, adjusting the lay of the mail across Rowan's back.

"Heavier than I expected." Rowan moved his arms experimentally, testing the range of motion. "But good. Substantial."

"That's about forty pounds of steel you're wearing." Ben grabbed a leather belt and cinched it around Rowan's waist. Then he circled him, checking the fit. "The belt helps take some of the weight off your shoulders and redistribute it to your hips, but you're going to feel it by the end of the day."

"Worth it." Rowan grinned. "I look like an actual knight, don't I?"

"You do." Ben couldn't help but smile. There was something satisfying about seeing his work worn properly.

He moved to retrieve the hardened leather arm bracers, and as he buckled them on, Rowan spoke quietly. "So. You and Sir Mariel."

Ben's hands stilled for just a moment. "What about Charlie and me?"

"Come on, mate." Rowan's voice was warm, amused. "I've got eyes. I've been watching you two dancing around each other since last Saturday."

Ben focused on adjusting the bracers, not looking at Rowan's face. "We're... getting to know each other better."

"That's one way to put it." Rowan chuckled. "For what it's worth, I think it's great. She's brilliant. Terrifying, but brilliant."

"She is." Ben couldn't quite keep the softness out of his voice.

"Just like Viv," Rowan said, and something in his tone made Ben look up.

The actor's expression had gone serious, almost vulnerable. "I know what people might think—divorced less than a year, jumping into something new with the director of my show. But it's not like that. I didn't cheat." Rowan met his eyes. "And it's not a rebound."

Ben finished with the bracers. "You don't have to explain—"

"I want to." Rowan glanced over at where Viv stood with Charlie, the two women talking quietly. "My marriage was over long before the divorce. We stayed too long trying to make it work. By the time we finally called it, we were more relieved than heartbroken. Well, until the media decided to play judge, jury and executioner. It did get messy."

Ben nodded, understanding.

"Viv is..." Rowan's whole face softened. "She's everything I didn't know I was looking for. She's brilliant and fierce and she doesn't take shit from anyone—especially not from me. When I'm with her, I'm not Rowan McCrae the actor. I'm just... me. And she likes that version better anyway."

"Sounds like you've got it bad," Ben said, but he was smiling.

"Completely gone," Rowan admitted. "Head over heels. Absolutely ruined for anyone else." He paused. "Kind of like someone else I know."

Ben felt heat creep up his neck. "I don't know what you're talking about."

"Right." Rowan laughed. "Just like you don't spend half your time staring at Charlie when you think no one's watching. Just like she doesn't light up every time you walk into a room."

"It's complicated," Ben said quietly.

"The best things usually are." Rowan adjusted the chainmail, letting the belt take more of the weight. "But from where I'm standing? You two make sense together. Warrior recognizes warrior, yeah?"

Ben thought about Charlie at Loveland Pass, the way she'd looked at the mountains like she understood them. The way she'd let him see her vulnerability over dinner, the way she'd fallen asleep under his hands. The way she'd said *I can't wait* like it was both a confession and a promise.

Warrior, yes. But more.

Warrior Princess.

"Yeah," he said. "Something like that."

"Then don't overthink it." Rowan clapped him on the shoulder, the chainmail clinking. "Life's too short, and the good ones are too rare."

Before Ben could respond, Viv called over. "How's he look?"

Ben turned to see both women watching them. Charlie's eyes met his, and something warm passed between them.

"I look like a king," Rowan said, turning in a circle.

Viv beamed. "Perfect. Let's go make some magic."

THE MORNING SUN had climbed higher by the time the Faire gates opened, and the grounds filled quickly. Ben could hear the crowd's energy even from backstage—laughter, excited chatter, the periodic roar when someone won at the axe-throwing lanes.

Della's son Marcus was manning the forge for the day, which freed Ben up for this madness. He stood behind the main stage now—a permanent structure built to look like the front of a castle, complete with crenellations and painted stonework—and watched organized chaos unfold.

Viv had transformed. She wore a deep crimson gown with gold trim, her hair swept up under a delicate circlet. She looked every inch a medieval queen, which made sense given that she'd spent the last hour at Della's costume shop. Apparently, she and Della were now best friends.

"No, no," Viv was saying to the streaming crew's director. "Camera two needs to be stage left. We want to catch reactions from both the players and the audience." She gestured expansively. "And make sure you've got a tight shot ready for when—"

"Viv," the other director said gently. "I've got this."

"Right. Sorry." Viv smiled sheepishly. "Occupational hazard. I'll just... stand over here and be queenly."

Charlie stood nearby still in her tactical gear—dark pants, boots, fitted jacket over a black tee that allowed her to conceal-carry. But Ben had seen her face earlier when they'd returned to the costume shop so Viv could change. When Charlie saw that the Princess Evelaine dress was gone, Ben had caught the flicker of disappointment across her face before she'd masked it.

Ben smiled. *Yes, maybe the princess dress had been a stoke of genius after all.*

Now, watching her stand there in bodyguard mode while Viv glowed in her queen's gown, Ben found himself imagining Charlie in that dress. The way it would bring out the gold flecks in her eyes. The way her blond hair would look loose and curling over her shoulders instead of pulled back in that practical ponytail.

She'd be breathtaking.

He couldn't stop staring at her.

"Stop gawking," Shane muttered as he passed. "You're gonna trip over your tongue."

Ben ignored him.

"Well, well," a voice called out. "Quite the production you've got here!"

Ben turned to see Duke Holloway striding toward them, dressed as Caiden Bramble in dark leather and wool, a chronicler's satchel slung over his shoulder. He wore an easy smile, arms spread wide in greeting.

"Rowan! Looking properly kingly, mate." Duke clapped Rowan on the shoulder. Rowan's smile didn't quite reach his eyes, but he played along.

"Duke. Good to see you."

"And Vivienne!" Duke swept into an elaborate bow before Viv.

"Your Majesty. Absolutely stunning. You're going to break the internet in that dress."

"Thank you, Duke." Viv's voice was carefully neutral. Professional.

Duke's attention shifted to Charlie. "And who's this lovely lady? I don't believe we've met."

"Charlie King," Charlie said, her tone flat. "Viv's friend."

"*Friend*?" Duke's eyebrow quirked, but his smile never wavered. "Well, any friend of Vivienne's is a friend of mine. Pleasure."

Then he turned that thousand-watt smile on Maddie, who was standing at Viv's elbow. "Maddie, love! You look gorgeous today. New hairstyle?"

Maddie flushed pink. "Oh, yeah. Um, thanks for noticing."

"I always notice." Duke's voice was warm, intimate. He reached out and squeezed her shoulder. "You work too hard, you know. Have you eaten today?"

"I grabbed a protein bar—"

"Not good enough." Duke shook his head in mock disapproval. "After this is over, I'm buying you a proper lunch. My treat."

"You don't have to—"

"I insist." Duke winked at her.

Maddie looked absolutely flustered. She shot Viv a look that screamed SOS.

"Please stop harassing my assistant, Duke."

Duke laughed. "Someone sounds hangry. How about I buy you lunch, too?" He looked at Rowan. "Honestly, you need to feed these lovely ladies more often." He winked at Maddie again. "Ciao, bella."

Maddie kept her eyes on his as he walked away.

Viv shook her head. "The nerve." She put her hand on Maddie's shoulder. "I hate to give him the point, but you do need to eat something more substantial than a protein bar. Why don't you take a break until it's time for the joust? Grab something to eat, have a look around."

"Are you sure?"

"Absolutely! I'll text you if I need anything."

Maddie looked relieved. "Thanks, Viv. I'll be back before the game's over."

The stage manager appeared. "Five minutes, everyone. Let's do a quick run-through."

They gathered in a loose circle while the stage manager explained the setup. The game was called *Chronicles of the Realm*. It was a *BattleLore*-specific strategy card game where players took on character roles from the books. Ben would be the Game Master—the Chronicler's Voice, they were calling it—narrating and adjudicating the game. Duke would play Caiden the Chronicler of course. Rowan had King Aldric.

"Which of you ladies is playing Sir Mariel and which is Princess Evelaine?" the stage manager asked. He looked Charlie up and down. "As if I don't already know."

"Actually," Charlie spoke up. "If it's all right, I'd like to be Evelaine."

Yup. I made the right decision with the dress.

"Perfect! I wanted to play Mariel," Viv said.

"Fine." The stage manager made a note. "We'll pick the random audience member to play one of the Embersworn knights right off the bat. Now, play for drama and laughs. Engage with the audience. We've got cameras on everyone, and the livestream chat will be on the monitors stage right if you want to glance at reactions. Questions?"

No one had any.

"All right. Break a leg." The stage manager grinned. "Or, you know, don't. We need you all intact."

The curtain began to rise.

The roar from the crowd was immediate and deafening. The open-air theater was packed—every bench filled, people standing three-deep at the back.

Ben stepped forward to the Game Master's podium, and the crowd quieted. He slipped easily into Benjamin the Blacksmith mode—the persona he wore at the Faire, confident and theatrical.

"Good people of the Realm!" His voice boomed, amplified by the sound system. "Welcome to the Chronicles! Today, legends walk among us. Kings and humble chroniclers. Lovely princesses and bold warriors. And one lucky soul from among you will join their ranks!"

The crowd cheered.

"Who among you is brave enough to face the challenges of *BattleLore*?"

Hands shot up across the theater. Ben scanned the crowd, then pointed to a young woman in the third row wearing a homemade Embersworn tabard. "You! What's your name, brave warrior?"

"Beth!" she shouted.

"Sir Beth of the Embersworn, come join us!"

She practically floated up to the stage, beaming.

The introductions followed—each character stepping forward as Ben introduced them and narrated their role. Rowan as King Aldric drew massive applause. Viv as the Knight Commander got whistles and cheers. Charlie as Princess Evelaine prompted some good-natured catcalls that made her blush. Duke as Caiden got even louder cheers than Rowan.

He pretended to be surprised, then bowed low and shot Rowan a grin that said *Hear that? They love me.*

Everyone took their seats at the elaborately decorated game table —a beautiful piece painted to look like weathered stone. The cards were laid out, the tokens distributed as Ben explained the rules.

"Let the Chronicles begin!" Ben declared.

The game moved smoothly. Ben narrated the scenarios, the players bantered as they made their strategic plays, and the crowd laughed at every joke and reacted to every dramatic moment. Charlie was surprisingly good—calculating, strategic, playing Evelaine with quiet authority. Viv was aggressive, pushing for bold moves. Rowan played the steady, wise Aldric. Duke was... Duke. Charming, witty, making the crowd laugh the hardest with his commentary.

And then, twenty minutes in, it happened.

Rowan made a play that won him the game—Aldric formed an

alliance with Viv's Sir Mariel. The crowd loved it, cheering the partnership and the victory.

Duke leaned back in his chair, grinning. "Ah, forming intimate partnerships, are we? Funny how art imitates life, eh Rowan?"

Rowan's smile tightened slightly. "It was a good strategic move."

"Oh, absolutely." Duke's voice was warm, friendly. Nothing but good humor. "Though I have to say, stealing the director's heart is the best way to secure your role on the show." He laughed, like it was all a joke, like he was just ribbing a friend.

Viv's face went pale.

The crowd's reaction was confused—some laughter, some gasps.

"Wait, what?" someone called out.

Duke looked genuinely surprised. "Oh. Oh no." He put a hand to his mouth. "I assumed this was your public declaration!"

Viv's knuckles were white where she gripped her cards.

Duke turned to the crowd, apologetic. "My apologies, folks. I didn't mean to spill any beans. But yes—" He gestured between Rowan and Viv. "These two lovely people have been an item for months now. And honestly? I'm thrilled for them both. Congratulations!"

The theater erupted. Some cheers, but mostly gasps and shocked exclamations. Ben could see phones coming out, people already typing furiously.

On the monitor showing the livestream chat, comments exploded:

WHAT?

ROWAN AND VIVIENNE CROSS ARE TOGETHER???

Rowan found his voice. "Duke—"

"No, no, don't be embarrassed!" Duke was all warmth and support. "Love is beautiful. I'm happy for you both. Truly." He looked directly into the camera. "Though I suppose this explains some creative decisions, doesn't it? Maybe if I'd tried that strategy myself, Caiden would have a future in season three."

The implication hung in the air like poison.

Ben saw Viv's expression crumble, just for a moment, before she forced it back into place.

The crowd was buzzing, distracted. More phones came out. More comments popped up on the live feed.

IS THIS WHY SHE'S KILLING CAIDEN???

WAIT! SHE'S WHAT!?!?

#ThroneOfEmbarrassment

#KillOffVivienneCrossInstead

Duke leaned toward Beth, who looked absolutely lost. "I hope I didn't make things too awkward," he said, loud enough for the microphones to catch. "Sometimes I forget not everyone lives in our little bubble. But really—don't you think they make a lovely couple?"

Beth nodded, starstruck.

Duke flashed that megawatt smile. "And what about you, Beth? Anyone special in your life?"

She shook her head.

"No? Well, I can't believe that." He took her hand and kissed the back of it. "Thanks so much for playing today."

The game wrapped up quickly after that, the energy never quite recovering from Duke's bombshell. Ben kept things moving, trying to salvage what he could, but everyone's attention was on their phones now.

As the players stood and the curtain began to fall, Maddie came running up from stage left, tablet clutched to her chest, slightly out of breath.

"I just saw the end on the feed," she said, her voice tight. Tears shimmered in her eyes. "I can't believe Duke did that. He's such a jerk!"

Viv reached for her. "Maddie—"

"No, seriously!" Maddie's anger seemed genuine, protective. "He had no right to out you two like that. On a livestream! And then—" She gestured angrily toward where Duke was still chatting with Beth. "He shouldn't be hitting on her like that. It's so inappropriate. God, I can't stand him sometimes."

Charlie sidled up to Ben. They stood watching Duke.

"Do you think he's the leak?" Ben asked.

"What does it matter? If he wasn't before, he sure is now."

FOURTEEN

Charlie's phone buzzed for the fifteenth time in as many minutes. She didn't need to look to know what it was—more notifications, more hashtags, more strangers dissecting Viv and Rowan's relationship like it was public property.

#ThroneOfEmbarrassment

#KillOffVivienneCrossInstead

The last one made her stomach turn.

"Ignore it," Shane said quietly, falling into step beside her as they walked toward the jousting grounds. "Social media's gonna social media. That's just some cowardly asshole sitting in Mommy's basement a thousand miles away. Focus on what's going on here, King." He handed her a comm.

"I know." Charlie placed the comm in her ear while she kept her eyes forward, scanning the crowd that parted around their small group. Viv and Rowan walked ahead, carefully keeping their distance. Viv and Maddie spoke non-stop. Charlie figured they were trying to craft a public statement. "Doesn't mean I have to like it."

"Nobody does." Shane's jaw was tight. "But that's the job."

The jousting grounds came into view—a large oval arena ringed with wooden barriers and tiered seating already filling with spectators. Colorful banners snapped in the breeze. The smell of horses and hay mixed with funnel cake and roasted turkey legs.

Charlie's tactical brain kicked in automatically. Two main entrances. Emergency exits at the north and south ends. Crowd density higher than she'd like. Too many variables.

Ben appeared at her elbow, and her pulse jumped before she could stop it.

"Hey," he said quietly.

"Hey." Charlie found herself smiling despite everything—Duke's ambush, the social media storm, the professional voice in her head screaming that she needed to focus now more than ever.

But he was so close their shoulders almost brushed. She could smell cedar and forge smoke still clinging to him.

"Hell of a morning," Ben said.

"That's one way to put it."

"How are they holding up?"

Charlie glanced ahead at Viv and Rowan. "Rowan's furious. Viv's..." Charlie paused. "She's putting on a brave face, but she's pretty shaken. Can't blame her." Charlie's hand drifted unconsciously toward her sidearm. "Duke knew exactly what he was doing."

"Yeah." Ben's voice hardened. "He did."

They walked in silence for a moment. The crowd noise swelled around them—laughter, music from a nearby stage, vendors hawking their wares. Normal Ren Faire sounds. But nothing felt normal.

"Charlie." Ben's voice was low enough that only she could hear. "Are you okay?"

The question caught her off guard. She was supposed to be the one checking on everyone else. Making sure Viv was safe. Making sure the perimeter was secure. Making sure—

"I'm fine," she said automatically.

Ben gave her a look that said he didn't believe her for a second.

"Really," Charlie insisted. "I'm just—" She stopped, unsure how to finish that sentence. *Just what? Distracted by you? Worried that I'm going to get someone hurt? Feeling like everything's spinning out of control?*

Ben's hand found hers just for a second, a brief squeeze of reassurance before he let go.

It was enough to steady her.

"We're almost there," Shane said. "Charlie, you're in the Queen's section with Viv. I'll be mobile, coordinating with Faire security. Ben—"

"I'll be with them," Ben said. "Rowan might need help with the armor between rounds. I don't think either of us trusts Duke to squire right now."

Charlie nodded. "Stay sharp, everyone. After that shit show at the game, the crowd's going to be keyed up."

They reached the entrance to the jousting grounds. A handler in a stable keeper's costume waited with three horses already saddled—one for Rowan, two for the other jousters. The animals stamped and tossed their heads, picking up on the energy of the gathering crowd.

Viv turned back to look at their group. Her queenly composure was back in place, but Charlie could see the strain around her eyes. "Ready?"

"Ready," Rowan said. He reached for her hand and squeezed it. For a moment Viv looked alarmed, but then she softened.

"Fuck it. Everyone knows already." She turned, grabbed Rowan's shoulders, and kissed him, hard. "Now go get 'em, tiger. Make your queen proud."

Charlie watched Viv take a deep breath, straighten her shoulders, and lift her chin. The transformation was remarkable—from shaken woman to commanding queen in the space of a heartbeat.

She's stronger than she looks, Charlie thought. *They both are.*

"Let's give them a show," Viv said.

Maddie grinned. "You're going to be great. Both of you. Don't let Duke ruin this."

They got to the entertainer's entrance and Viv joined the Royal

Court. Charlie and Maddie would sneak into the box after the pageantry. The Court filed through the entrance and the crowd's roar washed over them as Viv approached the Queen's box—a raised platform with cushioned seats and a canopy to shade them from the sun. Scanning for threats, Charlie and Maddie skirted the inside of the ring while the Royal Herald announced the list until they stood behind Viv.

Ben stayed with Rowan and Duke near the horses, and Charlie found her gaze tracking him even as she positioned herself behind Viv's seat.

Focus, she told herself. *You're on the job.*

But when Ben looked up and caught her eye across the arena, that small smile just for her, focusing became the hardest thing in the world.

The Queen's box offered an excellent vantage point—Charlie could see the entire arena, both entrance gates, and most of the crowd from here. She positioned herself slightly behind and to the left of Viv's ornate chair, where she could move in any direction quickly.

Maddie stood on the other side of Viv. "The PR team wants a statement by tonight. I told them we'd have something finalized within the hour."

"Down, girl." Viv's voice was tight despite the smile she put on for the crowd. "We'll deal with it after the joust."

Charlie's eyes swept the crowd. Families with kids waving foam swords. Couples in elaborate costumes. Groups of college-aged fans wearing homemade Embersworn tabards. Most seemed excited, festive. But there was an undercurrent now—people whispering, phones out, fingers pointing.

At Viv. At Rowan.

Shane's voice crackled in Charlie's earpiece. "King, you copy?"

Charlie touched the small comm unit. "Copy."

"I've got eyes on the north entrance. Faire security's doubled up at all access points. They turned away two people in Caidansworn costumes already. Stay alert."

"Roger that."

Down in the arena, handlers were preparing the horses. Rowan stood with his mount—a massive gray gelding with white socks that must have been at least sixteen hands high—running a hand down its neck. He'd traded out his chain mail for plate mail. Duke had changed into his squire costume—Caiden's colors, dark leather and forest green. He carried Rowan's lance with easy confidence, spinning it once like a showman before planting it upright in the sand.

The crowd noticed. A ripple of reaction—some cheers, some boos.

Charlie's jaw clenched. She hated that Viv had been exposed on her watch. But on a personal level, it pissed her off how he'd just blown up Rowan and Viv's privacy on a livestream.

Duke waved and blew kisses at the queen's ladies-in-waiting, all charm and swagger.

"That son of a bitch," Maddie muttered.

Viv said nothing, but her hands gripped the armrests of her chair.

Down below, Rowan and Duke exchanged words. Charlie couldn't hear them, but body language said enough. Rowan's shoulders were stiff. Duke's gestures were expansive, apologetic. Playing the peacemaker for anyone watching.

Ben stayed close to Rowan, a solid presence. Charlie saw him say something to Duke—brief, sharp—and Duke stepped back with raised hands. *Message received.*

Good.

Before mounting, Rowan ran a hand along the horse's barrel and slid his fingers briefly under the girth strap—a quick, practiced check. Satisfied, he nodded to the handler and swung up onto the gray with the ease of someone who'd done it before.

Then Duke stepped in. Charlie couldn't hear what he said, but his body language was all performance—playing to the nearby crowd as he reached down and tugged the girth strap with a showman's flourish. Rowan looked down at him with an expression Charlie couldn't read from this distance. Duke stepped back and presented the lance with an elaborate bow.

Her eyes found Ben across the arena. He was watching Duke, not the crowd.

Focus, she told herself. *You're on the job.*

But she filed it away.

The herald—a barrel-chested man in crimson and gold—stepped to the center of the arena and raised a brass horn. Three short blasts silenced the crowd.

"Good people!" His voice boomed across the grounds. "Welcome to the Grand Tournament! Today, brave knights shall test their valor in the lists, for the honor of our gracious Queen Vivienne!"

The crowd roared. Viv stood and waved, every inch the regal monarch despite everything.

Charlie scanned faces in the front rows, looking for anyone who appeared too focused, too intense, too still. But everyone seemed caught up in the pageantry.

"Our first challenger," the herald continued, "is Sir Aldric of The Embersworn, defender of the realm, champion of the people!"

Rowan mounted and rode his horse to the center of the arena. The gray gelding pranced slightly, showing off. Rowan sat tall in the saddle, his armor gleaming, one hand raised to acknowledge the cheers.

He looked every inch a king.

Charlie's professional assessment noted his posture, his control of the horse, the way the armor moved. Everything looked right.

So why did her instincts keep screaming that something was wrong?

"Attending Sir Aldric," the herald called, "is his loyal squire, Caiden Bramble!"

Duke jogged into view, carrying the lance. He performed an elaborate bow that got laughs from the crowd, then presented the weapon to Rowan with a flourish.

Rowan took it without looking at him.

The second knight entered the arena on a black destrier, his armor gleaming silver. He took position at the opposite end from Rowan. Earlier, Ben had called him Sir Geoffrey. Local guy who had been doing this for years. A good rider who knew his stuff.

"And now," the herald announced, "let the tournament begin!"

The crowd erupted.

Charlie's eyes found Ben again. He'd moved to the sideline, arms crossed, watching. Even from here she could see the tension in his shoulders.

He felt it too. Something off.

Their eyes met across the arena. Ben's expression shifted to concern. He'd caught her watching him, and seen something in her face. They immediately shared the rapport that had kept them alive in the attack months ago.

Charlie gave the smallest shake of her head. *I don't know. Just... watch.*

Ben nodded once. *I've got your back.*

The herald raised a flag. "First pass! Riders, take your marks!"

Both knights spurred their horses to opposite ends of the list—the long wooden fence running down the center of the arena that kept the riders separated but close enough to joust without the horses running into each other.

Rowan settled into position, lance couched. Through the helmet's visor, Charlie could just make out his eyes. Focused. Ready.

The flag dropped.

"Charge!"

Both horses exploded forward, hooves thundering, sand flying. The crowd's roar turned deafening.

Charlie's heart hammered. She forced herself to breathe.

The knights closed the distance impossibly fast—forty feet, thirty, twenty—

Impact.

Rowan's lance struck Geoffrey's gritted grand guard with a crack that echoed across the arena. His lance shattered spectacularly. It was designed to break safely. Geoffrey's glanced off Rowan's guard.

"Five points for Sir Aldric!"

The crowd went wild.

Both riders circled back to their starting positions. Rowan tossed aside the broken lance. Duke ran forward with a replacement.

Charlie watched the exchange as Rowan took the new weapon and adjusted his seat in the saddle.

Was it her imagination, or did he shift his weight differently that time?

"Second pass!" the herald called.

The riders turned and faced each other again. Charlie noticed Rowan's posture had changed. Subtle, but there. He was sitting differently, compensating for something, the way someone adjusted when their chair wasn't quite stable, when their footing wasn't quite sure.

The saddle. Something's wrong with the saddle.

She saw it now—the way it sat slightly off-center on the horse's back, the way Rowan kept shifting his weight to compensate. The way the leather girth strap looked... wrong. Too loose? Too tight? She couldn't tell from here, but Ben had seen it and Ben *knew* horses and tack and—

The flag dropped.

"Stop!" Charlie heard herself shout, but the herald's voice drowned her out.

"Charge!"

Both horses launched forward.

Everything happened too fast and too slow at the same time.

Charlie's blood went cold.

Her gaze snapped to Ben.

He was already moving.

Ben vaulted the barrier—one hand on the rail as his legs cleared it in a single fluid motion that screamed Ranger training and immediate danger.

The herald turned, confused.

But Ben was already sprinting across the sand toward Rowan's end of the list, and Charlie's brain finally caught up to what her instincts had already screamed. On the edge of her awareness, she heard Viv asking what was wrong.

Rowan was committed. No way to stop a destrier at full gallop. The gray thundered down the list, Rowan's lance leveled at Geoffrey's grand guard, his body leaning forward in the saddle for maximum impact.

Ben was still running, still shouting something Charlie couldn't hear over the crowd's roar.

Charlie grabbed the railing of the Queen's box. "Rowan!"

Her voice cut through the noise—combat training, projection, the ability to be heard over gunfire and explosions and chaos.

Rowan's head jerked slightly. He'd heard her.

Ten feet from impact, Rowan dropped his lance. The weapon tumbled into the sand as both hands grabbed for the horse's mane, for anything solid, for purchase.

The crowd gasped, confused. This wasn't part of the show, was it?

Charlie watched the saddle suddenly coming loose, tilting, Rowan's weight shifting wrong, his hands fisted in the gray's mane but momentum carrying him forward and down as Rowan's saddle slid completely sideways. He was falling, going under the horse, about to be crushed beneath half a ton of panicked horse—

Ben hit them both at full sprint.

He didn't try to stop the horse. That would have been insane. Instead, he grabbed Rowan's armor—those careful hands that had buckled every strap, that had checked every fitting, now pulled Rowan away.

Ben's momentum combined with his grip yanked Rowan sideways out of the falling saddle. They went down together in a tangle of limbs and armor and sand, Ben taking the impact on his shoulder and rolling them both away from the horse's hooves.

The gray gelding, suddenly rider-less and terrified, veered away from the list. The saddle had fallen completely off and lay in the sand. The herald was frantically waving the abort flag. Geoffrey hauled back on his reins, his horse rearing as handlers rushed in from the sides to Rowan's panicked gray. Viv was screaming.

"Viv, Maddie, stay here!" Charlie was moving before she knew it —over the railing, dropping the six feet to the arena floor, landing in a crouch and coming up running. She reached Ben and Rowan in seconds. Both men were on the ground, Ben still gripping Rowan's armor. In her ear, Shane was calling for paramedics.

"Don't move," Charlie ordered, dropping to her knees beside them. "Rowan, can you hear me?"

"Yeah." Rowan's voice was muffled by the helmet. His chest was heaving. "Yeah, I'm—I'm okay."

"Ben?" Charlie's hands were already checking him for injuries, professional training overriding everything else. "You hurt?"

"Shoulder." Ben grimaced but pushed himself to sitting. "I'm good."

"The hell you are," Rowan said.

The crowd was on its feet now, a roar of confusion and concern. People were shouting. Phones were out, recording everything.

Viv appeared at Charlie's side, her queen's composure shattered. "Rowan!" She dropped to her knees in the sand.

"I'm okay." Rowan fumbled with his helmet, got it off. His face was pale, sweating, but his eyes were clear. "I'm okay, love. Ben got me."

Shane materialized with two Faire paramedics. "Clear the arena! Everyone back!" He looked at Charlie. "What happened?"

"Saddle failed."

Shane went to investigate.

Duke ran up, all concern. "My God, Rowan, are you alright? I had no idea—"

"Don't." Ben's voice cut like a blade. He was on his feet now, one hand on his shoulder but steady. "Not now, Duke."

Duke stepped back, hands raised. "I was just—"

"I said not now."

More security arrived. The arena was controlled chaos—handlers with horses, guards clearing spectators who'd jumped the barrier, the herald trying to calm the crowd with assurances that Sir Aldric was unharmed.

Charlie helped Rowan to his feet. The plate armor was heavy, and his legs were shaking. "Easy. You might be in shock."

"I felt it." Rowan's voice was quiet, just for her and Ben and Viv. "When I mounted up. The saddle felt wrong. I thought maybe I was just nervous, or the horse was skittish, or—" He stopped. "I felt it shift on the first pass. I knew something was wrong. I just didn't know what."

Charlie's stomach dropped. "You knew?"

"Not for sure. Not until—" Rowan looked at Ben. "You saw it. Before the second pass."

"Yeah." Ben's jaw was tight. "The girth was separating. I saw it start to give."

"And you ran onto the field without thinking." Rowan's voice held something like awe. "You could've been killed."

"So could you." Ben's voice was matter-of-fact. "Wasn't about to let that happen."

"King. You and Moose come here." Shane's voice sounded grim through the comm.

"Ben." Charlie pointed toward Shane, kneeling beside the saddle with an official. They walked over to him.

"Take a look at this."

Charlie and Ben knelt to examine the leather strap. It was still warm from the horse's body. She examined the break point, and her blood went cold.

The strap hadn't frayed. Hadn't worn through from age or use.

It had been cut.

Not all the way through—that would've been too obvious. But deep enough. A clean slice on the side against the horse's belly, hidden from casual inspection, weakened just enough that under the stress of a full-tilt joust it would fail catastrophically.

Charlie looked up at Shane and met his gaze. She saw her own understanding reflected back. They'd talk. Later. Privately.

THIS WASN'T AN ACCIDENT.

They made their way back to Rowan and Viv. Maddie stood with them, tears streaming down her face. "Oh my God, Rowan! Are you okay?" She looked horrified. "I can't believe this happened. Thank God you're alright. Thank God Ben and Charlie were watching!"

"Yeah." Rowan pulled Viv close. "Thank God."

Charlie looked around the arena. The crowd was being ushered out while the handlers took care of the horses. Duke, stood off to the side, looking shocked and concerned and completely innocent.

Someone had cut that strap, knowing it would fail, knowing Rowan would be on that horse, knowing the physics of a full-speed joust would send him under the animal's hooves.

Ben was watching her with that steady, knowing gaze. Warrior recognizing warrior. Both of them understanding what this meant.

The game had changed.

Someone wasn't just leaking information anymore.

Someone was willing to kill.

FIFTEEN

MONDAY AFTERNOON SUNLIGHT SLANTED THROUGH Riversong's windows. Ben sat at his usual table near the back, listening to old jazz—Sonny had won a coin toss earlier with April, so jazz it was for the afternoon. His coffee had gone cold twenty minutes ago.

Shane dropped into the chair across from him with his own mug—an Americano that smelled strong enough to wake the dead. "You gonna drink that, or just stare at it until it evaporates?"

"Lost track of time." Which was an absolute lie. Ben was counting the seconds until it was time to drive down to Denver and pick Charlie up at DIA. Ben pushed the mug away as he looked up at the giant wall clock, which seemed to have stopped. He could have sworn ten minutes had passed since he looked at it last, but it was only three.

"Want a fresh one?"

"Nah. I'm good."

Shane gave him a look that said he clearly wasn't good, but didn't push. Yet. "DCSO called this morning. Forensics confirmed the girth strap was cut. Clean slice, hidden on the underside against the horse's belly. Someone knew what they were doing."

Ben's jaw tightened. "Duke?"

"Alibi's solid. He arrived shortly before the card game, there's footage of him online signing autographs and talking to fans all the way to the jousting ring, and he was visible on the field the entire time as Rowan's squire, including at the girth before Rowan mounted. There wasn't time for him to go anywhere near the stable." Shane took a sip of his coffee.

"What about any Caidansworn?"

"Tack room had a dozen people with access—jousters, handlers, Faire staff. No one saw Duke or anyone suspicious there." Shane looked Ben in the eye. "Any chance one of the couldn't have been bribed?"

Shit. Ben tried not to be angry at the question. "I've known most of the stable hands for years. They wouldn't do this."

"Figured you'd say that. Unfortunately, there are no security cameras in the stables, either...so." Shane leaned back in his chair. "DCSO's treating it as attempted murder, but without solid evidence pointing to a specific person, they're stuck. Official word's that it was an accident. And Viv's production company is pushing to keep filming on schedule. LA office is handling Viv and Rowan's security now. We're off the hook unless they come back to Colorado."

"They will." Ben glanced at the clock again—four minutes had passed—then looked out the window at the red cliffs over the St. Vrain, watching the sunlight illuminate the sandstone. "Viv wants that avalanche scene. She'll be back in November or December when there's snow."

"Then we've got time to figure this out." Shane's phone buzzed. He glanced at it, then back at Ben. "Elissa's still digging into The Chronicler but not having much luck. You can imagine the fans are blowing up over this. It's chaos. Now he's even harder to find."

The front door chimed. Ben looked up to see Gabe walk in, hand-in-hand with Rochelle. They were both smiling. Gabe looked happier than he had in years. Ben smiled. He remembered when Gabe had been too nervous to talk to Rochelle, and when she'd run from the coffee shop after buying him that first coffee because her stutter got in the way. Now they were happily married.

Gabe's expression—pure contentment—made Ben's chest ache.

That's what he wanted with Charlie. Just being without her for two days was driving him crazy. The wall clock mocked him again. This afternoon was taking forever.

Gabe spotted Ben and Shane, raised a hand in greeting, and steered Rochelle toward the counter where April was already pulling shots for their usual orders.

"Sure I can't talk you into something new?" April asked Gabe. Her voice projected through the coffee shop. "Something with ice in it?"

"Why start now?" Gabe asked.

"Maybe because it's hotter than the devil's sweaty ass—"

"April. Language." April's father, Sonny turned from the espresso machine and gave his daughter a look that could blister paint off a wall.

"What?" April gestured around the coffee shop. "Nobody's here. Your farty old jazz chased everyone away."

Ben snorted as Shane raised his hand. "Uh, we're here, darling. Sweetheart. Love of my life. Hi."

April rolled her eyes. "You don't count because your drinks are free."

"She gets cranky when it's hot," Shane stage-whispered.

"I heard that." She dropped two spoonfuls of sugar into the bottom of a ceramic mug followed by coffee and one shot of espresso for Gabe, then made an iced mocha for Rochelle.

Ben laughed. Yeah, he wanted this with Charlie, too—easy, fun banter. He sighed.

"She lands at six," Shane said quietly.

Ben's head snapped toward him. "What?"

"Charlie. Her flight from LA lands at six." Shane smirked.

"You've checked that clock a hundred times since I sat down. You're not subtle, Moose."

Heat crept up Ben's neck. "I wasn't—"

"You were." Shane's smirk softened into something more genuine. "It's good, man. You two are good together."

"We barely know each other."

"Bullshit." Shane leaned forward. "Seeing you two at the Ren Faire, You guys move like you've been doing this for years."

Ben didn't have an answer for that.

Gabe and Rochelle approached their table, coffees in hand.

"Hey," Gabe said. His voice had that careful modulation of someone who'd trained themselves to compensate for hearing loss. "Mind if we join you for a minute?"

"Course not." Shane gestured to the empty chairs.

They settled in. Rochelle immediately pulled out a book but kept it closed in her lap. Her way of having an escape route if the conversation got overwhelming, Ben knew.

"How you holding up?" Gabe asked Ben directly. No small talk, no dancing around it. Just straight to the point.

"I'm fine."

Rochelle's eyes flicked up to his face, then back down. She opened her mouth, closed it, then tried again. "You saved someone's life." Her voice was quiet but steady. "That's not fine. That's... big."

Ben looked at her—really looked. Rochelle understood what it was like to feel different, to have people underestimate you, to build walls to protect yourself. She'd worked through her stutter, built confidence, found love with Gabe. She was a different woman from the shy, quiet one he'd first met, who barely spoke or made eye contact.

"Maybe," Ben admitted.

"And Charlie's okay?" Rochelle asked.

"She's good. Flying back today."

Rochelle's expression brightened. "We like her. A lot. When she comes back, we'll have to convince her to hang out with us."

"The gal squad has spoken," Gabe said with a grin. "Rochelle, Ellie, April, Wren, Arden, Frankie, even Stephanie—they've all given Charlie the stamp of approval."

Ben smiled softly. "I think she'd like that. She's..."

Rochelle held up her hand. "You don't have to explain quiet and reserved to me."

"How is Frankie?" Shane asked. "Last I heard, everything was going smooth."

"Really good." Rochelle smiled. "She's glowing. The pregnancy's been easy so far, thank God. After everything with the ch-chemo..." She trailed off, but they all knew what she meant.

Frankie's cancer had been brutal. Finding out she was pregnant barely three months after finishing chemo had been terrifying. But so far, everything was progressing normally. The baby was healthy. Frankie was healthy.

Small miracles, Ben thought. He couldn't have been happier for her.

"Waylon keeps rearranging the nursery furniture," Rochelle added. "Frankie says he's nesting like crazy."

That got a laugh from everyone.

April appeared at their table with a fresh coffee for Ben. "On the house," she said before he could protest. "You look like you need it."

"Thanks, April."

She squeezed his shoulder. "Charlie gets in at six, right?"

Ben blinked. "How did you know?"

"Honey, we *all* know. Shane's a blabbermouth. You all are." April's smile was warm. "You should pick her up. Surprise her."

"I was planning to."

"Good." April's expression turned serious. "She's special, Ben. Don't let her slip away because you're too much in your head about whether you're good enough."

Ben felt his ears go red. "I'm not—"

"You are." April patted his shoulder again. "Trust me. I know the signs. Just... trust what you feel, okay?"

Before Ben could respond, the door chimed and several customers walked in. Sonny's voice boomed from behind the counter. "April! Stop mothering the customers and get back to work!"

April rolled her eyes but was grinning. "Duty calls." She headed back toward the counter, calling out to the customers, "Welcome to Riversong! Thanks for braving the music."

They talked for a while longer, Ben's gaze straying to the clock over and over. Yup, it was definitely broken. No clock in the history of time had ever moved so slowly.

"We should go," Rochelle said, tucking her book into her bag. "Stephanie will have my head if I'm late for yoga."

"Yeah." Gabe stood, Rochelle following. "Good seeing you both. And Ben?" He waited until Ben looked up. "She's worth it. Whatever you're worried about—she's worth it. And so are you, brother."

They left, Gabe's hand finding Rochelle's as they walked out into the afternoon sun.

Shane drained the last of his coffee. "They're right, you know."

"About what?"

"All of it." Shane stood, stretching. "As long as I've known King, she's never been this interested in a guy. I don't know. I've never seen this side of her."

"What do you mean?"

"It's the way she looks at you, man. She goes soft."

Ben immediately felt defensive. "She's not weak."

"Dude, not what I said. That woman used to drink the rest of under the table and swear until the rest of us felt like nuns. Hell, half the time we forgot she was a woman." He grinned. "Maybe that's it."

"What?"

"You've never seen her as one of the guys." He clapped Ben on the shoulder. "Pick her up at the airport. Tell her how you feel." He met Ben's eyes. "Life's too short to waste time pretending you don't feel what you feel. Sean taught us that."

The mention of their friend hit like a punch to the chest. Sean, who'd always lived large, loved hard, and never held back. Sean, who should've been home with them.

On time, on target, never quit.

"Yeah," Ben said quietly. "He did."

Shane straightened. "I've got the investigation covered. DCSO will keep digging. We'll figure out who sabotaged that saddle. But right now? Charlie's coming home and she's got the week off. So go get your girl."

DENVER INTERNATIONAL AIRPORT was chaos at six PM on a Monday. Ben stood near the top of the escalators that brought passengers up from the trains, shoulder-to-shoulder with other people waiting for arrivals—twenty-somethings checking phones, grandparents with balloons, a limo driver holding a sign that said RODRIGUEZ BACHELORETTE PARTY.

Ben just held his breath.

He'd parked in the covered parking lot and walked in an hour early, unable to sit still in the truck. Now he scanned every face coming up the escalator, looking for hazel eyes and long, dark-blond hair pulled back in that practical ponytail.

There.

Charlie appeared at the top of the escalator, Flo on a leash beside her. Even from here, Ben could see the exhaustion in her shoulders, the way she carried herself like someone who'd been running on fumes for too long. Her tactical backpack was slung over one shoulder, her other hand gripping Flo's lead.

She looked tired. Drawn. Beautiful.

Charlie's eyes swept the crowd, searching. Professional habit, probably—assessing threats, locating exits.

Then she found him.

The transformation was instantaneous. Her face lit up—not the polite smile she gave strangers or the professional mask she wore for clients. This was pure, unguarded joy. Her whole body seemed to brighten. Her shoulders lifted as if her exhaustion melted away as she stepped off the escalator.

Ben's chest went warm.

She was still searching his face as she followed the crowd through the roped-off security area, like she couldn't quite believe he was real until she was standing in front of him, looking up into his eyes. Flo wagged her tail, recognizing him immediately.

"Hey," Charlie said, her voice soft.

Ben didn't answer with words. He just wrapped his arms around her, pulling her against his chest. She came willingly, easily, like she belonged there. Her backpack hit the floor beside them. Her arms went around his waist and she pressed her face against his shirt.

She smelled like the recycled air from the plane, but underneath it, he smelled warm, sweet ponderosa pine bark and that distinctive scent that was just *Charlie*.

"I've missed you, Princess," Ben murmured into her hair.

He felt her shiver—actually shiver—at that word.

"I missed you, too." Her voice was muffled against his chest. "So much."

They stood like that for a long moment, the crowd flowing around them like water around stones in a river. Flo sat patiently at their feet, tail thumping against the sparkling white floor.

Finally, Charlie pulled back just enough to look up at him again. "Thanks again. You didn't have to drive all the way down here."

"Yes, I did." Ben picked up her backpack and slung it over his shoulder. It barely weighed anything. That was his efficient Charlie. "Your coach awaits."

That got a tired laugh out of her. "My coach?"

"Big blue pickup truck. It doesn't turn into a pumpkin at midnight, I'm afraid."

"Good. I can use some normal."

She slipped her hand into his as if she'd done it a hundred times.

That sent his heart pounding in his chest and his cock twitching in his pants.

She was smiling as they walked toward the parking garage, Flo trotting beside her. They didn't talk much on the walk. Ben kept stealing glances at her—the shadows under her eyes, the tight set of her jaw that said she was holding something back. Worry, probably. Maybe guilt. He'd have to fix that.

"You got them home safely," Ben said as they reached his truck.

"I know. And if anyone can protect them, it's Malcom McCoy." Charlie opened the back passenger door for Flo, who hopped in without hesitation.

"Malcom McCoy?"

"Former black ops, built like a tank, could kill you with a look." Charlie's mouth quirked. "And completely wrapped around his wife Annalie's little finger. He's the best there is. They're in good hands."

"But you're still worried."

"Even though he wasn't my client, someone tried to kill Rowan on my watch." Charlie closed the back door and leaned against it, her eyes on the concrete floor of the parking garage. "I should have caught it earlier. Should have seen—"

"Charlie." Ben stepped close, bracketing her against the truck with his arms. "You did catch it. We both saved him. That's how it works."

She looked up at him through those dark lashes. "Shane said the same thing."

"Shane's a smart guy."

"Sometimes." A ghost of a smile. "When he's not being an idiot."

"Want to grab dinner?" Ben asked, even though what he really wanted was to take her home and hold her until that tension in her shoulders finally released.

If he was being honest, he wanted to do so much more than that. He thought of all his fantasies, and how each one of them would remove every last bit of tension as she moaned his name.

Charlie's lips parted ever so slightly as she met his gaze. Her cheeks flooded with color and he noted her breaths speeding up.

"No. Just take me home," she whispered.

Ben opened the passenger door for her. "As you wish, Princess."

CHARLIE LED Ben up three flights of stairs to her apartment. Just before they went in, a door across the hall opened and a woman who looked at least a hundred poked her head out. She had perfectly coiffed dyed red hair and sharp, curious eyes that immediately locked onto Ben.

"Oh! Charlene, dear, you have a guest!" The woman's smile was warm but calculating.

Charlie sighed. "Hi, Mrs. Calhoun. This is Ben. Ben, this is my neighbor, Mrs. Calhoun."

"A gentleman caller!" Mrs. Calhoun clasped her hands together. "How wonderful! I've been telling Charlene she needs to meet a nice young man. You look very nice, dear. Are you nice?"

Ben's mouth twitched. "I try to be, ma'am."

"Wonderful! Well, I won't keep you two. I'm sure you have... plans." She winked and ducked back into her apartment.

Charlie groaned quietly as she unlocked her apartment door. "I'm so sorry. She means well, but—"

"She's going to ask you all about me next time she sees you," Ben finished as he walked into Charlie's apartment.

"Exactly." Charlie looked mortified as she closed the door behind them. "She's the building gossip, but she's harmless. Just very... interested in whether I've 'met a nice gentleman yet.'"

Ben grinned. "Have you?"

Her expression softened. "Yeah. I think I have."

Charlie's apartment was exactly what Ben expected.

She lived on the second floor of a well-maintained building in a quiet neighborhood. The security was good—locked entry, cameras, solid doors with deadbolts. Charlie unlocked hers and held it open for him, Flo padding inside first. Charlie took her shoes off and put them on a low wooden rack. Ben followed suit.

"Let me get Flo settled, then give me five minutes to change into something that doesn't smell like a two-hour plane ride."

The space was small but efficient. Living room with a couch and a recliner, both in denim blue. Kitchen visible through a doorway. No clutter, no dishes in the sink, throw pillows precisely aligned on the couch. Everything was military neat.

Except for the dining table near the window.

A large Moleskine sketchbook lay open, its pages filled with a sketch of the St. Vrain. Terracotta-colored Conte crayons broken into different-sized pieces and shapes were scattered across the surface. Fine-tipped pens and markers stood in a cracked mug with brushes of all sizes.

And tacked to the wall above the table, a single drawing.

Ben moved closer while Charlie got Flo settled with fresh water and food. The drawing was done in colored pencils, the strokes confident and sure. It showed the St. Vrain River near Riversong, late afternoon light turning the cliffs red and the water golden. Green and brown Cottonwoods lined the near side of the bank. A small figure sat on a rock by the water's edge.

The detail was incredible. Ben could almost hear the water, smell the summer heat, feel the stones under his hands.

"That's—" He stopped, throat tight.

"The St. Vrain." Charlie came to stand beside him. She'd taken off her jacket, was down to a black t-shirt and tactical pants. Somehow she looked both more vulnerable and more herself.

"It's beautiful," Ben said.

"It's home." Charlie's voice was soft. "Or it's starting to feel like it." She turned her head as she slipped her hand into his again.

"Charlie."

Ben turned her in his arms and looked into her hazel eyes only for a moment before he closed the distance between them.

He poured everything he'd been holding back into his kiss—relief that she was safe, gratitude that she'd invited him into her home, desire that had been building since the moment she'd smiled at him from that escalator.

Charlie made a small sound against his mouth and her hands came up to fist in his shirt. She kissed him back just as fiercely, with just as much hunger.

When they finally broke apart, both breathing hard, Ben rested his forehead against hers.

"Still want those five minutes to change clothes?" he asked, his voice a rough laugh.

Charlie's laugh was breathless. "No."

"Good." Ben swept her up off her feet and she wrapped her legs around his waist with a surprised gasp that turned into another laugh.

"Ben! No one's ever picked me up before."

"Bedroom's that way?" He nodded toward the open door.

"Yes."

"Good." He was already moving, Charlie in his arms. "Because I've been thinking about this for two days and I'm done waiting."

"Me too," Charlie whispered against his ear. "Me too."

Ben carried her through the hall and into her bedroom. He kicked the door closed behind them, and laid her gently on the bed. He stopped thinking about anything except the woman looking up at him with those hazel eyes full of trust and want.

"Hi," she said softly.

"Hi, Princess." Ben smiled down at her. "I've got you."

"I know." Charlie pulled him down to her. "I know you do."

SIXTEEN

No one had ever picked Charlie up like she weighed nothing, like she was something dainty.

As Ben carried her through the doorway into her bedroom, she should have felt self-conscious—she was tall, strong, probably bigger than any other woman he'd been with. His arms flexed around her body and he looked at her like she was the most beautiful thing he'd ever seen.

Ben laid her gently on the bed, his weight settling over her, careful not to crush her even though she wanted to feel all of him. He kissed her slowly, thoroughly, like they had all the time in the world.

"Before we go any further—are you on birth control? I have condoms if we need them, but I need to know what you want."

The question cut through the haze of desire just enough to ground her. "I'm on birth control. And I haven't been with anyone in over two years."

"Neither have I." Ben kissed her. "So...we're good?"

Charlie nodded. "We're good."

She listened to his heavy groan. "Can I touch you?" His voice was rough, strained.

"Yes. God, yes."

"Tell me what you want," he murmured against her mouth. "Tell me what you need, Princess."

Charlie's breath caught. *Princess.* He kept calling her that, and it sent heat straight through her core every time. She'd never been anyone's princess. Never been soft or delicate or treated like something to cherish.

"You," she managed. "I want you."

"You have me." Ben's hands found the hem of her t-shirt. "May I?"

She nodded, lifting her arms so he could pull it off. Her sports bra followed, and then she was bare from the waist up, her breathing quick and shallow.

Ben sat back on his heels, just looking at her. Charlie fought the urge to cover herself. Old insecurities rose up—*too tall, too muscular, not feminine enough*—but the expression on Ben's face stopped those thoughts cold.

Wonder. That's what she saw there. Pure wonder.

"Beautiful," he whispered. "So damn beautiful, Charlie."

He leaned down and kissed her between her breasts, right over her racing heart. Then his mouth found her nipple and Charlie arched off the bed with a gasp.

"Sensitive," Ben said with obvious satisfaction. "Good to know."

His tongue circled her tight nipple, then he sucked gently. Heat shot straight to her core and she fisted her hands in his hair.

"Ben—"

"I've got you." His hand slid down to the waistband of her tactical pants. "These need to come off."

Charlie helped him, lifting her ass, then shimmying out of her pants and underwear in one motion. Before she could second-guess or talk herself out of the best night of her life.

She was naked on her bed with Ben Massey looking down at her like she was a feast and he was starving.

Ben's warm, callused hands skimmed up her thighs. He traced

patterns on her skin, taking his time, exploring. When his fingers brushed the crease where her leg met her body, Charlie whimpered.

"Do you need something?" That teasing edge in his voice made her even wetter.

"You know what I need."

"Tell me anyway. I want to hear you say it."

Charlie's face flushed hot. She'd never been good at this—asking for what she wanted, being vulnerable, admitting need of any kind. But Ben was looking at her with such warmth, such patience, such *desire* that the words tumbled out.

"I want you to touch me. Please. Everywhere."

He brushed his hand lightly across her belly, making her insides flutter. "So soft, so *delicate*," he breathed into her ear.

I believe him, she realized with a great deal of astonishment.

"Does my lady like this?"

"Oh, yes." Charlie's voice quavered.

Is that me speaking?

He stroked her belly again, feather-light. "Now, spread your legs for me, Princess."

She did, and he gently bent her knees.

"I'm going to spread them wider. Is that all right?"

Charlie nodded and he spread her farther, until she felt entirely exposed.

"That's it. This is going to make you feel so good." Before he touched her, Charlie watched Ben study her body, his eyes dark with desire. She felt herself swell and grow wet under his gaze. She'd never been so turned on.

"That's it. That's my girl. Keep your legs spread wide for me." Ben slid his fingers up through her folds to her clit. She closed her eyes and bucked against his hand. His gruff laugh only turned her on more.

Then he settled between her thighs, his massive shoulders keeping her legs spread.

"Perfect." His breath ghosted over her wet heat and Charlie shivered. "Now relax, Princess. Let me take care of you."

His first touch was feather-light—just his fingertips tracing through her folds, learning her shape. Charlie bit back a moan.

"Don't hold back," Ben said. "I want to hear every sound you make."

Then his mouth was on her and Charlie stopped thinking entirely.

Ben's tongue circled her clit, then flicked directly over it.

"You taste so good."

When she gasped and bucked her hips, he did it again, harder.

"That's it," he murmured against her. "Show me what you like, princess."

He slid one finger inside her and Charlie cried out.

"Do you know how hard that makes me to hear you?" He ground against her mattress, which made her wetter. When he crooked his finger to find that perfect spot inside her she saw stars.

"More," she gasped. "Please, Ben, that feels amazing."

He added a second finger, stretching her while his tongue worked magic on her clit. The dual sensation overwhelmed her. Her pleasure built and built until she was right on the verge of coming.

Ben must have sensed how close she was because he slowed down, and that was the sweetest torture she'd ever known.

"Not so fast, Princess." He gave her one long, slow lick. "I want you on the edge until you can't take any more."

Charlie closed her eyes as her head fell back against the pillow. She'd never felt so hungry. Ben sped up gradually, bringing her close again, then slowed and she bit her bottom lip. She opened her eyes when he groaned. He looked up at her, his eyes dark and hot.

"Come for me, Princess. Want to feel you come on my fingers."

That was all it took. Charlie went over the edge into ecstasy. Ben stroked her through it, his fingers gentling but not stopping until she collapsed back against the mattress, trembling and utterly satisfied.

"Holy shit," Charlie breathed.

Ben crawled up her body, pressing kisses along the way. When he reached her mouth he kissed her deeply, and she could taste herself on his tongue.

"You're still dressed," she pointed out, tugging at his shirt.

"Easily fixed." Ben sat up and pulled his shirt over his head in one smooth motion.

Charlie's mouth went dry.

All that muscle, all that strength, and the way he was looking at her like she was the only thing in the world that mattered.

She reached up and traced the planes of his chest, the ridges of his abs. When her fingers found the waistband of his pants, she looked up at him. "Can I?"

"Please."

Charlie undid his belt, then his button and zipper. She pulled his pants and boxer briefs down together like he'd done to her. His cock sprang free, thick and hard and already wet at the tip.

Oh.

"Too much?" Ben's voice held uncertainty for the first time.

"No. Not at all. My turn to touch you." Charlie wrapped her hand around the shaft of his cock—he was hot and heavy in her palm. "You're perfect." She stroked him once, twice, and Ben groaned deep in his chest.

"Charlie, if you keep doing that, this is going to be over embarrassingly fast."

"Can't have that." But she stroked him one more time just to watch his eyes flutter closed.

Ben caught her wrist and stilled her hand. He reached between them and circled her entrance with one finger, teasing. "Already so wet again. You want this, Princess?"

"Yes. God, yes."

He pushed inside her—one finger, then two—and when he found that perfect spot again she couldn't hold back her moan.

"That's it. Don't hide from me. Show me what you like." Ben's thumb found her clit while his fingers worked inside her. "I want to watch you come apart for me again."

The pleasure built faster this time, sharper, and Ben wasn't slowing down. Charlie grabbed his shoulders, needing something to hold onto as he drove her higher and higher.

"Ben, I'm—"

"I know. I've got you." He increased the pressure and speed until Charlie climaxed for the second time, crying out his name as she clenched around his fingers.

When she came back to herself, Ben was kissing her softly, murmuring praise against her lips. "So beautiful. So perfect. My perfect princess."

Charlie pulled him down for a deeper kiss, wrapping her legs around his waist. She could feel his cock pressing against her, hot and hard.

"I need you inside me," she whispered. "Please, Ben."

"Are you sure? We can wait—"

"I'm sure." She looked into his eyes. "I want this. I want *you*."

Ben positioned himself at her entrance, the head of his cock pressing against her. "Tell me if it's too much or if I'm being too rough."

She nodded. No man had ever asked her before. No man had treated her with such attentiveness, afraid he'd hurt her.

"Tell me if you need me to stop."

"I won't." Charlie tilted her hips, trying to take him in. "*Please*."

He pushed inside her slowly, giving her time to adjust. The stretch was intense—he was bigger than anyone she'd been with before. But it felt *right*. Like her body had been waiting for this, for him.

"Okay?" Ben's voice was strained, his muscles trembling with the effort of holding still.

"More than okay." Charlie lifted her hips, taking him deeper. "Don't you hold back."

Ben groaned and thrust the rest of the way in, seating himself fully inside her. They both gasped at the sensation.

"So tight," Ben breathed. "So damn good. Fuck, Charlie."

He started to move—slow, deep strokes that rebuilt her heat with every thrust. Every withdrawal left her aching for him to return.

Charlie wrapped her arms around his neck, her legs around his waist, holding him as close as possible. She'd never felt this connected to anyone, never felt this *safe* while being so completely vulnerable.

"Harder," she whispered. "I won't break."

Ben's control snapped. He thrust harder, faster, one hand gripping her hip while the other braced beside her head. The sound of skin on skin filled the room, mixed with their harsh breathing and Charlie's increasingly desperate moans.

"Touch yourself," Ben commanded. "Want to feel you come around my cock."

Charlie slid her hand between their bodies and found her clit. The added stimulation was almost too much—she was so sensitive, so overwhelmed.

"That's it, Princess. Come for me one more time."

The orgasm hit her like a tidal wave. Charlie cried out, her body clenching around Ben's cock as pleasure whited out everything else. She felt Ben's rhythm falter, felt him thrust deep one final time as he groaned her name.

They collapsed together, both shaking, both gasping for breath. Ben stayed inside her and rolled to the side, immediately pulling Charlie against his chest.

She'd never felt safer in her life.

"You okay?" Ben sounded concerned.

Charlie nodded against his chest. "More than okay."

"Good." He pressed a kiss to the top of her head. "Because I'm never letting you go."

And for the first time in her life, Charlie believed those words.

"Good," she whispered. "Because, Ben? I want you to stay."

SEVENTEEN

Ben woke to soft gray light filtering through Charlie's bedroom curtains and the warm weight of her body pressed against his side.

I want you to stay.

After they'd made love, after she'd come apart in his arms three times, she'd curled into him and whispered those five beautiful words like she was afraid he might disappear in the night.

Not a chance in hell, Princess.

Now she was sound asleep, her hair spilling across his chest, one leg thrown over his thigh. Her breathing was slow and even and her expression was the most peaceful he'd ever seen on her face.

Ben carefully shifted so he could see her better. Without that professional mask she wore during the day, she looked younger. Softer. Her lips were slightly parted, her lashes dark crescents against her cheeks.

My Princess.

Charlie stirred, making a small sound. Her hand slid across his chest and lower over the top sheet, brushing against his morning erection.

Ben sucked in a breath.

Charlie opened her eyes slowly. Hazel eyes, still hazy with sleep, focused on his face. A slow smile curved her lips.

"Morning," she said, her voice rough.

"Morning, Princess." Ben tucked a strand of hair behind her ear. "Sleep okay?"

"Best sleep I've ever had." Her hand was still resting dangerously close to his cock tenting the sheet. She had to see how hard he was. "You?"

"Same."

Charlie's smile turned wicked. She shifted her hand deliberately, cupping his cock over the thin sheet. "Is this for me?" She licked her lips.

Ben groaned. "You don't have to—"

"I want to." She pushed herself up on one elbow, and looked down at him. Her breasts were bare, nipples tight with excitement, he hoped. "I wanted to last night, but you wouldn't let me."

"Last night was about you."

"And this morning is about *you.*" Charlie threw back the sheet and Ben's cock stood at attention, hard and aching.

She wrapped her hand around his shaft and stroked once. Ben's hips jerked involuntarily.

"Sensitive," Charlie said, echoing his words from last night. Her smile was pure satisfaction.

She leaned down and licked the tip of his cock. Ben's hands fisted in the sheets.

"Charlie—"

"Relax, Ben. Let me take care of you now. It's my turn." She took him into her mouth, her tongue swirling around the head.

The wet heat was almost too much. Ben groaned, one hand moving to tangle in her hair. "*Fuck.*"

Charlie made a satisfied sound that vibrated his cock. She took him deeper, her hand stroking the base. She found a rhythm that made his toes curl as pleasure built at the base of his spine.

"Not gonna last," Ben managed. "You're too good at this."

Charlie pulled off with a wet pop. "Good." She stroked him faster. "I want to watch you come."

The combination of her hand and those words sent him over the edge. Ben came with a groan, spilling across his stomach as Charlie worked him through it.

When he finally caught his breath, Charlie was grinning at him.

"Satisfied?" she asked.

Ben pulled her up for a kiss. "Very. But now I need to return the favor."

"You don't have to—"

"I want to." Ben rolled them over until Charlie was on her back beneath him. He kissed down her neck, her chest, stopping to lavish attention on her breasts.

Charlie arched into his mouth, her hands in his hair.

Ben continued his path downward, kissing across her belly, her hip bones, the inside of her thighs. When he spread her legs, she was already wet.

"And is all *this* for *me*?" Ben teased.

"Getting you off got me hot." Charlie's cheeks flushed pink. "That okay?"

"That's perfect." Ben settled between her thighs. "Now spread your legs wider, Princess. I'm hungry."

He started slowly this time, long licks through her folds, circling her clit without directly touching it. Teasing. Learning every sound she made, every twitch and gasp that told him what she liked.

When he finally sucked her clit into his mouth, Charlie cried out.

"Yes. Right there. Don't stop," she gasped.

Ben had no intention of stopping. He worked her methodically, building her pleasure stroke by stroke, lick by lick.

"Ben, I'm close—"

He increased the pressure and Charlie came with a sharp cry, her thighs clamping around his head. Ben gentled his touch but didn't stop until she pushed at his shoulders, oversensitive.

He crawled back up her body and kissed her deeply. Charlie wrapped her arms and legs around him.

"Again," she whispered against his mouth. "I want you inside me again."

Ben's spent cock twitched with interest. "Give me a minute."

"We have time." Charlie ran her hands down his back to his ass, pulling him closer. "We have all morning." She looked at him shyly through her lashes. "I have all week, actually. If you're interested in spending it with me."

If he was interested? God, she was killing him.

No work, no obligations, nothing but each other and this bed and the gray morning light turning gold.

"I am. Just try and keep me away."

Ben kissed her slowly, thoroughly, letting his body recover while he explored hers. He mapped every freckle, every scar, every sensitive spot that made her gasp or moan.

By the time he was hard again, Charlie was writhing beneath him.

"Please," she begged. "Ben, I need you."

He positioned himself at her entrance. "Tell me what you need, Princess."

"You. Deep. Hard. Everything. All of it."

Ben pushed inside her in one smooth thrust. They both groaned at the same time.

"So wet," Ben said. "So perfect for me."

He set a steady rhythm, hitting deep with every stroke. Charlie met him thrust for thrust, her nails digging into his shoulders.

"Want to feel you come around me, baby."

Within seconds she was gasping, trembling on the edge.

"That's it. Come for me, Princess. Let me feel it. I've got you."

She clenched around him as she came, and that was all it took. Ben thrust deep one final time and followed her over. He'd never come so hard.

"I should take care of Flo," Charlie said without moving.

"In a minute." Ben pulled her closer. "Just want to hold you a little longer."

Charlie snuggled into his chest. "Okay. A little longer."

BEN INSISTED on making Charlie breakfast.

"No, it's rude of me to have you over and not cook for you." She tried to reach past him for a pan on the stove.

Ben laughed as he grabbed her wrist gently. "As if I didn't want to be here." He kissed her and patted her ass. "Go. Take Flo for a walk, wash your hair, watch TV, whatever you want to do."

"I want to make you breakfast."

"Anything except that." He kissed the tip of her nose. "Let me spoil you."

Her eyes turned misty and she blinked hard. She was clearly—*clearly*—not used to being spoiled.

All that was about to change.

"Thank you," she whispered.

"Anything for you."

She smiled and turned.

"And, Charlie?"

She looked back at him. "Yeah?"

"Just so you know, making breakfast for you is not spoiling you. That's baseline care in my book."

She bit her lower lip as she looked away.

He thought he heard her say, *not in mine* as she left the kitchen.

Charlie took Flo for a quick walk. Ben loved hearing her talking to the dog before and after. She hadn't had Flo for long, and already she was her baby. And it was clear that Flo loved her right back. She wagged her tail as Charlie sat on the floor with her, scratching her ears.

"Did you have a dog growing up? Ben asked.

"No."

"Cats?"

Charlie paused. "No pets." She stood up and walked to the kitchen table.

Dammit. He'd stepped in it somehow.

Charlie settled down to sketch at her kitchen table while Ben fried half a dozen eggs and baked a pound of bacon on a sheet pan in the oven. He sneaked peeks at her as he cooked. She was completely focused on her drawing, but the intensity of her gaze left her looking peaceful. All of the tension from just a few minutes before had melted away. She tilted her head and smiled down at the paper, and started humming. Ben took that as satisfaction with her work.

I could do this for the rest of my life.

Only, he pictured Charlie in the Victorian he'd so carefully restored. He'd set up one of the spare bedrooms—the one that got the best light—as her studio. Or even build her one beside his forge.

Whatever his Princess wanted.

When the toast popped up, Charlie looked up, then cleared off the table and set all her art supplies on the coffee table in front of the couch. She appeared in the kitchen a minute later.

"Let me at least set the table." She pulled plates down from a shelf beside the fridge.

"Set those on the counter and go sit," Ben said with a smile. "Do I have to teach you how to be spoiled?"

Charlie actually giggled. "Maybe?"

"Well, I will." He leaned forward and kissed her. "For as long as it takes."

Her eyes went misty again, and Ben could only wonder to himself.

Who hurt you so badly, Charlie?

While they ate breakfast, Ben's curious gaze kept drifting to the sketchbook on the coffee table. He'd only seen one sketch and the drawing of the St. Vrain the night before. Charlie tilted her head.

"I can't wait to see what else you've done. If it's all right?"

She grinned as she fed Flo a piece of bacon under the table.

"Sure," she said quietly. She slid the sketchbook across the coffee table toward him.

Ben considered it a victory.

He turned the pages slowly, careful with them. They were landscapes. Mountains, mostly, and several of the St. Vrain, the peaks above Lyons, and a sweeping panorama of the Front Range. All of it was rendered with the same quiet precision she brought to everything else she did.

"These are extraordinary, Charlie."

She ducked her head over her coffee. "They're just rough sketches."

"No," he said. "They're not. They're beautiful."

They loaded Charlie's art supplies and Flo into Ben's truck. As they were closing the tailgate, Mrs. Calhoun appeared on her balcony with a watering can.

"Good morning, Charlene! And good morning to your nice gentleman friend!" She waved enthusiastically. "I'm glad to see you came back this morning."

Charlie tried not to laugh as she waved back. "Yes, he did. Morning, Mrs. Calhoun."

"Going somewhere exciting?"

"Just a day trip to the mountains," Charlie called up.

"How lovely! You two have a wonderful time!" Mrs. Calhoun beamed at them, then stage-whispered loud enough to be heard across the parking lot: "He's a keeper, dear!"

Charlie's face went pink as they got in the truck.

Ben was grinning. "She's something."

"Yeah, she's something all right. Everyone in the building probably knows about you by now."

"Is that a problem?"

Charlie looked at him, considering. "No," she said as she broke into a huge grin. "No, I don't think it is."

AS THEY DROVE along through the mountains, Charlie took out her Moleskine notebook and flipped it open. Her packet of colored pens and pencils came next, and soon she was sketching something. Ben assumed she was drawing the distant peaks that came into view over the treetops every time they came around a bend.

"We can stop for a few minutes if you'd like. There are several scenic views along here and you could snap a photo for later."

"No thanks. I can see what I'm drawing just fine from here." She smiled at him.

He couldn't wait to get to Loveland Pass, just so he could see what she'd been drawing. He loved her quick sketches even more than the bigger pieces she worked on at home. Her sketches held life and movement in their quick pen strokes. She'd have to draw quickly, since her subject kept appearing and disappearing from view. Unless she was sketching the road, but even then, it twisted and turned, changing shape like a sidewinder crossing a dusty plain.

She hummed quietly to herself, which meant she was happy with whatever she was capturing on paper. Her whole demeanor softened the atmosphere in the truck, making him so comfortable, he forgot to be self-conscious. As much as he wanted to get there and see what she'd drawn, he wanted to keep driving forever, keep the easy, golden, satisfied feeling in his chest, knowing she was happy, in her element, and he could just exist with her in the world. That was more than he'd ever expected in a relationship.

But roads didn't always go on forever, and eventually, he saw the sign for the turnoff.

Be grateful for what you have. A perfect two hours with Charlie happy beside you. The memory of this feeling will be with you always. Always.

He eased into a parking spot. Charlie straightened and blinked as she looked out the windshield.

"We're here?" she asked, sounding surprised as she closed her sketchbook and tucked it into her bag.

"Yes," Ben answered. "I would have thought you'd seen the signs since you were sketching. You were so engrossed, but I guess you were too busy focusing on the landscape in the distance and not things up close."

"That's not what I was looking at or sketching."

"No? So you were sketching the road itself?"

"No," she laughed lightly. "You really don't know, do you?" Her voice had turned soft, threaded with wonder. "Would you like to see?"

"Of course. I've been wondering what had your rapt attention for an hour."

She grinned and reached back into her bag. She took out the Moleskine and flipped through several pages until she came to the latest sketches. She gazed at them fondly for a moment before those gorgeous hazel eyes looked back up at him through her lashes. She flipped the cover closed, her thumb bookmarking the pages, and handed over the book.

Ben slid his thumb between the pages as he took the Moleskine. He flipped it open and stared for a moment at the sketches, dumbfounded.

"These are...these are all of me."

Ben shook his head, his eyes never leaving the book. She'd done several of him, some from the side, some in three-quarter view. Ben staring straight ahead and gripping the wheel. Ben with his mouth slightly open as he sang along to the radio. Ben smiling, glancing at her. Snapshots of their drive up, one after the other, after the other. And they were...flattering. She'd somehow captured the way he'd felt —at peace, happy, content.

"Is this how you see me?" he asked softly.

"Sorry, I'm not good at portraiture..."

"I'm absolutely...you made me look...attractive."

Charlie widened her eyes for a moment, then laughed. "That's because you are, Ben. How can you not know that?" Some of the laughter faded from her eyes, replaced by a quizzical look. "You really don't know, do you?"

"Know what?"

"How attractive you are."

Ben stared at her. No one had ever looked at him the way Charlie was looking at him right now—like he was someone worth keeping.

His chest went tight. Words crowded in his throat, three simple words that wanted out so badly he could barely breathe around them.

"I—" He stopped. Swallowed hard. "I think you're—"

Charlie's expression softened. She reached up and touched his face, her thumb brushing his cheekbone. "I know," she said quietly. "Me too."

She understood. She felt it too. And she wasn't running.

Ben let out a shaky breath and pulled her into his arms. Not yet. The words would come when the time was right. But this—holding her, knowing she felt the same—this was enough for now.

Ben and Charlie got out of the truck. Flo hopped down after them, immediately sniffing the air. Up here at nearly twelve thousand feet, the wind was sharp and cool despite the relentless summer sun. Charlie pulled on a hoodie and grabbed her art supplies.

"This way," Ben said, leading her to a flat outcropping of rock that overlooked the valley below. The view was spectacular—jagged peaks in every direction, patches of late-summer snow clinging to the shadowed slopes, and far below, the winding ribbon of highway they'd just driven.

Charlie stood at the edge, taking it all in. Ben watched her face light up with that artist's eye, already composing the scene.

"It's even more beautiful than I remembered it," she said quietly.

"I'm glad you think so." Ben set out a couple of folding chairs and a collapsible table he'd brought from the truck. "You can work here. I'll keep Flo entertained."

Charlie settled into one of the chairs and opened her Moleskine. She untied a waxed canvas roll that held her pencils, pens, and other art supplies and grabbed a drafting pencil. Within minutes, she'd switched to her colored pencils and was lost in her work, her hand moving across the page in quick, confident strokes.

Ben sat nearby with Flo, throwing a Kong Charlie had brought along. The dog bounded after it, happy to run in the mountain air. But Ben's attention kept drifting back to Charlie.

She was completely focused. Every few minutes she'd look up, study the landscape, then back down to capture what she saw.

Beautiful.

After a while, Ben moved closer. "Can I watch?"

Charlie glanced up, startled out of her concentration. Then she smiled. "Sure."

Ben took the chair beside her, careful not to block her light. On the page, mountains were taking shape in layers of blue and purple and gray. She'd captured the depth of the valley, the way distance softened edges and lightened colors until they almost faded into the azure sky.

"You're really good at this," Ben said.

"Thanks." Charlie added dark blue to a shadow. "Sean used to watch me sketch sometimes."

Ben's chest tightened at the mention of his friend. "Yeah?"

"Yeah. Remember at dinner, when I said the river was what brought me to Lyons? That's only partly true."

"What?"

She added some crosshatching to one of the Seven Sisters. "Sean told me I'd love it here, that it was the St. Vrain that made him want to join the Navy. He wanted me to draw it for him." Charlie kept working, not looking at him. "From a photo of you all as teenagers horsing around in the river."

"I know the one you're talking about. We all have a copy of it." Ben remembered that day. Hot summer, cold river water, the kind of perfect afternoon that only existed when you were young and stupid and invincible.

"I thought about that photo a lot after Sean died. I was suffocating in San Diego. The Navy, the memories, everything. I needed somewhere that felt like hope instead of loss. Shane recommending me to Kyle was a lifeline."

"So that's why you came out. For Watchdog."

"No. The job just made things convenient." Charlie grinned at him. "I came out because one guy in particular in that photo caught my attention."

"Elias, right?" Ben said, his mouth quirking.

Charlie laughed. "That pretty boy? Nah."

"Must have been Bear then."

"Wrong again. He was quite a bit smaller in that photo than now. I like them bigger. More rugged. The kind who remembers coffee orders and pulls out chairs for a woman."

"Yeah?"

"Yeah." Charlie leaned over and kissed him. She pulled back and held his gaze as she stroked his cheek. "It wasn't just the photo of you that got my attention. Sean told me about each of you. Bear was the quiet one. Elias and Waylon were the troublemakers. Gabe never met a stranger. Of course I already knew Shane as a smartass." Charlie laughed.

Her gaze grew soft and warm. "You were the gentle giant who everyone underestimated."

"Sean said that?"

"He did." Charlie said. "He also told me you were the best artist he'd ever seen, even back then. Clay, wood, metal, didn't matter. You could make anything beautiful with your hands."

Ben looked away, throat tight. "He was a good friend."

"The best." Charlie's voice went soft. "I miss him. Every damn day."

"Me too."

They sat in silence for a moment. The wind whistled past the rocks. Flo chased a butterfly.

"Sean would've liked this," Charlie said. "You and me."

"I agree, Princess."

Ben wrapped his arm around her shoulders while she worked. He watched the whole scene before them come alive on the page.

"There," she said finally, setting down her pencil. "What do you think?"

"I think it's incredible." Ben kissed her temple. "You captured it perfectly."

Charlie closed the sketchbook and turned. "Thank you for bringing me here."

"Thank you for coming with me."

"I'd go anywhere with you, Ben." She said it simply, like it was just a fact. "You know that, right?"

Ben's heart pounded in his chest. "Yeah. I know. "Come here." Ben pulled her onto his lap.

They sat together, wrapped in each other's arms, while Flo dozed in the sun and the wind carried the scent of pine and stone and summer.

Right now, in this moment, Ben had everything he ever wanted.

EIGHTEEN

KNOCK KNOCK KNOCK.

Charlie sat straight up in bed before her eyes were even open. Ben stirred next to her.

Ben blinked up at her. "What—"

"Fuck. I think that's Mrs. Calhoun. She never uses the buzzer." Charlie slapped her hand over her mouth. She was pretty sure that was the first time she'd ever said fuck in front of Ben.

Ben chuckled as he rubbed his eyes. "She's an early riser, I see."

"Yeah. Probably checking to see if you're still being a gentleman."

Ben gave her one of his panty-melting smiles. "Am I?"

"Pffft. After what you did to me last night, you're more of a knave." She leaned down and kissed him, lingering until another knock sounded, this time a little louder. Charlie pulled away reluctantly and with an eyeroll. She got out of bed and threw on her robe.

"Wait in here," she said quietly as she put her index finger to her lips. "Back soon."

"Oh, I'll be waiting." He stretched his massive arms and put his hands behind his head as he leaned back against the headboard and

Charlie damn near went back to bed, gossipy Mrs. Calhoun be damned.

I hope she didn't see that Ben spent the night again. I'll never hear the end of it.

There was a third polite but insistent knock when Charlie was halfway across the living room.

But of course she did.

"Coming, Mrs. Calhoun, coming." Charlie tightened her robe around her as she turned the deadbolt, hoping Mrs. Calhoun had no concept of sex hair, and opened the door.

"Charlene, honey, look who I ran into in the lobby! He looked lost, so I asked him who he wanted and then I brought him straight up. Isn't this nice?"

Mrs. Calhoun's voice faded as a dull roar filled Charlie's head. Standing behind her neighbor was Charlie's father.

The man Charlie never wanted to see again. The man she'd avoided for over a decade.

"Charlene." Her name came out of his mouth in a wheeze.

"What the hel—what are you doing here?" She tried not to hold anything against Mrs. Calhoun. How was she supposed to know that the last person Charlie ever—*ever*—wanted to see in this lifetime was the man who treated her like dog shit, like his own personal maid, and encouraged his sons to do the same.

"Sorry for the short notice—"

"Try *no* notice. How did you find me?"

Then she remembered the phone message from Joey. The hesitancy in his voice had been totally fake. He'd found her and ratted her out.

Mrs. Calhoun looked between the two of them like she was watching a tennis match, no doubt looking forward to spreading the gossip.

As her father literally pushed past her into the apartment, Mrs. Calhoun bought a clue and said, "I'll let you two catch up. Too-daloo." She crossed the hallway to her apartment and disappeared inside.

Charlie didn't close her door, but turned to the man who dared to call himself her father and said quietly, evenly, "Get the hell out, now."

"Nice way to greet your old man. I brought you something." He reached into his pocket, pulled out a bag of peanut M&Ms, and held it out to her at arm's length.

She stared at him. "Are you serious?"

"They're your favorite."

"No, I hate the peanut ones. Get out." She pointed back out into the hall.

He put them back in his pocket. "Charlene. Come on. I've come all this way. Just give your old man a minute."

"No."

"Not even one minute to catch his breath?" His voice had turned almost charming, but she wasn't falling for it. She'd *never* fall for it.

God, why today? Why, when she had Ben waiting in her bedroom, would her father darken her door?

Hide what you love.

Charlie dropped her head. The only way out was through. She prayed Ben had drifted back off to sleep and wasn't listening at the bedroom door. She kept her voice low, hoping her father would, too.

"Fine. One minute and then you leave." She glanced at the wall clock. "Starting now." She reluctantly closed the door and folded her arms.

"Your place looks good," her father said, looking around. "You're keeping it nice."

"Clock's ticking."

Then he saw the drawing of the St. Vrain on the wall.

"You draw that?" he asked casually as he pointed at it.

Charlie felt like she'd been gut punched. "Are you being serious right now?" she choked out. An old familiar feeling of panic set in. Memories threatened to overwhelm her. Memories of her father ripping up all the drawings Charlie did as a little girl, all the drawings of her mother—

Hide what you love from him.

"It's real pretty. You always were a good artist."

"Time's up. Get out." Her voice sounded so small. She felt small. It always happened around her father. It didn't matter how old she was or how tall she'd grown—Charlie was always the smallest person in the room when her father was in it, too. So she added, "Desmond."

His eyes flickered with surprise, registering that she'd just used his first name. That gave her a little strength back.

He tried a different tactic. "Louise left me." He gave her a hangdog look.

Charlie rolled her gaze to the ceiling and huffed out a breath. "Wife number three, or is it four now?"

"Three. I don't want another. Too expensive."

Charlie snorted. "So what does any of this have to do with me?"

His gaze swept around her apartment until it settled on the drawing of the St. Vrain again.

"Need you to come home."

If Charlie hadn't closed the door behind her, she would have fallen backward through the doorway. "No fucking way, are you serious? Is that why you had Joey try to find me?"

Her father looked confused. "Joey? I haven't talked to that little shit in ten years."

Charlie hid her shock. So Joey hadn't been working on her father's behalf?

Desmond continued. "Louise is gone. She took half my money. I'm not in the best of health anymore."

Charlie just stared at him, knowing what was coming next and still unable to believe it.

"I don't know how to cook and I don't have the money to eat out all the time. I can't hire a housekeeper. You always did all that for us. Who's gonna take care of me if you don't come home?" he whined.

"The devil himself, for all I care. Or maybe your worthless sons."

"Baby girl—"

Charlie reared back. "Don't you *ever* call me that," she hissed. "Mum called me that."

"Right up until the day she left you," Desmond said. "Worthless bitch up and left her husband, her kids."

"And I can't blame her." Charlie gestured at her father. "Look what she had to deal with."

Staring at her father, at his red, swollen nose, his small, cruel eyes, the bitter frown lines around his mouth, she understood her mother's choice.

"Can't believe you're still taking her side, Charlene. She left you and went and got herself another family. You ever hear from her?"

No.

"That's none of your business."

He barked out a laugh. "Yeah, that's a no." He walked to the couch and sat down, settling in like he owned it. Owned her. "I'm the one who kept a roof over your head, kept you and your brothers fed, took care of you—"

"Oh now that right there is a lie." She pointed at him. "You never cared for me, for any of us. I'm the one who cared. I'm the one who shopped and cooked and cleaned and made sure my little brother had his homework done, right up until he turned on me, too." That had hurt almost as much if not more than her mum's abandonment. "I took her place. No twelve-year-old child should have to do that. And now I can't believe you're asking—no, *telling* me—to do it again."

She realized she was raising her voice and glanced quickly toward the bedroom. No sign of Ben. *Good.*

Hide what you love, or he'll take it away.

"It's a child's duty to respect and obey her father—"

"Then it's a good thing I'm not a child anymore, if I ever was."

"—and a woman's duty to manage the home. So I'm not taking no for an answer, Charlene."

Charlie opened the front door. "Get off my couch and get out of here. Your minute's up, old man."

He didn't move. If anything, he settled in.

"You never were much of a woman, though, were you?" He looked her up and down, making her skin crawl. "Women are supposed to be dainty. What the hell happened to you?"

He'd told her that ever since she hit a growth spurt at thirteen. *What's wrong with you? Girls are supposed to be dainty. No man's ever gonna want you for a wife.* Over and over until she believed it.

Charlie sized him up, remembering all the times he yelled at her, belittled her, hit her with his belt when she didn't make what he wanted for dinner, or the house wasn't clean enough, or just because he'd had a bad day and she was a convenient target. He'd tower over her as he slipped the belt out of its loops one by one. If she cried, he'd tell her to toughen up.

When her brothers ganged up on her, he'd laugh. *Toughen up.*

Even when she was tall enough to look him straight in the eye, he'd always seemed so much bigger than her, so much more powerful.

Not anymore.

Now she could see him through adult eyes, eyes that had seen combat. He was out of shape, flabby, and almost twice her age. The way he was wheezing, she'd be surprised if he didn't have emphysema. She could literally kick his ass out of her apartment, through the hall, down the stairs, and across the parking lot to his car.

He glared back. "Just look at you right now. You look like a man, Charlene. Sizing me up, thinking you can take me. You never could and you never will. I came all this way, thinking you gave a damn about me." He sneered. "You owe me, Charlene. You still have a duty to me."

"I don't owe you shit."

Desmond stood up, hands opening and closing at his sides the way they did right before he took off his belt, like they just couldn't wait to inflict pain. "You think because you were in the Navy, you're tough now? That you can take me?"

Charlie's stomach twisted. "How'd you know I served?"

"Found out when I looked you up. I shouldn't have been

surprised. Why'd you enlist? You think because you're big as a man, you are one?" His voice rose, "Or are you just a slut who wanted to be around a bunch of men who were forced to be around you?"

Now she heard movement—the bedroom door opening, footsteps.

Ben. Please, no. Stay hidden.

Her father turned toward the sound. "You got someone here?" He made a wheezing sound that barely passed for a laugh. "Can't wait to see who's desperate enough to want you."

Because if he can't take away what you love, he'll piss on it until it's ruined.

Ben appeared at the front of the hall, taking up most of the entryway. He'd put on pants and a t-shirt which stretched across his chest, highlighting every muscle. Flo stood at his side, hackles raised, growling.

The sight of Ben wiped the mean smile right off Desmond's face.

"I'm going to give you one chance. My lady said you need to leave, so you'd better leave."

Desmond sneered. "Your lady? My daughter's no *lady*, she's a fucking moose—"

Ben thundered across the room toward Desmond. He took one step back, his calf hit the couch, and he would have fallen backward if Ben hadn't grabbed his shirt collar and hauled him up.

Charlie stood frozen in place. The concept of someone defending her from her father was making her brain tilt.

"I'm not going to waste my breath telling you to show some respect for your own daughter," Ben growled through clenched teeth, his face inches from Desmond's. "Because it's obvious you're too stupid for that." He started walking backwards, dragging Desmond with him. Desmond clawed at Ben's hands but had no chance of making him let go.

"I have emphysema."

"I don't give a shit." Ben reached for the doorknob behind him and turned it. He threw it open and dragged Desmond into the hall.

Charlie unfroze and ran to the door. She stopped just shy of going out into the hall, standing in the doorway instead.

"Now, do I have to drag you all the way down to the lobby? Because I'm more than hap—"

Desmond took a swing at Ben.

"Well, I guess I do." Ben turned Desmond around and frog-marched him to the stairs. Charlie couldn't see her father past Ben's broad shoulders as they disappeared down the stairs.

Mrs. Calhoun's door opened slowly and she poked her head out. She looked at the disappearing men, then looked at Charlie.

"Keeper."

Charlie could only nod.

If he comes back.

MAYBE IT WAS A MINUTE LATER. Maybe it was an hour, or an entire day later—Charlie had no concept of time in her current state—but Ben came back.

Charlie was standing just inside her apartment, eyes squeezed shut, trying to process... everything.

She listened to him lock the door, then cross the room and sit down on her couch, the creak of the wood hidden somewhere under the upholstery sounding like tired old bones. She felt so much older than she really was, and at the same time she felt like a helpless little girl who'd been caught doing something she shouldn't have but that might not be her fault and then the room was spinning, spinning spinning and she tried to push it all back down inside, deeper than the bottom of the ocean, down in the cold dark—

"Come here."

His voice cut through the deep fathoms of where her soul had sunk to. Her shame. Her secret.

"Charlie."

But she couldn't move. Couldn't open her eyes. She couldn't turn and face him. Couldn't let him see the devastation on her face. The weakness. The broken fortress.

"Princess. Come here."

A bolt of pink light shot down through the midnight blue fathoms and found her.

"Come here, Princess."

She tried to ignore his voice. If she stood here perfectly still long enough, he would leave. And then she could quietly put the fortress back together stone by stone, and make sure the mortar was twice as thick as it was before so that this could never happen again.

Her mother taught Charlie to put on armor and hide what she loved.

She loved Ireland, her homeland more than she loved us, I guess.

She'd left Desmond, went back, married her childhood sweetheart, and never sent for her children like she'd promised.

Charlie heard the couch creak again and knew he was standing, and soon he would walk past her out the door again. He would open it and she would stare at the floor, and he would turn the knob and she would count the rings in the wood and he would close it behind him and she would be alone again and she could put the armor back on in peace.

She felt his weight behind her before he touched her. Before he reached out and put his hand on her shoulder and his hand was so big she couldn't believe it was real. Was she shrinking? Was she somehow collapsing into herself?

Ben scooped her up and she curled into his chest. She'd never felt so small. She should have felt terrified but she didn't. He walked with her in his arms down the hall to her bedroom and settled her in. Why was she shaking so hard when it was the end of August? Flo jumped onto the bed and curled against Charlie's legs, a warm, solid presence. Ben wrapped the covers around her and crawled onto the bed. Then he pulled her into his lap and held her until the shaking stopped.

And all the while, he sang to her. *The Lady of Shalott. The Bonny*

Swans. The Sheep Beneath the Snow. Ben had a fine voice. And not once did he stutter.

Another minute, another hour passed—maybe, she didn't know—before she could speak.

"I'm sorry."

Ben stopped singing. "N-no."

"I am."

"*No*," he said, firmer. "You will never apologize, to me or to anyone, for that pathetic excuse of a human being."

He stroked her hair.

He started singing again.

"You have a beautiful voice, do you know that?" she asked after a while.

He stopped, nuzzled the top of her head, and sighed.

"No one's ever told me that."

"That's because you sing under your breath, where no one can hear you."

"Except for you."

Charlie nodded. "That makes me lucky." She looked up into his face as best she could. "No one's ever called me a princess."

"That's because no one ever saw the woman under the armor." He shifted until he could look into her eyes. "But I can see both—the warrior and the princess. Because you've shown me both. And that makes me a lucky man."

A tear slid down Charlie's cheek. Ben was smart enough to let it fall freely.

"How much did you hear?"

He closed his eyes. "I should have come out sooner."

"No." She shook her head. "I didn't want you to. I didn't want—" She took a shuddering breath. "I wanted to be strong and handle it myself. I wanted to hide you. From him. The way I've always hidden the things I love from him."

She went stiff as she realized what she said.

"I love you, Charlie." Ben brushed a lock of hair off her forehead. "I love all of you."

"I love you, too, Ben."

He held her close.

"When you're ready," he said, "I want you to pack your art supplies, and anything else you want for the rest of the week, and I'm taking you to my house."

"That sounds good." Right now, her apartment felt polluted. And what if he decided to come back?

She knew Ben understood.

NINETEEN

THE KITCHEN SMELLED LIKE COFFEE AND THE FAINT SWEETNESS of maple syrup from the pancakes Ben was keeping warm in the oven. His princess was still sleeping and he didn't want to wake her just yet.

In spite of everything, he was nervous about today. He wanted it to be perfect.

Charlie had been living with him for two weeks now, ever since Desmond went off like a nuke in her apartment. The first few days she'd been cautious, afraid to move anything or claim space. She asked if it was okay to make coffee. Asked before she opened the fridge. She'd practically asked permission to use the bathroom.

Ben had fixed that by rearranging his own furniture one morning, moving her art supplies into the spare bedroom himself, and hanging her St. Vrain drawing in the living room where he could see it every day.

Now she was settling in. Her coffee mug sat next to his above the coffee pot. Her sketchbooks littered the sunroom. Her tactical backpack hung on the hook by the door next to his forge apron.

It felt *right*.

He just had to convince her to make it permanent. He hoped today would go a long way toward that.

The bedroom door opened and Charlie appeared, sleepy-eyed but undoubtedly drawn by the scent of coffee. Flo trotted out behind her, tail wagging, and headed straight for her full food dish. Charlie's hair was sleep-mussed, gorgeous. She wore one of his old t-shirts that hit her mid-thigh, which absolutely delighted her. She'd told him it made her feel dainty.

"Morning, Princess," Ben said.

Charlie made a sound that might have been words and headed straight for the coffee pot. Ben had already poured her a mug. He handed it to her and she took it like a drowning woman grabbing a life preserver.

"You're perfect," she mumbled into the steam.

"You say that every morning."

"And I'm right every morning."

He chuckled at their usual routine as he opened the oven.

She took a long sip, then another. Finally her eyes focused. "What time do we need to leave?"

"We have an hour. Faire opens at ten, but I want to get there early for setup. Hope you don't mind eating bachelor-style in the kitchen." He set two plates of pancakes on the counter. "Eat up."

"With pleasure." She opened a drawer and took out two forks and knives while he grabbed the syrup and butter.

Charlie took a bite, closed her eyes, and groaned. "So good."

"Thank you. Glad you approve."

As Charlie woke, she looked Ben up and down approvingly. "I do love that kilt."

Ben felt his cheeks heat. He knew just how much she loved it every time she sneaked into the backyard forge to watch him work while he wore it. He was surprised he didn't have to pick her jaw up off the floor each time.

"I don't suppose you have any spare armor lying around I could wear this time?" she asked, half-joking. "I wasn't exactly dressed for it last time."

Ben's mouth curved. "Sorry, I've pretty much sold out of everything, like I always do by the last weekend."

"Figures." She pretended to pout.

"But... I have something else."

Charlie looked at him over the rim of her mug, one eyebrow raised. "Yeah?"

Ben set his own coffee down and moved behind her.

"What are you doing?"

He covered her eyes with his hands. "Trust me?"

"Always."

He guided her through the kitchen, down the hall, into the sunroom. The first morning light poured through the windows, turning everything to molten gold.

Except for one spot of moonlit sliver.

Ben grinned. "Okay." He dropped his hands.

Charlie's breath caught.

The dress was on a dressmaker's form he'd borrowed from Della. Princess Evelaine's gown—blue velvet bodice with silver embroidery, the full skirt in silver and blue silk, the waist fitted.

"Ben," Charlie whispered, shocked. "That's—"

"Princess Evelaine's dress from the Faire." He moved to stand beside her.

Charlie reached out and touched the gossamer fabric, her fingers trembling slightly. "You bought this for me?"

"Weeks ago. I've been waiting for the right time to give it to you."

"How...how did you know?"

"I saw how you looked at it when you took Viv to the costume shop. I knew you had to have it."

"But there's no way I can wear it. It can't possibly fit."

"Of course it can. I had Della alter it to fit you." He moved to stand beside her. "She added pockets, too. Said no woman should suffer a dress without pockets."

Charlie shook her head. "It might fit, but it won't...*fit*. Not me. I'm..." She gestured over her body. "This."

Ben cupped her face in his hands.

"You know, the books never actually describe Princess Evelaine as petite," Ben said.

Charlie blinked, confused. "Of course they do. She's an Elven princess. She's 'willowy as a slender sapling' and 'her hair shines like starlight on the sea' and her eyes are 'the color of an early morning sky in spring' and..." Charlie frowned as she mentally went through all the descriptions of Evelaine in the books.

Ben grinned. "And?"

"She's...she's got to be petite."

"Why?"

"Because she's beautiful. The most beautiful princess who ever lived."

Ben stopped her there. His hands gently curled around her arms just above her elbows. Charlie suddenly found herself face to face with him, and having to tilt her head up to meet his eyes.

"She is the most beautiful princess who ever lived. And I've always pictured her as tall and formidable. Strong. Determined. Loyal." He lifted his hand and brushed his thumb across her cheek then tucked a lock of her hair behind her ear. "Not petite."

Charlie's hazel eyes went misty.

"I don't know what to say."

"Say you'll wear it today."

"Yes." She laughed, the sound breaking slightly. "God, yes. Thank you!"

"There's one more thing." Ben picked up a carved wooden box from the table where he made jewelry. The surface was still covered in tools—pliers, files, a magnifying glass on a stand, wire-rimmed glasses he wore when he worked on delicate pieces.

He handed her the box.

Charlie opened it carefully. Her eyes lit up again.

Inside, nestled on black velvet, was a silver necklace. Delicate filigree work formed a pendant set with three pale blue stones that matched the dress.

"Ben." Her voice was barely a whisper. "This is—"

"I started it the day I bought the dress. Finished it last night." He took the necklace from the box and moved behind her. "May I?"

She lifted her hair and he fastened the clasp. The pendant settled perfectly at the hollow of her throat.

Charlie turned and looked up at him. "No one's ever—" She stopped, swallowed. "Thank you."

Ben cupped her face in his hands. "Go put on the dress, Princess. I want to see you in it."

TWENTY MINUTES LATER, Charlie emerged from the bedroom.

Ben forgot how to breathe.

The dress fit her perfectly. Della had taken in the bodice to follow Charlie's athletic build, adjusted the sleeves so they sat properly on her shoulders. The blue brought out the gold in her hazel eyes. The necklace gleamed against her skin.

She'd left her hair down, loose around her shoulders.

"Well?" Charlie did a slow turn, the skirt swirling. "What do you think?"

Ben couldn't speak. He just stared.

Charlie's confidence faltered. "Does it look weird on me? I can change—"

"No." Ben found his voice. "God, no. Don't you dare change. You're—" He crossed to her, pulled her close. "You're the most beautiful woman I've ever seen."

Charlie's cheeks flushed pink. "You're biased."

"I'm honest." He kissed her forehead. "My princess."

THEY DROPPED Flo off at Watchdog's kennels then drove down to the Faire. The parking area was already filling with vendors and performers setting up for the last weekend of the season.

Charlie drew stares the moment she stepped out of the truck. Ben loved it.

Let them look. Let them see my princess.

"I feel like I should curtsy or something," Charlie muttered as they walked through the gates.

"Just be yourself." Ben took her hand. "You're perfect."

The Faire was in full setup mode. Vendors arranging their last pieces of merchandise, food stalls firing up grills, musicians tuning instruments. Ben spotted the costume shop—Della's booth was still packed with garments despite it being the last weekend. She always over-stocked and always sold well anyway.

"Ben!" Della waved from behind her counter. When she saw Charlie in the dress, her face lit up. "Oh my stars, look at you! It's perfect! I knew the three-quarter sleeves would work better on you than the original. And that *necklace*!" She clasped her hands together. "Did you make that, Ben?"

"Finished it last night."

"Gorgeous work. Both of you look absolutely stunning together." She winked at Charlie. "Keep him, honey. The good ones are rare."

BEN'S last demonstration of the year drew a solid crowd. He worked the forge, heating steel to glowing orange, shaping it on the anvil with practiced strikes. Charlie watched from the front row, her eyes tracking every movement.

Afterward, Ben offered Charlie his arm. They moved through the Faire.

"Have you heard from Viv?" Ben thought of the chaos of their last visit.

"Yes. No more attacks, though the online backlash is still brutal.

Poor Maddie's doing overtime trying to quash it, but it seems to get worse the more she tries."

Ben nodded. "Rowan said the same thing. But, there's a silver lining. If anything, the pressure has brought him and Viv closer together."

But Charlie's attention had snapped elsewhere. Ben grinned at her smile.

"Would you like to meet them?" he asked her.

She looked at him with unbridled, innocent excitement. "Can we?"

Ben led Charlie to a large, open ring where Jerry and Linda kept their elephant and camel. The elephant, a gentle giant named Jasmine, stretched her trunk toward Charlie, hoping for treats.

"She likes you," Linda said. "Animals always know good people."

"Where do you keep her?" Charlie asked.

Jerry grinned. "We winter in Arizona with these two, spend summers here in Colorado. When we're up here, we stay with Linda's dad outside Castle Rock. He's a microbiologist with twenty acres. Says elephant manure makes the best fertilizer."

"And he's not wrong," Linda added. "His garden is legendary."

They visited more friends—the perfumers, the glass blowers, Foxglove who made flower crowns and insisted on making one on the house for Charlie despite her protests.

Finally, as the afternoon sun slanted golden through the trees, Ben screwed up his courage and found Patrick, the harpist.

"Got time for one more song?" Ben asked.

Patrick's eyes lit up. "For you? Always. What are we playing?"

"Black Is the Color." Then he leaned in and whispered in Patrick's ear while Charlie looked on, bemused.

A crowd gathered as Patrick re-tuned his harp. Ben stood in the center of the clearing, found Charlie's face in the crowd, and began to sing:

Hazel are the eyes of my true love, Charlie,
Soft as summer rain on the mountain pines.

Her laugh can break the dark like morning, darling,
And peace comes over me when her hand's in mine.

Charlie's hand went to her mouth.

Her hair, it holds the sunlight when she's laughing,
Gold and chestnut tangled by the breeze.
And every time she looks at me, I'm steady—
My wandering heart remembers how to breathe.

Ben's voice didn't stutter. Not once. The words came clear and strong, carrying across the clearing.

I'll take her where the cold wind never finds her,
We'll stand where the storm breaks on the ridge.
And if the night grows heavy on her shoulders,
I'll lift it off and swear she's never left alone again.
Hazel are the eyes of my brave love, Charlie,
Bright as firelight 'gainst the falling snow.
If she would walk beside me through the shadows,
There's not a path on earth I'd fear to go.

Patrick's harp rang out the final notes. The crowd burst into applause.

Ben crossed to Charlie. Tears streamed down her face.

"You wrote that for me," she whispered.

"Every word." He wiped away her tears with his thumb. "Every single word."

She pulled him down and kissed him in front of everyone. The crowd cheered louder.

When they finally broke apart, Charlie laughed through her tears. "I love you so much."

"I love you too, Princess."

Charlie's phone buzzed. She pulled it from her pocket—bless Della for adding those—and looked at the screen. Her expression changed.

"It's Wren. Frankie's in labor."

Ben felt his own heart jump. "Now?"

"Now." Charlie was already texting back. "They're heading to the hospital."

Just then, Ben's phone buzzed.

"Ben! Frankie's—"

"I know. Wren just texted Charlie. How are you holding up?"

"I'm terrified, brother. What if she—"

"Listen to me." Ben kept his voice steady. "Frankie's the strongest woman I know besides Charlie. She's got this. And you've got this. You just need to be there for her. Tell her she's amazing. That's all you can do."

"What if something goes wrong? Brother, as an EMT, I've seen—"

"You won't. You've been preparing for this for months. You've got the best medical team, Frankie's healthy, the baby's healthy. All you have to do is show up and love them both. Can you do that?"

Another pause. "Yeah. Yeah, I can do that."

"Good. We'll come by the hospital later if visiting hours allow. If not, we'll see you tomorrow."

"Thanks, Moose."

"Anytime, Ram. Now go be with your girl."

Ben hung up and looked at Charlie. She was watching him with soft eyes.

"What?" he asked.

"You're a good friend."

"Waylon's family. We take care of family."

Charlie slipped her hand into his. "Yeah. We do."

They walked back through the Faire toward the truck, the sun setting behind them, casting everything in gold and amber light. Charlie in her princess dress, Ben in his kilt, both of them heading home together.

It felt right.

It felt like forever.

TWENTY

After another week in Ben's house, it was starting to feel like Charlie's home, too.

Charlie stood in front of the bathroom mirror, wrestling with the clasp on her beautiful silver necklace. Behind her, she could hear Ben moving around in the bedroom, the now-familiar sound of him getting dressed. She'd moved more of her things in three days ago. In addition to everything in the bathroom, her art supplies had taken over the spare bedroom. Her Moleskine collection lined a gorgeous wooden bookshelf Ben had made years ago as if he'd known what would someday fill it. Her favorite *BattleLore* coffee mug sat next to his on the kitchen shelf above the coffee pot.

He'd made room for her. And now, their lives were fitting together.

Ben appeared in the bathroom doorway. "You ready?"

Charlie turned and forgot what she was doing entirely.

He was wearing the kilt.

Solid dark green, falling to just below his knee. A white linen shirt, open at the throat. He'd left his hair loose, which he almost never did. He looked like someone had pulled him directly out of a *BattleLore* illustration—massive and devastating.

"Yeah," she managed to croak out of her suddenly dry mouth. "I'm ready."

Ben's lips curved into a wicked smile. "You asked me to wear it."

"I know I did." Charlie turned back to the mirror, her cheeks warm. "I stand by that decision."

She felt him move up behind her, close enough that she could feel warmth radiating from his chest. He gently took her necklace and fastened the clasp.

"There," he said. His hands rested on her shoulders for a moment. In the mirror, they looked right together. Her and this enormous, gentle man who pulled out her chair and remembered her coffee order, who wrote her a song, made her a necklace, and had given her a studio with the best natural light in the house.

No princess could ever be happier.

"Thank you." She turned and straightened his collar just to have an excuse to brush her fingers across the top of his chest. "You look incredible."

He dropped his gaze, this gorgeous man who still amazingly had no idea. "You always say that."

Charlie tilted his chin up. "And I'm always right."

He kissed her. Softly and slowly, knowing exactly what she liked as if he'd been doing it for years.

"Come on," Ben said, grabbing his keys from the hook by the door. "We're going to be late."

ARDEN'S Victorian ranch house looked welcoming when they pulled up. Charlie could hear voices and laughter through her open window from the driveway. She sat for a moment after Ben cut the engine, looking up at the house.

"You okay?" Ben asked.

"Yeah." She was. Completely. That was the strange part. "I've been to parties here before. But this feels different."

"Different how?"

Charlie turned to look at him. "Last time I came to one of Arden's parties, I was unsure that I belonged. That, even though everyone had shown me nothing but kindness, I was still an outsider."

Ben waited.

"Tonight I'm coming in with you." She held out her hand. "That's all."

He took her hand, lifted it, and brushed his lips across her knuckles. "That's not all, Charlie. It's not just because of me. It's that you're ready to let them in."

Charlie gave him a wondering smile. How could anyone know her so well?

He squeezed her hand. "So let's go in and celebrate with our family."

They got out of the truck and Ben opened the back door. Flo bounded out, tail wagging, already sniffing the air for familiar friends.

The sound of barking came from behind the house—Camo's deep woof, Pete's enthusiastic yipping, and at least three other dogs whose barks Charlie recognized from Watchdog.

"Sounds like the pack's already assembled," Ben said.

As if on cue, Alex appeared from around the side of the house with Camo at his heels. The black-and-gold Lab went straight to Flo, the two dogs greeting each other like old friends.

"I've got them," Alex called, waving. "Everyone's out back. Chickens are secure, alpacas are curious, barn cats are judging us all."

"Thanks, Alex!" Charlie called back.

Flo took off with Camo around the back of the house where the chaos of happy dogs echoed across the property. Charlie and Ben went up the porch steps and into the house.

The great room was already full. Charlie spotted Kyle by the fireplace. Elias and Wren sat side by side on the couch. Rochelle was curled up in the window seat—her favorite, naturally—listening to

Wren's latest crazy story, then scooted over for Gabe when he brought her a drink. Bear stood toward the back of the room with baby Star in a sling on his chest, slowly rocking back and forth.

Frankie sat in the best armchair in the room. She looked exhausted and luminous in equal measure, dark circles under her eyes, but her skin glowing otherwise. Waylon perched on the arm of her chair, hovering over her. Every few minutes he leaned down and said something that made Frankie laugh.

And in her arms, a small bundle in a pale yellow blanket.

"The man of the hour," Ben murmured.

"He's so tiny," Charlie said.

Ben nodded. "He's a little miracle."

He steered Charlie toward the kitchen first, where Arden had staged enough food to feed the entire Watchdog roster. Arden, April, and Gina were in there talking, Fleur standing right beside Gina and looking up adoringly, hoping for scraps, which she got a moment later. Shane had a plateful of food and a biscuit in his mouth as he scootched past the women. He mumbled something to Ben and Charlie that Charlie took as a greeting.

Arden spotted Charlie the moment they walked in. Her silver-grey eyes warmed and she pulled Charlie into a hug that was surprisingly easy to return.

"I'm so glad you're here," Arden said. She looked between Charlie and Ben with a smile that said she knew exactly what she was looking at. "Both of you."

"Ben!" Kyle called out. "I have a question for you. I'm replacing some of the old scallop shingles and I have no idea what I'm doing."

Arden smiled up at Ben. "Please, save me and go talk to my husband before he destroys my home."

Ben grinned at Arden and squeezed Charlie's shoulder. "Will do." He grabbed a cookie and made his way out of the kitchen. Arden was a step behind.

"Excuse me, ladies, but it's my turn to hold the baby," Arden said.

Gina smoothly stepped beside Charlie as if it had been planned.

"Come on," Gina said. "I want to introduce you to someone." She pointed toward a woman in a spectacular deep red dress, holding a flute of champagne. Her gleaming white hair was swept up in an elegant twist. She was sitting in a wing back chair, holding court among four people.

Charlie frowned. "What do you mean? I've met Stephanie....wait. Is that...?" Charlie discreetly pointed at the handsome man sitting beside her, laughing at something she'd just said.

"Dr. Boyfriend, in the flesh." Gina's smile turned fond. "He showed up at Thanksgiving and we still barely know anything about him. He's very quiet." She glanced at Charlie. "You'd think someone like Stephanie would wear him down, but somehow he holds his own."

Charlie had been invited to Thanksgiving, but she'd politely turned down the invitation, thinking that Arden had only invited her to be nice.

So many good times I've denied myself. So many friendships.

No more.

"Oh, I've got to meet him."

They crossed the room, Fleur leading the way. Stephanie clocked Charlie from ten feet away and opened her free arm.

"Charles! You gorgeous creature." Charlie grinned at the nickname. She was officially part of the Guy Name Club along with Stephanie and Frankie who called each other Steve and Frank.

Stephanie stood and pulled Charlie into a hug that smelled like Chanel. "I heard you finally made an honest man out of that handsome blacksmith."

"I'm not sure who made an honest person out of who," Charlie said.

Stephanie laughed. "Oh, I like that." Then she gestured to the quiet, silver-haired man beside her who had also stood up. "*This* is Dr. Boyfriend."

The man extended his hand with the patience of someone who had long since accepted his fate. "William Blakely."

"He insists," Stephanie said, waving her champagne glass. "I find it lacks panache."

"Nice to meet you, William," Charlie said.

He gave her a smile that suggested he was used to being the straight man and had made his peace with it. "You as well, *Charles*."

"Smart man," Stephanie told him, then she kissed his cheek.

Gina pulled Charlie away before Stephanie could reel them in. They made their way to the massive leather couch where Wren was sitting, close to Frankie's armchair. Frankie had her head turned and was talking to Rochelle. She didn't notice them until Charlie sat down across from her.

"Hey, you," Frankie said, beaming. "Moving in going okay?"

"Yes, thank you." Charlie glanced toward the fireplace where Lachlan Campbell was approaching Ben and Kyle. She watched Lachlan look Ben over with a raised eyebrow.

"Nice skirt, lad."

"Skirt?" Ben replied, eyebrows raised. "It's an Irish kilt."

"Oh dear, here they go," Gina said, shaking her head with a soft smile. "We've lost them."

"What do you mean?" Charlie asked.

"Oh, just listen. This'll be hilarious." She tilted her head, considering. "So long as they don't come to blows."

Charlie's eyebrows rose. "Really?"

Gina put her finger to her lips and gestured with her golden eyes toward the men. Charlie tuned into their conversation, Gina grinning beside her.

"I'm not saying that Ireland's kilt tradition rivals Scotland's," Ben was saying. "But it does have a legitimate history."

"Uh-oh," Gina whispered.

"Legitimate history? Only if you're talking the nineteenth and twentieth centuries," Lach rebutted.

"The léine predates your Great Kilt by centuries—"

Lach snorted. "A léine is practically a dress—"

"It's a long tunic and a precursor—"

Charlie looked at Gina. "How long does this usually go?"

"Last time? Forty-five minutes." Gina sipped her wine. "Kyle had to physically separate them."

"They're not going to—"

"No, no. They're great friends." Gina smiled. "Lach is the same way with Kyle about whisky versus Irish whiskey with an E."

"And when he's not arguing with Ben about kilts, it's about mead," Arden said, appearing at Charlie's elbow with a tiny bundle in her arms. Her grey eyes were soft and warm. "Do you want to hold him?"

Charlie looked at the baby. She hadn't held a baby since—since her little brother was an infant. She looked at Frankie.

"It's fine if you want to." Frankie answered her unasked question with a smile.

"Yeah," Charlie said, surprising herself. "Okay."

Arden settled the baby carefully into her arms. Charlie adjusted automatically, cradling the small weight against her chest.

He was so small. He had Frankie's dark hair peeking out from under his beanie and Waylon's nose. Charlie couldn't help herself—she nuzzled his forehead.

"He smells incredible."

"Right?" Frankie smiled from the armchair. She looked like she might cry, but in a good way.

"New person smell, just like new car smell," Wren said. Both Charlie and Frankie laughed.

Charlie looked down at the baby. He blinked up at her with dark, unfocused eyes, completely unbothered. "Hello there, Danny."

She felt something shift in her chest, quiet and enormous, like a door opening into a room she hadn't known was closed off.

She felt watched and looked up. Ben was mid-sentence, telling Lachlan, something about pre-Norman textile traditions, but his gaze was on her.

He went completely still.

Then he smiled—warm and wondering and completely unguarded.

Charlie felt her eyes go misty as she smiled back.

Wren leaned over and murmured, "That man is absolutely gone over you."

"Yeah," she said quietly. "I know."

Charlie looked back down at Danny. "The feeling's mutual."

"Good!" Wren said. "Because we're planning on keeping you."

Charlie's head shot up. "Keeping me?"

"Isn't she already ours?" Frankie asked. "I mean, she is in the Guy Name Group. I think Steve would fight us if we didn't keep her."

"Who am I fighting?" Stephanie shouted from across the room.

"Nobody, Steve," Frankie shouted back. "I'm just telling Charlie —I mean, Charles—that she's one of the gals."

"Goes without saying," Stephanie shot back.

Charlie laughed as she handed Danny back to Frankie.

"What's so funny?" Wren asked.

Charlie sat back. "I can't tell you how many times I've been called one of the guys." Charlie's smile softened. "And I can't think of a single time I've been one of the gals." She grinned at Wren. "I like it. A lot."

She was still smiling when she slipped out the front door onto the porch, needing just a moment of fresh air. Through the screen door, she could still hear Lachlan and Ben going at it, Gina's laughter threading through the debate. The mountains were behind the ranch, but she could still sense their presence the way she always could in Colorado.

She heard the door open behind her and turned. Arden stepped out, two glasses of wine in hand, and offered one without a word.

"Thank you." Charlie took it and turned back to the front garden.

They leaned against the porch railing together, not needing to fill the quiet. That was the thing about Arden—she never pushed. She just made space and waited to see what came into it. Charlie guessed that was what made her so good with her young clients on the ranch.

"Can I talk to you about something?" Charlie said.

"Of course." Arden gave her a gentle smile that warmed her silver-grey eyes.

"When I was holding Danny tonight, I thought about Joey." The name felt strange in her mouth, like a word in a language she used to speak fluently. "My youngest brother. After my mum left us, I raised him. Until he turned mean on me, just like our older brothers. I left home when I turned eighteen and didn't look back." She paused. "He left a voicemail for me at Watchdog a few weeks ago. Said he wanted to talk. I thought it was because our father put him up to it—wanted him to talk me into coming back and taking care of him." She exhaled slowly. "Turns out that's not the case. I think Joey just wants to reconnect. I haven't called him back."

She looked at Arden for a moment. "Sean." Charlie said his name carefully, watching Arden's face. "You two had a falling out before he died. I know it's not my business—"

"It's okay." Arden said. "We disagreed about something that mattered to both of us. And then before we could fix it, he was gone." She was quiet for a moment. "I've made my peace with it. Mostly."

"Mostly," Charlie repeated softly.

Arden looked at her. "If he'd just been estranged? Still out there somewhere?" She didn't hesitate. "I'd have called him. Even if he'd hung up on me. Even if it took ten tries." Arden gave her a small, sad smile. "I'd have kept calling if there was the smallest chance we could fix things."

Arden reached out and touched her arm. Then she nodded toward the door.

"Come on. Ben's losing the kilt argument. He needs moral support."

Charlie laughed and followed her back inside, knowing now what she was going to do about Joey.

TWENTY-ONE

Three Months Later

Ten PM on a freezing night in mid-December, and Loveland Pass looked the way it was supposed to—like the mountain where Lord Darkfell's Keep held both the Embersword and Princess Evelaine hostage. The Seven Sisters loomed above them, massive avalanche chutes loaded with more snow than Charlie had ever seen. Heavy snow had been falling in the high country since the end of November. An especially brutal December, Ben said.

Perfect for what Viv needed to film.

CDOT had closed the road hours ago. Now the film crew was at a fantastic vantage point for watching and filming, just waiting for the signal.

Charlie pulled her coat tighter as she looked at the Seven Sisters, thankful for the avalanche beacon strapped under her vest. She did another visual sweep of the area. Flo and Pete were warm and comfy and probably napping in Viv's trailer. Shane had the fun part of being with CDOT when the fireworks went off. She was with the rest of the cast and crew—Viv, Rowan, Duke, and the filming unit—well clear of the avalanche paths.

Ah yes, and the Embersworn Knights.

The twenty or so extras recruited to play the courageous band trying to rescue Princess Evelaine and reclaim the Ember Sword from Lord Felldark—stood near the equipment trailers, already in full costume.

The best part? Viv and Rowan had kept in touch with Charlie and Ben, and Viv had seen the photo of the guys in the St. Vrain and insisted they act as Embersworn. Bear looked enormous in chainmail and leather. Gabe, Elias, Waylon were all in medieval armor and matching Embersworn capes, grinning like kids despite the cold. Ben had teased them about becoming bigger *BattleLore* nerds than he was.

Ben.

Charlie's chest went warm just looking at him. Six-foot-seven of blacksmith in an Embersworn Knight costume. He'd delivered the Embersword yesterday—she could still picture Viv's face when she saw the finished blade, the way Rowan had tested its weight and balance, Duke asking technical questions about the forging. The PR photos had taken an hour, but Ben had been patient through all of it.

He caught her looking at him and smiled. She smiled back, then forced herself to scan away. Professional. She was working.

But God, am I happy.

Living with Ben for the past few months had been... everything. Every morning better than the last. Thanksgiving at Arden's with all their friends, Frankie and Waylon and baby Danny, Ellie, Bear and Star, who was now toddling around and beginning to talk. And of course, all the dogs. The whole chaotic, wonderful family they'd built made her happier than she'd even been.

Christmas was in a week. Their first Christmas together. Ben had been working on something in the forge, secretive and pleased with himself. That was fine—Charlie had her own surprise planned.

Maddie appeared at Viv's elbow, tablet in hand. "CDOT just radioed. They're detonating in ten minutes."

"Perfect." Viv turned to her cinematographer. "Final positions, everyone!"

The plan was simple. CDOT would trigger the avalanche and cameras would capture it from multiple safe angles. Later, they'd film the Embersworn Knights getting "hit" by the avalanche using a combination of practical effects, like controlled snow drops.

And there would also be the heartbreaking scene with Aldric and Caiden—Caiden reassuring Aldric before the final push up the mountain to Lord Felldark's Keep. The loyal friend steadying the hero, not knowing he was about to make the ultimate sacrifice.

The reality was so different. Though, according to Viv, things were better than they had been.

Charlie watched the crew move into position. Cameras locked down at safe distances with long lenses. Everyone well clear of the avalanche paths, positioned where CDOT had designated as secure.

Duke stood off to the side with Rowan, both of them in costume, reviewing lines quietly. They'd been professional all day. Distant, but professional. Maddie moved through the staging area, checking equipment, confirming camera positions, her usual efficient self, but wound tight as a spring.

"Five minutes!" someone called.

The mountain waited above them, cold and patient and loaded with snow.

Charlie did one more sweep. Everyone in safe positions. Escape routes clear. Emergency avalanche protocols reviewed.

Everything was ready.

"Positions!" Viv called out.

The crew moved with practiced efficiency. Charlie watched the cinematographer check his equipment one last time, cameras locked down at carefully calculated angles. The snow and wind prevented them from using drones tonight. CDOT had mapped every inch of the avalanche paths. Everyone knew exactly where the snow would go.

In theory.

Charlie's tactical brain noted the wind picking up and there was snow in the air. The temperature was dropping another few degrees. The snow on the Sisters seemed to shift in the darkness, restless.

"Two minutes!" someone shouted.

Ben and the other Embersworn Knights stood and watched—they'd film reaction shots later, but for now they just needed to stay clear and enjoy the show CDOT was about to put on. Ben stood with his arms crossed, looking up at the mountain with the kind of respect you only got from years in the backcountry. Gabe, Elias, Waylon, Bear, and the other extras—all of them had gone quiet, their earlier joking gone.

They understood what they were about to witness.

Charlie positioned herself where she could see both Viv and the mountain. Her hand rested near her sidearm out of habit, even though the threat tonight was snow, not bullets.

"One minute!"

"Thirty seconds!"

The mountain went silent. Even the wind seemed to hold its breath.

Charlie counted down in her head. *Twenty. Fifteen. Ten.*

At five seconds, someone hit the lights on the cameras.

At zero, the world exploded.

The *boom* came first—deep, percussive, more felt than heard. Then another. Then a third. The charges going off in sequence up the Sisters.

For a heartbeat, nothing happened.

Then a white wave of snow rose and the mountain moved.

Charlie had seen avalanches on video and watched footage during the safety briefing. She'd read reports and studied statistics in preparation for tonight.

None of it prepared her for this.

The snow didn't fall. It *flowed.* A wall of white twenty feet high, maybe thirty, rushing down the chutes with a sound like a freight train mixed with thunder. Boulders vanished. Everything in the path simply ceased to exist under the weight of thousands of tons of snow moving at highway speeds.

The ground shook. Charlie felt it through her boots, up her legs, into her chest.

"Jesus," someone breathed.

The avalanche hit the runout zone and kept going, spreading out like a massive white hand across the base of the Sisters. Slower now but still moving, still grinding everything beneath it into nothing. Viv couldn't have asked for better footage.

Charlie's brain was automatically calculating—velocity, mass, destructive force. Anyone caught in that wouldn't have a chance. The snow would hit like concrete. Bury you in seconds. Even with her beacon, even with the best search and rescue team in the world—

She forced the thoughts away. Everyone was safe. Everyone was in position.

The avalanche finally stopped, settling into new formations across the landscape. The sound faded to a hiss, then to silence.

Absolute silence.

No one spoke. No one moved.

Then Charlie heard Viv's voice, quiet and awed. "Did we get it?"

"Got it," the cinematographer confirmed. His voice shook slightly. "All cameras. Every angle."

A cheer went up from the crew. They'd just captured something incredible.

Charlie watched the dust settle, watched the snow drift in the work lights—beautiful and terrifying in equal measure.

Ben appeared at her side. "You okay?"

"Yeah." She was. "That was..."

"Intense."

"That's one word for it." Charlie looked up at him. "Remind me never to take the mountains lightly."

"Never take the mountains lightly," he said mock-dutifully. Then, quieter, "You're shaking."

She was. Adrenaline, probably. Or maybe just the cold finally getting through.

Ben pulled her close, wrapped his arms around her. "It's over. Everyone's safe."

Charlie leaned into him for just a moment. Everyone else was cheering and giving each other high-fives. Viv and Rowan were safe. Professional distance could wait another thirty seconds.

"Yeah," she said. "Everyone's fine."

THE CREW STARTED BREAKING down equipment, voices echoing in the cold air. Viv pulled Charlie aside, away from the main group toward where half a dozen snowmobiles were parked.

"Can we talk security for the next scene?" Viv asked as she took out her canister of O2. But her expression wasn't all business. She was glowing.

"Of course." Charlie scanned the area automatically. "What's the setup?"

Viv inhaled from her canister, then put it away in the front pocket of her puffer jacket. "Caiden's 'You've always been the true king' speech to Aldric."

Charlie smiled. That was one of the most quoted passages from the books. "It's going to be a tearjerker."

"That's the hope. And it's why I want to get up there with Duke and Rowan ahead of the crew for a final rehearsal to make sure they nail it. Can we do just the four of us on snowmobiles—you, me, Rowan, and Duke?"

Charlie nodded. "As long as CDOT clears it."

"There's a flat area CDOT set up for us and just declared it safe. We'll use that." Viv hesitated, then smiled. "Can I tell you something?"

Charlie's nerves prickled. "Sure."

Viv took off her glove and held out her left hand. A simple platinum band with a small diamond caught the light. "Rowan proposed last week."

Charlie felt her face break into a genuine smile. "Viv, that's wonderful. Congratulations."

"We're announcing it tomorrow, after filming wraps." Viv's eyes were bright. "I wanted you to know first. You and Shane have been... well, you kept us safe when things were bad."

"I'm really happy for you both." Charlie meant it. After everything—the joust, the threats, the chaos—they deserved this. "How are things with Duke? It seems better." Malcom McCoy had said it was in the briefing he gave Charlie when he turned Viv back over to her, but Charlie wanted to hear it from her directly.

"So much better." Viv's relief was palpable. "Ever since he landed the lead for *Family of Serpents*, the whole dynamic's shifted. Duke wouldn't have been able to take the role if I hadn't killed off Caiden—it's a huge opportunity for him. Big budget, multi-season deal." She grinned and winked. "But if you ask me, I think he's doing it for the action figure."

Charlie laughed. "That's great."

"It is. The fans have gotten less salty since he talked about how happy he was getting the part. He even thanked me." Viv laughed. "Oh, *and* he's dating his new costar." Viv laughed. "Rowan and I are engaged. Duke's moving on, no hard feelings—well, maybe a few. Everyone's getting what they want. It's like the universe finally aligned."

Don't jinx it like that. Charlie felt that slight unease again, The joust was still unresolved. Duke had an alibi. DCSO had investigated the stable hands and come up empty. They'd never figured out who cut that strap. At least there hadn't been any other attempts on Rowan's life.

Maybe I'm just being paranoid. But paranoid had kept her alive in the past.

"That's really good to hear," Charlie said. "I'm glad it all worked out."

Maddie appeared at Charlie's side. "Coffee, anyone? Thought we could all use something warm so I grabbed some from craft."

Viv smiled. "Maddie, you're a lifesaver. Thank you."

Charlie took a cup, grateful for the warmth. She studied Maddie. The usually-chipper assistant was dragging just a little bit. Her eyes looked glassy.

"Hey, Maddie? You okay?" Charlie asked quietly.

"Fine." Maddie's voice was clipped. "Just cold. I'm going to check on the equipment for the next scene."

"Take a break," Viv said.

"No, I'm good." She set down the coffee carrier and walked away, her movements stiff.

Charlie watched her go. "What's wrong with Maddie?"

"Oh, I don't know. She's been working too hard," Viv said, shaking her head. "I caught her staring off into space the other day. I'm giving her a big Christmas bonus. She's been incredible through all of this."

"Yeah," Charlie said slowly. "Incredible."

She made a mental note to keep an eye on Maddie. Maybe she just needed someone to talk to.

TWENTY MINUTES LATER, Charlie straddled a snowmobile and checked her radio one more time.

"Elk, you copy?"

"Copy, King. You're clear to head up."

"Roger. Maintain position at base."

Shane would coordinate the main crew and equipment while Charlie took Viv, Duke and Rowan up. With Duke's new show and the tension resolved, the threat level had dropped. Plus, the real danger today was nature, not people.

"You good with this?" Shane had asked before they left.

"Four people, cleared route, ten minutes up, then the full crew in Snowcats. I've got it."

Shane grinned. "And the pups are good in Viv's trailer. Radio check when you arrive and if anything's wonky. We'll be up in an hour."

"Copy that."

If something happened at base, Shane could coordinate with CDOT. If something happened at up the mountain, Charlie could get Viv, Rowan, and Duke out with the snowmobiles.

Not that anything was going to happen. CDOT had cleared the route. The avalanche had already been triggered. They were going to a safe, flat area to practice and then film a scene.

Viv mounted the snowmobile beside her while Rowan and Duke took two others. Four machines, ten-minute ride up toward the Sisters. Simple.

"Stay close," Charlie said before she started the engine. "Single file. I lead, you three follow."

They headed up the mountain in a line, headlights cutting through the darkness and falling snow. The trail was clear enough, packed down by CDOT vehicles earlier. Charlie kept her speed moderate, checking over her shoulder every thirty seconds to make sure the others were keeping up.

The cold bit through her jacket. Wind picked up as they climbed higher, exposed to the elements. Charlie's tactical brain noted the risks—communication could get spotty, avalanche chutes above them freshly triggered but the mountain still loaded with snow in other areas.

Ten minutes felt like twenty.

Finally, Charlie saw the markers CDOT had left earlier in the day—reflective posts marking the safe zone. She slowed, guided her snowmobile into the flat area, and killed the engine.

Silence rushed in. Just wind and the distant sound of the crew down below.

The others pulled up beside her. Viv climbed off first, already looking around with her director's eye. "This is perfect. Rowan, Duke, stand over there so we have the slope behind you."

Charlie dismounted and did a quick perimeter check. The area was maybe forty feet across, relatively flat, backed by a steep slope on one side and open to the valley below on the other. The Seven Sisters loomed above them, massive and dark against the sky, but the snow was undisturbed.

Charlie tried her radio. "Elk, you copy?"

Static, then Shane's voice, faint and breaking up: "...opy... signal... weak..."

Great. Mountains were interfering with the signal. Not unusual, and not ideal.

"We're at the location," Charlie said clearly, hoping he caught it. "Beginning scene walk-through, over."

More static. She couldn't tell if he'd heard.

Charlie moved to where she could watch both the approach trail and the area where Viv was positioning Rowan and Duke. The two actors were professional, focused, discussing the emotional beats of the scene—Caiden's final speech to Aldric, the loyal friend telling his king the truth before the end.

Viv took a puff on her O2 canister. "Camera will be here," Viv said, pointing. "Wide shot first, then we'll move in for close-ups. Duke, when you say, 'You've always been the true king,' I want you looking right at him. Eye contact. Make it hurt."

Duke nodded. "Got it."

Rowan pointed at Viv's O2. "I've got one if that's running low."

"Thanks. I'm okay."

Charlie scanned the darkness beyond the snowmobile headlights they'd left on. Nothing but snow and rock and wind.

Then she heard it.

Another snowmobile. Engine growing louder. Coming up the trail.

Charlie's hand moved to her sidearm. "Viv, we expecting anyone else?"

Viv looked up, confused. "No. Everyone's supposed to stay at base until they're ready."

The sound grew closer. A single headlight appeared on the trail.

"Elk, you sending anyone up early? Over."

Nothing but static, then "...Maddie there. Over."

Charlie relaxed a little. "It's Maddie. Did you forget something?"

Viv looked confused. "I must have, but I can't think what." She looked at the men. "Either of you forget something?"

Rowan shook his head. Duke grinned and shrugged. He said something but his voice was lost beneath the sound of the snowmobile.

Now Charlie wondered, *What could be important enough that it couldn't wait for the rest of the crew?*

As Charlie started toward Viv, Maddie parked the snowmobile next to the others, killed the engine, and climbed off. She kept her helmet on.

"What did I forget?" Viv called.

"Nothing," Maddie said calmly. "Absolutely nothing."

"Maddie." Charlie said. "What are you doing up here?"

"Sorry, Charlie," Maddie said, then made a sound like a laugh crossed with a hiccup, or maybe a sob.

"Stop right there. What's going on?"

Maddie stopped about eight feet away and faced the men.

"You said you loved me. But you're with *her* now."

Is she talking to Rowan or Duke? Charlie's hand moved to her sidearm. "Maddie—"

"I loved you," Maddie said, her voice breaking. "I did what you asked. I turned them all against her." She gestured wildly toward Viv.

"Maddie, honey—"

"Shut up, Viv!" She turned her attention back to the men. "I did everything for you."

Duke's eyes went round. "Maddie, what—"

"And then you got your new show." Maddie's voice rose. "And your new girlfriend. Like I never existed."

"Maddie," Duke said carefully, "we were just friends. I never said I loved you—"

"Liar! You *did*!" Her voice cracked. "Every time you complained about Viv. Every time you said they were ruining the show. Every time you told me I was the only one who understood. I was The Chronicler. For you. I riled up the fans. For you. You're the perfect Caiden."

Her voice dropped, low and menacing. "I cut that saddle strap for you. So Rowan would get hurt, Viv would fail, and you'd keep being Caiden."

Duke's face went white. "Maddie, I never asked you to—"

Maddie drew a gun and pointed it directly at Duke's chest.

Charlie's weapon came up as she moved, putting herself between Maddie and Duke.

"Gun down. *Now*."

"I don't care what happens to me anymore." Maddie's eyes were dead. Empty. Her finger moved to the trigger.

Charlie lunged. The gunshot cracked across the mountain.

Followed by a roar above them. A wide, white plume of snow rose and blotted out the sky.

TWENTY-TWO

BEN WATCHED CHARLIE DISAPPEAR UP THE MOUNTAIN, HER snowmobile's taillight vanishing into the darkness and falling snow. Three more lights followed—Viv, Rowan, Duke.

His chest felt tight. She was working. This was her job.

But he still wanted to be up there with her.

"You're staring, Moose," Elias said, appearing at his elbow with two steaming cups of coffee. They seriously clashed with his medieval-style armor. "Want one?"

"I'm good." He took it anyway.

"You're not good. You're pining." Elias grinned. "When are you going to pop the question?"

Ben felt his ears go red. "Christmas."

"Finally." Elias clapped him on the shoulder. "About damn time."

Gabe, Bear, and Waylon drifted over in their Embersworn Knight costumes minus the helmets. They were having the time of their lives.

Nerds, Ben thought with a smile. *Next, I'll have to get them into playing* Chronicles of the Realm.

"What are we talking about?" Gabe asked.

"Moose is getting married," Elias boomed.

"We know," Bear said. His deep voice was warm with approval. "Made the rings already, didn't you?"

Ben nodded. "Finished them last week."

Waylon's face split into a grin. "Brother, You've made them for all of us. It's about time you made yours."

I never thought I'd be making rings for my own wedding.

Ben's throat felt tight. "Making a ring for Charlie, knowing what it means..."

"That's love, brother," Bear said quietly. "It's the most important ring you've ever made."

Gabe nodded. "She's lucky to have you. You're both lucky."

"Yeah." Ben looked back toward the mountain where Charlie had disappeared. "Yeah, we are."

"We'll all be up there filming in an hour," Waylon said. "Stop worrying."

"I'm not worrying."

"You're absolutely worrying." But Waylon's smile was understanding. Then he looked at his brothers. "Come on, let's get coffee before we freeze our asses off."

The group headed toward the craft trailer where the warmth of the work lights and equipment created a bubble of relative comfort in the freezing night.

Ben started to follow when he noticed Maddie walking past, heading toward the snowmobiles. She'd looked unhappy all night. Now her body language told him she was absolutely devastated.

"Hey, Maddie," Ben called. "You okay?"

She stopped and turned. Her face looked strange in the work lights—pale, drawn. Then she managed a small smile.

"Just tired."

"Long day." Ben nodded toward the crew area. "You should grab some coffee, warm up."

"I can't. Viv...needs something fixed. So do I." She looked past him toward the mountain, then back. Her expression shifted—something vulnerable breaking through. She looked down at her gloves. "My boyfriend and I broke up. I thought he felt the same way I did, but..." She trailed off. "He lied to me."

"Maddie, I'm sorry," Ben said. "That's hard. And you of all people. You don't deserve that treatment."

She looked up at him, heartbreak in her eyes. "You're lucky. With Charlie. Don't take it for granted."

"I don't."

"Good." She gave him a smile that didn't reach her eyes. "Because you never know when things can change and you lose the one you love."

She turned and walked toward the snowmobiles before Ben could respond. He watched her climb onto one of the snowmobiles and start the engine.

"Maddie!" someone shouted. "Where are you going?"

She didn't answer. Just gunned the engine and headed up the trail after Charlie and the others. Ben watched her taillight disappearing into the darkness, feeling awful for her.

He also wished he'd jumped on the back of the snowmobile with her, just to be with Charlie sooner. Maybe it was what Maddie said, or the weather, or seeing an avalanche and knowing Charlie was up there right now that made the hair on the back of his neck prickle.

Ben turned back toward the crew area where his brothers were still joking around. Elias was taking photos with his phone. Bear was trying to adjust Waylon's chainmail.

"Let me do that before you hurt yourself." Ben stepped in and adjusted Waylon's belt. "Better?"

"Much. This shit is *heavy*. I don't know how you nerds walk around in it all day."

"I'd explain the physics, but it might sprain your tiny brain."

"Har har!"

Ben chuckled as he poured himself another coffee from the craft services table, then checked his watch. They'd all be heading up there in a Snowcat in another few minutes, depending on how quickly the crew could pack everything. They'd watch Rowan and Duke do one of Ben's favorite scenes, then it would be their turn to pretend to march up the mountain and die beneath Lord Felldark's snowy wrath.

Then back down and to a hotel in Georgetown. One day closer to Christmas and proposing to Charlie.

"Moose!" Elias called. "Come settle this. Bear says my cape is on upside down."

"It is," Bear rumbled.

"It's a cape! How can it be upside down?"

Ben walked over, grateful for the distraction. He helped Elias adjust the cape—which wasn't upside down, but was inside out—while Gabe took videos for their extremely jealous women waiting back home.

Then he wandered to the crew, who were packing the last of the equipment from the avalanche shoot into a Snowcat. Four others stood empty, waiting to transport personnel. Ben checked his watch. Charlie and the others had been gone almost twenty minutes now.

Shane appeared at Ben's side, radio in hand. "Have you seen Maddie?"

"She took a snowmobile up to the site."

"When? She was supposed to wait and go with the rest of us."

Ben checked his watch. "About ten minutes ago. She said Viv needed something fixed."

"Fixed? What could be broken? They didn't take any real equipment up there."

Shane's radio crackled just then. It was Charlie's voice, broken by static.

"Elk... send... early? Over."

"Dammit. Mountains are blocking the signal," Shane muttered. He keyed his mic. "King, confirm. Is Maddie there. Over."

Nothing.

"Shit," Ben said. "Unless it's one of the snowmobiles. But, why would Maddie go up? This makes no sense."

Shane looked at Ben. "Did Maddie say anything else to you? Before she left?"

Ben thought back. *You never know when things can change.*

"She told me her boyfriend broke up with her," Ben said slowly. "She seemed... off."

"Yeah, Charlie mentioned she was acting stressed." Shane tried the radio again. Still static. "Who was her boyfriend? Did she say?"

"No." But even as Ben said it, pieces were clicking together in his mind.

Maddie's reaction when Duke had flirted with that fan.

Her eyes looked the same right before she walked away from Ben a few minutes ago.

Fuck.

And, she was the biggest insider of all, at Viv's side nearly twenty-four seven.

Glued to her tablet.

She could have easily been feeding fans all sorts of things without ever logging directly into sites. And if she was secretly dating Duke, that would be plenty of motive to keep him on the series.

But now he'd moved on to another show. What if he didn't need her anymore and had moved on from Maddie as well?

The sabotaged saddle strap.

Maddie had been away at lunch just before the joust.

But what if she wasn't at lunch?

Ben's blood went cold.

"Duke. I think Maddie's boyfriend was *Duke*."

Shane's face went white. "Oh shit." He keyed his radio. "King, do you copy? *Charlie*!"

No response. He radioed CDOT next.

Bear joined them, Waylon, Elias and Gabe right behind him. "What's wrong?"

"Maddie. We think she's the one who cut the saddle strap. She's going after Duke."

"And Charlie's with them," Elias said.

A CDOT supervisor ran from a trailer. "What's happening?"

"We have a potential active threat situation—four individuals plus suspect at upper staging area—"

The supervisor was on his radio before Shane finished.

"Dispatch, Loveland Pass CDOT. Possible armed suspect, avalanche terrain. We need law enforcement and S&R—"

A sharp crack bounced and echoed across the mountain.

Ben's heart froze. He'd never mistake the sound of a gun in the mountains.

"Was that—" someone started.

Then came a deep, percussive roaring from above.

Everyone knew what that was because they'd just listened to it less than an hour ago.

It was the sound every person in these mountains learned to fear.

Ben looked up and saw it—the white mass cracking and breaking loose high on the Seven Sisters. Moving. Accelerating.

Heading straight for where Charlie was.

"*No!*" Ben was already running for the snowmobile, Shane on his heels.

The CDOT supervisor shouted after him.

"Sir, stop! You can't go up there during an active slide—"

Ben threw himself into the seat and started the engine.

Shane grabbed his arm. "Moose, wait for S&R—"

"Charlie's up there!" Ben wrenched free.

Bear was suddenly beside him, reaching for the snowmobile.

"Then we're going, too—"

"No one is going anywhere!" The CDOT supervisor stepped between them and the machine. "That mountain is still moving. You go up there now, you'll get caught in a secondary slide. You'll die up there."

Ben looked the CDOT supervisor in the eye.

"Then I die."

Ben gunned the engine. He shot forward before anyone could stop him.

He left chaos behind him. Shane shouting. The CDOT supervisor calling for backup. Bear and the others scrambling for the Snowcat.

Ben didn't look back.

He raced up the trail, following snow mobile tracks. His heart hammered against his ribs. *Charlie. I have to get to Charlie.*

The grade grew steeper. Ben's headlight cut through the blowing snow. Ben pushed the machine as fast as he dared, maybe faster. Snow flew up from the treads.

Come on. Come on.

The avalanche had stopped. The mountain had gone silent. But secondary slides could come at any moment. The whole slope was unstable.

Ben didn't care.

The trail got harder to follow. Fresh avalanche debris covered everything. The original snowmobile tracks disappeared under feet of new snow. Ben's headlight swept across the staging area.

Gone. All of it.

Just a massive field of churned snow and debris. The work lights they'd set up—buried. The snowmobiles—gone. No markers. No reference points.

Nothing.

Ben killed the engine and jumped off. "*Charlie*!"

The silence was absolute. Just wind and the settling squeak and creak of snow.

He ran to where he thought the center of the staging area had been and dropped to his knees. Started digging with his bare hands, throwing snow aside.

"Charlie! Can you hear me? *Charlie*!"

Nothing.

Three feet down. That's what they always said. Most avalanche victims were buried three feet down.

But three feet of avalanche snow and debris was like digging through concrete. The snow had been compressed by the force of the slide, packed so tightly his fingers could barely penetrate it.

He clawed at it anyway. Threw handfuls aside. Moved two feet to the left and dug again.

Nothing.

"*Charlie*!" His voice cracked. "Princess, please—"

He moved again. Dug. Found nothing but more snow.

His hands were already numb. His chest heaving. Tears froze on his face before he could wipe them away.

Where is she? *Where is she*!

The debris field was massive—maybe a hundred feet across, thousands of cubic yards of snow. She could be anywhere. Anywhere at all.

He could dig in the wrong spot forever and never find her.

Ben kept digging anyway. Because what else could he do? Stop? Give up?

Never.

He moved again. Dug again. Nothing.

"Charlie," he whispered. "Please. Please hold on."

Then—engines. Lights cutting through the darkness.

Snowcats.

The one carrying his brothers, followed by CDOT and Search and Rescue vehicles. They pulled up to the edge of the debris field and doors flew open.

Shane jumped out first, avalanche beacon receiver already in his hand, scanning. His face went tight as he swept the device across the debris field.

"Charlie's beacon. I'm not getting a signal."

"What do you mean?" Ben's chest constricted. "She was wearing one—"

"I know." Shane scanned again, adjusting the settings. "Nothing. Either it's buried too deep or—"

"Or it's not transmitting," Bear said quietly.

Ben felt like the ground had disappeared beneath him. No beacon. No way to find her quickly.

"Then we grid search," he said, his voice hard. "Every inch. She's here. We're going to find her."

Bear jumped out with shovels and avalanche probes. Gabe was right behind him with more equipment. Waylon grabbed additional gear from the Snowcat.

And then two dark shapes leaped out before anyone could stop them.

Flo and Pete hit the snow and immediately went to work. Noses down, moving across the debris field in frantic patterns. Flo barked once, sharp and urgent, then started digging at a spot thirty feet from where Ben had been searching.

"Flo!" Ben ran toward her.

But the dog was already moving to another spot, then another. She knew Charlie was here. Somewhere. But there was too much snow, too much disruption, scents scattered by the avalanche's violence.

Pete was doing the same—running, sniffing, digging, moving. Neither dog could pinpoint a location.

"Here." Bear thrust a shovel at Ben. "We need to grid search. Systematic."

"No time—" Ben started toward where Flo was digging.

"Moose." Bear's hand on his shoulder, firm. "We do this right or we don't find them at all."

Ben wanted to scream. Wanted to dig everywhere at once. Wanted to tear the mountain apart with his bare hands.

But Bear was right.

"Okay," Ben said, his voice breaking. "Okay. Tell me what to do."

"Start here." Gabe was already setting up a grid pattern with the probe, working methodically from the uphill edge. "We probe every two feet. When we get a hit, we dig."

Shane kept scanning with the beacon receiver, moving across different sections of the debris field. Nothing. No signal at all.

They spread out. Five men with probes, working in a line, systematically checking the debris field.

Flo and Pete kept searching, their patterns less organized but no less desperate. Flo would stop, dig frantically for a few seconds, then move when she found nothing.

Ben forced himself to work methodically. Probe. Step. Probe. Step. Each thrust of the probe might be the one that found her. Or might be another second wasted while Charlie ran out of air.

If she's even alive.

No. Don't think that. She's alive. She has to be alive.

"Focus, Moose," Bear said quietly. "Stay with us. We'll find her."

Probe. Step. Probe. Step.

Then Pete started barking. Sharp, urgent, insistent. He started digging frantically at a spot near the uphill edge of the debris field.

"Over here!" Gabe shouted. "Pete's got something!"

They converged on the spot. Ben dropped the probe and grabbed a shovel. Started digging.

Three feet down, his shovel met resistance.

"Careful!" Bear said. They slowed down, using their hands now.

Cloth. Then a hand.

"I've got someone!" Ben's heart hammered. "Charlie—"

The face that emerged wasn't Charlie's.

Rowan.

Gasping, covered in snow and ice, but alive. His eyes were wild, disoriented. Bear and Gabe pulled him free, laid him on the snow.

"Rowan," Bear said. "Can you hear me?"

Rowan coughed hard. "Wh-wh-where's V-viv? The ava-valanche separated us—" He was shaking so violently he could barely speak. "Sh-she had her oxy-ge-gen. I had m-mine—" He held up a small portable canister, still clutched in his pale hand.

Bear looked at his watch. "How long ago did it hit?"

"Twenty minutes," Ben said. "Maybe twenty-five."

"Then they could still have air," Bear said. "If she still has the canister. If they're together."

"Charlie?" Ben grabbed Rowan's shoulders. "Was Charlie with Viv?"

"I th-th-think—I d-d-d-on't know. Charlie was—" Rowan's teeth chattered. "Ch-ch-charlie was shot. M-m-addie."

Oh fuck. Fuck!

"Cha-charlie tr-tried to throw hers-s-self over Viv. R-r-right before it h-h-it."

They're together. Charlie's with Viv.

Relief and terror warred in Ben's chest. If Charlie was with Viv, and Viv had oxygen—they had a chance. But where were they?

"Hey!" Someone shouted from down the slope. "I hear something! Someone's calling for help!"

"Charlie?"

Elias ran toward the voice. "It's coming from down there. It's Duke! Duke! Can you hear me?"

Ben's heart fell. Why that bastard and not his Charlie?

"Waylon, take two others and get Duke," Bear ordered. "The rest of us keep searching for Viv, Charlie, and Maddie."

They spread out again. Ben, Bear, Gabe, Elias. Rowan tried to help but Bear made him sit down before he collapsed.

Flo was still running in frantic circles, barking, digging, moving. She knew Charlie was here. Somewhere.

Probe. Step. Probe. Step.

Hold on, Princess. I'm coming. Just hold on.

Ben's probe hit something. He froze. "Here! I've got something!"

They converged. Started digging carefully.

It was Maddie.

Her face was peaceful. Eyes closed. Like she was sleeping.

But she wasn't breathing.

"She's gone," Bear said quietly.

Ben felt nothing. No pity, no anger. Just urgency. "Keep searching."

They moved to the next section of the grid.

Flo barked again, pawing at a spot.

Ben's chest was tight. His hands numb. The cold seeping through his gloves.

Please. Please let it be my princess.

Please let her be alive.

TWENTY-THREE

MADDIE PULLED THE TRIGGER AS CHARLIE LUNGED.

The gunshot cracked across the mountain.

The impact hit Charlie's left side like a sledgehammer. Her beacon—the hard rectangular device strapped to her chest under her vest—exploded. Shards of plastic and metal drove into her shoulder through the vest's gap.

Charlie went down, gasping. Pain spread like fire through her shoulder and chest. She heard Viv scream, Duke and Rowan shouting until a roaring filled her ears and drowned them out. She thought it was her own blood at first.

Until she could feel the vibrations throughout her entire body.

She looked up the mountain at the massive white plume filling the night sky.

Oh dear merciful God. No.

An avalanche.

A massive wall of white—twenty feet high, maybe thirty—rushed down one of the Seven Sisters straight toward them.

Charlie's training kicked in, driving out the pain in her shoulder. One thought, pure and absolute.

Get to Viv.

Charlie stood. Viv was frozen in shock, the oxygen canister still clutched in her hand. Rowan was reaching for her from the other direction. Duke stumbled backward, his face white with terror.

And then there was Maddie.

She stood perfectly still staring up at the avalanche coming toward them. Her face was calm. Peaceful.

Then she turned and gave Duke a triumphant smile that said *I don't care if I die as long as you die too.*

"Move!" Charlie yelled.

Her shoulder screaming and her vision blurring, she grabbed Viv and threw her body over her principal, trying to get them both down, trying to create any kind of shelter.

"Arms over your face and deep breath now! Swim! Here we go!"

Charlie filled her lungs as the avalanche hit.

The force was unimaginable.

Like being hit by a truck. A freight train. The fist of God.

Charlie felt her body lifted, twisted, tumbling. She held onto Viv with everything she had. Her shoulder wound screamed bloody murder but she didn't let go. Would never let go.

The world turned to gray-white chaos and crushing force and the sound of the mountain tearing itself apart.

Air pocket. Need to maintain an air pocket.

Charlie got one arm up over Viv's head, the other over her own face, creating a small space between them as the snow tried to rip them apart.

Then the snow compressed.

Everything stopped.

Silence. Absolute silence.

Charlie was completely buried. The snow pressed against her from all sides, packed tight by the avalanche's force. She couldn't move her legs at all or move her arms more than an inch or two. The air pocket she'd created was maybe the size of a basketball, shared between her and Viv.

Her left shoulder was on fire. Wet warmth spread—her blood.

But I'm alive.

"Viv?" Charlie whispered through her clenched teeth while still holding her breath, acutely aware of not wasting precious oxygen. Her voice sounded strange in the tiny space. Muffled.

Dead.

"Viv, can you hear me?"

Viv made a tiny movement against Charlie's chest.

"Charlie?" Her voice was barely audible.

"I've got you." Charlie's relief almost overwhelmed her. "Hurt?"

"I don't... I don't know. I can't move. Charlie, I can't move—"

"It's okay," Charlie soothed. "We're alive. Someone will find us."

Please let someone find us.

Charlie tried to assess their situation in the crushing darkness.

The air pocket. Basketball-sized. Maybe enough air for both of them for ten minutes. Maybe fifteen if they stayed calm.

My shoulder. Gunshot wound to left shoulder. Bleeding but not arterial. Her tactical vest had deflected the worst of the bullet, but the shattered beacon had done damage. Her ribs hurt—cracked, maybe broken from the avalanche impact. Her left leg was pinned. She couldn't feel her feet.

Viv's condition. Breathing rapidly. Conscious. Pressed against Charlie's chest in the tiny space they shared.

Our position. No idea. They could've been three feet under or fifteen. Hard to know which direction was up.

The beacon.

There was only pain where the beacon should be and warm liquid.

Blood.

The bullet had hit the beacon. Destroyed it.

No signal. They won't be able to find us with the beacon. Ironic that the thing that probably saved me will now cause us to die.

Panic tried to claw up Charlie's throat. She forced it down.

Stop thinking that way. Ben is here. He will find you.

"Charlie?" Viv whispered. "What's wrong?"

"Nothing. Just checking something." No point in scaring Viv. "We're okay."

But they weren't okay. Without the beacon, Ben and Shane would have to grid search. That took time. Time they might not have.

The temperature was already dropping around them. The snow was so cold on her back. Charlie could feel it leeching the heat from her body, but it would have been much worse if they didn't have each other's body heat.

Then she felt something hard pressing against her ribs between her and Viv.

The oxygen canister!

Right. Viv had been holding it when the avalanche hit.

"Viv," Charlie whispered. "The oxygen. Can you open it and hit the button?"

Charlie felt Viv's hand shifting. "Yeah. I... I think I can."

Hope blazed through Charlie's chest.

"Got it."

There was a faint hiss followed by the smell of pure oxygen.

Charlie felt tears of relief freeze on her face. "Small breaths. We need to conserve it until we're found."

"You breathe deep," Viv said. "You're hurt—"

"Viv—"

"You threw yourself over me. You took a bullet." Viv's voice was firm despite the fear. "You're losing blood. You first."

Charlie didn't have the strength to argue. She tilted her face down and she heard the oxygen hiss out of the bottle as Viv pressed the button.

The oxygen was clean and pure. Life.

"Your turn," Charlie said, then held her breath.

They took turns in the darkness. Seconds stretched into minutes that felt like years. The oxygen helped but Charlie could feel her body still shutting down from the cold, the blood loss, the shock.

"Rowan—" Viv's voice cracked. "Where's Rowan? Is he—"

"Viv," Charlie said quietly. "I need you to stay calm. Breathe slowly. We need to make this last."

Viv sobbed.

"Rowan's smart. He had oxygen too. He'll get himself out or they'll dig him out."

Please let that be true.

TIME BECAME meaningless in the darkness.

Charlie counted her breaths. Slow. Steady. In for four counts, hold for one-hundred twenty, out for ten. She tried to use as little oxygen as possible while keeping Viv calm.

Her shoulder throbbed with every heartbeat. The blood didn't feel warm which meant she must have stopped bleeding. That was good. Less blood loss.

But bad for other reasons.

The cold was seeping deeper. Into her bones. Into her core.

"Charlie?" Viv's voice was small. Scared.

"I'm here."

"Are we going to die?"

Charlie wanted to lie. Wanted to say *of course not, we'll be fine, help is coming.*

But Viv deserved the truth.

"I don't know," Charlie said quietly. "But I'm not giving up. And neither are you."

"I'm scared."

"Me too." Charlie adjusted slightly, trying to ease the pressure on her ribs. Pain shot through her side. "But we're still breathing. That means we still have a chance."

Silence for a moment, punctuated only by another hiss of oxygen. How much more did they have?

Then Viv whispered, "Tell me something. About you and Ben. Something happy."

Charlie closed her eyes in the darkness and calculated keeping Viv from panicking and hyperventilating versus spending her breath on talking.

"He made me a necklace. Silver filigree with blue stones. Took him weeks."

"Are you wearing it now?"

"Yeah." Charlie could feel it against her throat, the metal warm from her skin. "He gave it to me with that Evelaine dress at the Ren Faire. Called me his princess."

Viv was quiet for a while.

"He's going to come for you," she finally said. "You know that, right? He's up there right now, digging for you."

"Yeah." Charlie barely kept her voice from breaking. "I know."

THE AIR WAS GETTING STALER.

Charlie could feel it. Each breath was a little harder. The oxygen in their small pocket was depleting despite the canister. Carbon dioxide was building up.

How long has it been? Twenty minutes? Thirty?

Charlie's thoughts were getting fuzzy and she wasn't sure if she hadn't drifted off. The cold seeped deeper.

My body's starting to shut down, she thought without emotion. Then, *When was the last time I heard the O2 hiss?*

"Viv?" Charlie whispered. "You still with me?"

"Mmm." Viv's voice was faint. Slurred. "Getting... sleepy..."

"No. Stay awake. Stay with me." Charlie tried to move, to jostle Viv awake, but she couldn't move enough. "Viv. *Viv*. Hit the button, Viv."

"Tired, Charlie..."

"I know. Me too. But we have to stay awake." Charlie's own voice was fading.

The canister hissed but it sounded weaker.

We're running out of time.

Charlie's training told her what was happening. Hypoxia. Carbon dioxide poisoning. Hypothermia. The deadly combination that killed avalanche victims even when they had air pockets.

Ben. Please. Please find us.

"Charlie?" Viv's voice was dreamy now. Distant. "If this is it... if we don't make it... I need to tell you something."

"Save your breath—"

"No. Listen." Viv took a shallow breath. The oxygen hissed weakly. "You saved my life. At the joust. And just now. You threw yourself over me. You could have run. Could have saved yourself."

"That's my job—"

"It's more than a job." Viv's voice cracked. "You're... you're family, Charlie. You know that, right?"

Charlie's eyes burned. "Yeah. I know."

"And Ben loves you so much. The way he looks at you... that's real. That's forever."

"Viv—"

"If I don't make it, tell Rowan I love him. Tell him... tell him I'm sorry we didn't have more time."

"You're going to tell him yourself," Charlie said fiercely. "We're both getting out of here."

But she could feel herself fading too. The cold. The lack of oxygen. Her body shutting down.

This is what dying feels like.

The hiss of oxygen was getting fainter.

"Charlie?" Viv's voice was barely audible. "I think... I think it's almost empty."

Charlie's heart sank. They'd stretched it as long as they could. Thirty minutes, maybe more. But now—

"I pressed it, Charlie, but it didn't make any noise that time."

The canister was empty.

"Okay," Charlie said, trying to keep her voice steady. "Okay. They're coming. They have to be close by now."

But the air in their pocket was so stale. Thin. Each breath harder than the last.

"Charlie?" Viv whispered. "What's heaven like? Do you think... do you think we'll know we're there?"

Charlie thought about it. About Ben. About the life they were supposed to have.

"I think," Charlie said slowly, "heaven is anywhere Ben is. That's my heaven. Him and me and our life together. That's all I need."

"That's beautiful."

"What about you?"

"Rowan. And making movies. And...and all of you. The whole family we built." Viv's breath hitched. "I don't want to leave yet, Charlie. We were supposed to get married. Have kids. Make a hundred more seasons of *BattleLore*..." She slurred her words.

"You will." Charlie's voice was fierce despite her fading strength. "You will, Viv. I promise."

But the darkness was closing in. The cold absolute. The air gone.

Charlie forced her thoughts to stay on Ben. His smile. His hands. The way he called her Princess. At least she'd die with his necklace on.

I'm sorry, Ben. I'm so sorry.

"Charlie?" Viv's voice was barely audible now. "I can't... I can't breathe..."

"Me neither."

This is it. This is how it ends.

THEN—

A sound. Distant. Muffled.

Metal on ice. Digging.

"Did you hear that?" Charlie whispered.

"Hear what?"

The sound again. Closer.

Someone's digging.

"They're here," Charlie said. "Viv, they're here. Stay with me. Just a little longer—"

The digging got louder. Closer. Frantic.

A dog barked happily. Flo.

Then faint light that grew brighter.

Finally brilliant, blinding light piercing the darkness.

Cold air rushed in like an answered prayer.

"Charlie!" Ben's voice. Desperate. Raw. Broken. "Charlie! I've got you, Princess."

"Here," Charlie tried to say, but her voice wouldn't work. "Ben..."

Then he was there, his face filling her vision. Tears streamed down his cheeks.

"I've got you, Princess. I've got you."

"Get Viv first," she whispered. Charlie gasped, coughed, tried to breathe. Her lungs wouldn't work right. Everything hurt, but dully and far away. "Viv," she managed. "Viv—"

"We've got Viv, Charlie." Bear's voice. "She's alive."

Charlie actually relaxed. Viv was safe.

Then Ben's strong arms were lifting her so carefully. The weight of the snow was gone. Cold, fresh air filled her lungs.

Ben was carrying her across the snow, then wrapping her in something warm. His coat. She could smell him—metal and cedar smoke and Ben.

"Stay with me," Ben said. His voice was shaking. "Charlie, stay with me—"

"Always," Charlie whispered.

Then the world went dark.

TWENTY-FOUR

Charlie was trying to save people from an avalanche. Digging with her bare, frozen hands. Calling their names. But the snow kept falling, burying them deeper, and her hands wouldn't work right, and she couldn't breathe. At the same time somehow, people were trying to dig her out of the snow.

Charlie's throat was dry and her voice came out rough. "Tell Kyle. Next time, beacons on all the principals."

"Well, I would, but I don't work for him."

Ben's voice cut through the dream like a lifeline.

"Ben?"

"Wake up, Charlie."

I'm dreaming.

I'm not buried. I'm not dead. I'm safe.

Charlie's eyes flew open.

Fluorescent lights. White ceiling. The antiseptic smell of a hospital, though surprisingly, it was almost drowned out by the smell of flowers.

Ben saved me.

Her chest heaved as she tried to catch her breath. Everything hurt from a distance, thanks to pain meds—her shoulder, her ribs, her leg, her hands—but she was breathing. Real air. Fresh air.

"Easy, Princess. You're okay. You're safe."

Ben was there, his hand warm around hers. His face was drawn, exhausted, but his eyes were full of relief.

Charlie blinked against the too-bright lights.

Ouch. But I'll take it. Along with all that sweet, fresh air.

She squeezed his hand. "You found me," she croaked.

"Always." His voice cracked. He lifted her hand and pressed it to his cheek. "God, Charlie. I thought—"

"I know." She did know. She'd felt the same terror when the avalanche hit, and again when the oxygen ran out.

The terror of thinking she'd never see him again.

"But you found me."

Ben reached for a giant plastic cup with a wide straw and brought it to her lips. She sipped on the cold water and it tasted like ambrosia.

"Twenty-eight minutes." Ben's jaw was tight. "You were under the snow for twenty-eight minutes. Without that oxygen canister—" He stopped. Swallowed hard. "Viv's oxygen saved both of you."

Charlie's heart clenched. "How is Viv?"

"She's ready to make a superhero show all about you, that's how she is."

"I was just doing my job."

Ben squeezed her hand. "Viv is fine. Hypothermic, bruised ribs, shaken up, but fine."

"So a superhero series?"

Ben's smile was genuine this time. "I think her exact words were 'a six-foot-tall badass female bodyguard who scares avalanches.'"

Charlie huffed out a laugh, then winced. "Ow. Don't make me laugh."

"Sorry."

Charlie took inventory of herself. Her left shoulder was bandaged and immobilized. Her ribs were wrapped tight. Her left leg was elevated in some kind of brace.

"How bad do I look?" she asked.

"You look beautiful."

She knew he was biased, but at the same time, he looked like he wanted to memorize every detail of her face, so she believed him.

Ben's expression turned serious. "Gunshot wound to your left shoulder. The bullet hit your beacon first, so the vest caught most of it, but fragments from the beacon casing caused lacerations. You needed surgery to remove the shrapnel and repair the damage to a tendon. Three cracked ribs. Moderate frostbite on your left foot and minor on your fingers. You'll make a full recovery, but it'll take time. Hypothermia. You were at ninety-two degrees when we pulled you out."

Charlie absorbed that.

It could have been so much worse.

"Rowan?" she asked.

"Rowan's fine. Hypothermic and bruised, but he got lucky—ended up closer to the surface and he had an oxygen can. He says he's forever in your debt for saving his fiancée, by the way." Charlie smiled, then she grew serious.

"Duke?"

Ben's expression darkened. "Duke's battered but alive. His armor protected him from the worst of it. He rode a tree like a surfboard and ended up close to the edge, in shallower snow."

Charlie took a deep breath and steeled herself.

"And...Maddie?"

"Dead." Ben's voice was flat.

Charlie closed her eyes. She saw that triumphant smile all over again. "She never even tried to save herself. Just... stood there and let it take her. Maddie had wanted to die as long as Duke died with her."

"It turns out," Ben said quietly, "she wasn't lying about Duke. He did use her. Told her he loved her. Strung her along while she did his dirty work." He paused. "Doesn't let her off the hook for what she did, but... Duke's no longer seeing his costar, though he probably won't lose his new role."

Charlie opened her eyes. "It would be funny if there were an anonymous online campaign—"

"Elissa's already on it." Ben's smile was grim. "She's very creative when she's angry."

"That she is." Charlie felt a wave of exhaustion wash over her. Her eyes drifted closed.

"Sleep, Princess," Ben said softly. "I'll be right here when you wake up."

"Love you," Charlie whispered.

"Love you too. Always."

CHRISTMAS EVE, Charlie sat curled up on Ben's—no, *their*—couch, with her left leg propped on an ottoman and her shoulder still in a sling. She wore one of Ben's oversized sweaters and thick wool socks. Flo was pressed against her good side, warm and solid.

The Victorian was decorated like something out of a Dickens novel.

A real tree—a massive blue spruce that Ben had cut himself—stood in the corner by the window, covered in handmade ornaments and strings of cranberries and popcorn. Live balsam garlands draped the mantel and wound up the staircase banister. The whole house smelled like a magical forest.

Charlie had never bothered with a Christmas tree before. Never saw the point when it was just her.

This was beautiful, and she wanted it every year. Ben was going to have a fight on his hands if he so much as hinted at taking it down before Valentine's Day.

Fine, maybe February first.

"Here we go." Ben walked into the room carrying two flutes of bubbly, light-golden liquid. "Dry hard cider. Made it myself with champagne yeast."

Charlie took a flute carefully with her good hand. She sniffed it and the bubbles tickled her nose just like champagne. "You made this?"

"Fall before last. It's been aging." He settled beside her on the couch, careful not to jostle her arm or leg. "I was saving it for a special occasion."

"Christmas?"

"Something like that." He winked as he lifted his glass. "To life."

Charlie clinked her glass against his. "To life."

The cider was crisp and bright on her tongue, with just a hint of sweetness. *Perfect.*

As much as Charlie had wanted to spend Christmas with their family—and they'd all visited her in the hospital, showering her with flowers and art supplies and Moleskines and terrible jokes—she was grateful to be here. Just the two of them. Quiet. Safe. Home.

"I have something for you," she said.

"Charlie, you just got out of the hospital—"

"It was finished before the avalanche. Shane brought it from my apartment where I was hiding it."

"You mean the same apartment you're giving up at the end of this month?" Ben grinned.

"The very same." She nodded toward the large flat package leaning against the wall. "Can you get it?"

Ben retrieved the package. "I might know what it is, judging by the size and shape and your talents."

"You might. Or, you might not know completely what it is."

Ben raised his eyebrows, eyes sparkling. He carefully unwrapped it.

Then he went completely still.

It was the St. Vrain photo—the one of him and his brothers as teenagers, horsing around in the river. But Charlie had recreated it in colored pencil and charcoal, every detail perfect.

Except she'd also added Sean.

Standing in the background on the riverbank, watching his

brothers with that quiet smile he had in photos. Like he was still there with them. Like he'd never left the river.

Ben's throat worked. His eyes were bright with unshed tears.

"Charlie," he whispered. "This is—"

He couldn't finish. He set the drawing down carefully and pulled her into his side, his face buried in her hair.

"Thank you," he said, his voice rough. "Thank you."

They sat like that for a long moment. Charlie pressed against his chest, listening to his heartbeat.

Finally Ben pulled back. He wiped his eyes. "I have something for you, too."

"Ben, you don't have to." His fingers went automatically to the pendant at her throat. "My necklace is worth all the Christmas presents for the next hundred years."

"I'm hoping you'll feel differently about this one." He reached into his pocket and pulled out a small wooden box—dark walnut, polished to a shine, with delicate filigree carved into the lid—the smaller twin to her necklace's box.

Charlie's breath caught.

Ben opened the box.

Two rings sat nestled in light-blue velvet. Silver, delicate but strong, with tiny swords and filigree flowers wrapped around the bands. Small blue stones—the same color as her necklace—set into the centers of the flowers.

They were the most beautiful things Charlie had ever seen.

"I finished them the week before the avalanche," Ben said. His voice shook slightly. "I was going to wait until Christmas morning, do this whole elaborate breakfast in bed thing, but—" He stopped. Swallowed. "I almost lost you, Charlie. And I'm done waiting."

He slid off the couch and knelt in front of her. Then he took her good hand in both of his.

"Charlie King," he said. "My strong princess. My lovely warrior. The bravest person I've ever known." His eyes were bright. "Will you do this humble blacksmith the greatest honor and marry me?"

Charlie's vision blurred with tears. "Oh, Ben. Yes. God, yes."

Ben slipped the smaller ring onto her finger. It fit perfectly. Of course it did—he'd made it for her so it was perfect.

She wiped her eyes with her free hand. "Put yours on. I want to see."

Ben's smile was radiant as he slid the larger ring onto his own finger.

Yes. Perfect. They were absolutely perfect.

Charlie leaned forward and kissed him. Careful of her shoulder, but fierce in her certainty.

"I love you," she whispered against his mouth.

"I love you too, Princess. Always."

Someone knocked at the door. Flo lifted her head and gave a soft whine.

Ben pulled back with a frown. "Are you expecting anyone?"

"If I still lived in my apartment, I'd say it was Mrs. Calhoun. But this would be an awfully long walk for her."

The knock came again, followed by singing.

"God rest ye merry gentlemen, let nothing you dismay—"

Charlie started laughing from pure joy—which hurt her ribs but she didn't care. Those were some very familiar voices. And dog howls.

Ben got up and opened the door, Flo right at his heels, tail wagging a mile a minute.

Their entire family stood on the broad porch. Stephanie was front and center, wearing reindeer antlers and an ugly Christmas sweater with knitted tire treads across it. She was leading the caroling with dramatic hand gestures. Behind her stood Dr. Boyfriend—William—looking amused.

I guess he's part of the family now too, Charlie thought.

Behind him were Arden and Kyle. Gabe and Rochelle. Bear with Star sitting on his shoulders and Ellie at his side. Elias and Wren. Shane with April and their son, Kevin. Waylon and Frankie with baby Danny bundled in a little red snowsuit and Santa hat. Gina and

Lachlan. Alex and Sylvie. Hannah, and Sandra, and Nettie. Flint and Harper, Badger and Brianna. Jodie, and Mac, and Colin, all from Watchdog.

And a whole lotta dogs.

Stephanie stopped singing mid-verse. "Benjamin Massey, did you really think you could get away with proposing to our Charlie without all of us?"

Our Charlie.

She could have died of happiness right there and then.

"Yes, actually, I thought I could," Ben said.

"Well." Stephanie's eyes sparkled. "Shows what you know."

"Don't worry," Arden said, holding up several insulated bags. "We're just feeding the lovebirds, and then we'll be on our way."

"Wouldn't mind some of that cider I know you brewed gallons of though," Elias said, already pushing past Ben into the house.

"And I wanna see that ring, girlfriend!" Wren pushed right in behind her husband.

"Make yourselves at home," Ben said, his voice drier than the cider. "*All* of you."

But of course he was smiling. And Charlie was smiling. And suddenly the Victorian was full of noise and laughter and love.

Stephanie commandeered the kitchen, directing Arden and Rochelle in laying out enough food to feed an army. Kyle built up the fire. Bear settled into the armchair with Star, while Frankie perched on the couch next to Charlie with Danny.

"Let me see it," Frankie demanded, as Wren stood behind the couch pursing her lips and snapping her fingers like demanding royalty.

Charlie held up her hand. The ring caught the firelight, the blue stones glowing.

"Oh my God," Wren breathed. "Ben, I love the rings you made for Elias and me, but this? It's your best work."

"Of course it is," Stephanie said, appearing with a plate of colorful sugar cookies. "The man's a romantic. Who knew? Don't answer that."

Ben's ears went red but he was grinning.

Shane raised his glass of cider. "To Ben and Charlie. The couple who survived an avalanche and still said yes."

"To Ben and Charlie!" everyone chorused.

The evening dissolved into warmth and chaos. Food and drink and laughter and happy dogs underfoot. Baby Danny grabbed at Charlie's necklace with his tiny fists. Star toddled over to Flo, patted her very gently...and calling her Spot Skunk. Someone turned on some music and Brianna, April, and Hannah did their best Sixties Girl Band impressions. Elias and Lachlan argued about whether or not Die Hard was a Christmas movie, to which Charlie shouted, "Of course it is!" and Arden hugged her for that. Stephanie regaled everyone with the story of how she knew Charlie and Ben were meant for each other the moment she met them.

At one point, a line streaked through the house, ending under the mistletoe.

Eventually, as midnight approached, people started bundling up to leave. Hugs and congratulations and promises to help plan the wedding were plentiful. Arden especially told her that they should get together between Christmas and New Years.

"I'd love that," Charlie told her friend.

Finally, it was just Ben and Charlie again. Flo snored quietly on her dog bed by the fire. The tree lights glowed. The house smelled like balsam and cinnamon and fresh Christmas cookies. Charlie sat with the ring on her finger and the fire dying down and Ben dozing lightly against her good side, and she thought about Joey.

It's late, she told herself. *It's Christmas Eve. He's probably with friends, or his wife, or—*

She stopped.

His wife. She didn't even know if he was married. She didn't know anything about him.

She eased herself carefully off the couch, trying not to wake Ben. Flo lifted her head.

"Stay," Charlie whispered. "I'll be right back."

Flo ignored her for once, got up, and trotted beside her. Charlie grinned down at the dog who knew what was best for her.

She padded to the kitchen in her wool socks and pulled up the contact she'd copied onto her phone from the Watchdog voicemail months ago. She still hadn't attached Joey's name to it.

It's almost midnight. This is a terrible idea.

She hit call.

It rang three times. Four. She was about to hang up when he answered, slightly breathless, clearly distracted.

"Yeah, hang on—is this the driver? Because I said the blue house with the—"

"Joey."

Silence.

"It's—it's Charlene."

The silence stretched so long she thought the call had dropped.

"Charlie." His voice came out strange and small, then louder. "Oh my God. *Charlie.*"

"I'm sorry it's so late, I shouldn't have... I can call back tomorrow—"

"Don't you dare hang up." His voice cracked. "Don't you dare."

She pressed her hand over her mouth.

"I've been wanting to talk to you for years," he said, and he sounded wrecked, and young, and like the little kid she'd left behind. "After you left, Dad said...he told us you wanted nothing to do with us. That you hated us. Patrick and James believed him, they just, they went along with it, but I never... Charlie, I never believed that."

"I didn't hate you," she managed through her tears. "Joey, I *never* hated you. Not for a single second."

He exhaled shakily. "I wouldn't blame you if you did. I was terrible to you when I got older."

“It doesn’t matter.” Charlie felt a tear slip down her cheek. Flo nuzzled her and she stooped to pet her.

“It does matter, Charlie. It does. And I’m sorry. I’m so, so sorry.” Joey choked up before he continued. "So, you’re in Colorado. Are you okay? Are you safe?"

"I'm really good, actually." She looked through the kitchen doorway at the fire, at Ben's sleeping silhouette. Then she looked the ring on her finger. "I'm happy, Joey. I found my home and my family."

He was quiet for a moment.

"I just got engaged," Charlie said to fill the space. "Tonight, actually. About two hours ago."

Joey made a sound that was half laugh, half sob. "Are you serious? Tell me everything."

So she did.

And he told her everything too. He'd joined the military straight out of school and he was in San Diego now. “So you weren’t calling me late at all.”

He'd met his wife out there and they'd been married two years. His voice turned serious.

“I called Watchdog because I’m gonna be a dad.”

“What? When?”

“She’s just over four months along. I tried calling you right after we got the news. I wanted you to know you were going to be an aunt.”

Charlie had to sit down on the kitchen floor for that one and hug Flo.

“So, you just got engaged? Who is he?" Joey asked.

"He’s a former Ranger turned blacksmith. He's enormous and gentle and he makes chainmail and he sings folk songs and he's the best man I've ever met and he loves *BattleLore*."

"He’s a blacksmith who loves *BattleLore*." She could hear the grin in Joey’s voice. "Of course he is. Of course *my* sister ends up with a guy like that."

My sister. The words hit her somewhere she hadn't known was still tender.

"So, I'm on leave until the new year. Maybe," Joey said carefully, like he was afraid of pushing too hard, "we could—if you wanted—maybe we could meet up? No pressure. I just... I really want to meet your blacksmith. And you could meet my wife."

Charlie pressed her back against the kitchen cabinets and stared at the ceiling.

"Yeah." Her voice came out rough. "Yeah, Joey. I really want that too."

They talked for another hour, until Charlie heard a woman's voice the background asking if everything was okay because the food was getting cold and Joey said, his voice warm and proud, "It's *Charlie.* It's my sister calling me back. We're gonna meet up, baby. She's excited for us."

After they finally said goodnight, Charlie sat in the dark kitchen for a long moment, the phone still warm in her hand, Flo's head on her leg. She thought briefly about her mum and wondered if she'd ever be brave enough for that particular phone call.

Not tonight. But maybe someday.

Especially since it looked like Joey was back in her life. Maybe they could reach out to their mother together.

She got up and went back to Ben.

He stirred as she settled against him. "Everything okay?" he murmured without opening his eyes.

"Better than okay." She tucked herself carefully into his side and looked at the ring on her finger. "I'll tell you in the morning."

He pulled her closer.

"Merry Christmas, Princess," he said softly.

"Merry Christmas, Ben the Forger of the Ember Sword."

She looked at the ring on her finger, then at the drawing of her friend Sean and his brothers propped on the mantel. Looked at the man in her arms—her blacksmith, her gentle giant, her home.

"I love you," Charlie whispered.

"I love you too." Ben pressed a kiss to the top of her head. "Always."

Outside, snow began to fall. Soft and gentle and nothing like an avalanche.

Just gentle and beautiful.

The beautiful beginning of their always.

TWENTY-FIVE

"Are you *sure*, Kyle?" Arden's voice trembled. Her silver-grey eyes darkened and she reached for the fireplace mantel to steady herself.

"Affirmative, baby. Once you see it, you can't unsee it."

Arden dropped her chin forward. A tear fell straight down and splashed onto the bricks.

"Why didn't I *know*?" She bit her lip almost hard enough to draw blood. "Why didn't—"

"Come with me," Kyle said. "We'll talk it out."

More tears splashed onto the bricks. Arden squeezed her eyes shut so tightly she saw stars.

She felt Kyle's hand on the small of her back.

"I've got you, baby," he whispered. "Let's go."

Kyle guided her out to the SUV. Normally, they'd make the walk down to Watchdog's main office, but Arden's legs wobbled so much she didn't think they were up to the task.

Jodie said nothing to them as they walked through the lobby. She sat there looking almost as stunned as Arden felt.

But that would be impossible. No one—*no one*—was as shocked as she.

By the time they got to the conference room, Kyle was practically carrying Arden. She leaned on him as he turned the knob and opened the door.

The woman sitting in the conference room looked terrified—no, *haunted* might be a better word. But Arden only gave her a cursory glance.

It was the young girl sitting on her lap who captured all of Arden's attention.

Specifically the eyes—which, as Kyle had warned her, could not be denied once seen.

They were Arden's silver-grey eyes.

Or, more specifically, her dead brother Sean's eyes.

"Please," the woman pleaded. "I'm so, so sorry about this, but my niece and I need your help..."

Read about Maren and Colin in *Shadows on the Mountain – Watchdog Mountain Division Book 7*

AFTERWORD

If you haven't met me in person, you probably don't know that I'm under five feet tall.

Shorty, half-pint, short stuff, Hobbit, pixie, elf—I've been called all of these. To get stuff off tall shelves I use a short-person extender, AKA a stepstool. Tall shelves being a relative term; sometimes my husband and both my boyos don't have to stretch their arms to get what I need. But, the upside is that I have ample legroom in planes, even in the crampiest of cramped economy seats.

So, it was a lot of fun to write about two people who have the opposite problem that I do, but are still highly aware of how their bodies are perceived and how they take up space. Outliers like me, but at a different altitude. I got to ride up a little higher for a few months to see out of their eyes.

I hope all my tall readers see themselves portrayed lovingly and accurately, at least as far as height goes. I had a very tall roommate once who joked that we should buy identical pants so that when I cut off the bottoms so they don't drag behind me, she could sew them to hers so her pants went below her ankles. I learned a lot from her and it all went into this book.

As far as Charlie and Ben's reading tastes go, I didn't have to do any research at all. I've been a lifelong fan of fantasy and romantasy and Ren Faires, and this was my chance to dive into all of that fun sword and sorcery. Who knows? Maybe I'll write a full-on romantasy one of these days. I have ideas, oh-so-many ideas for a series...

Now Charlie, believe it or not, got her start about eight years ago, in the first draft of a romantasy book I was hoping to turn into a series (I still have that hope). She was a bodyguard trying to distract a group of fans from a pair of actors in disguise. If that sounds familiar, the whole scene ended up in *More Than Words Can Say*. Charlie was just too good to leave unwritten, and not only did she find a home with Watchdog, I think she's one of my favorite heroines so far.

Going over some old notes, I see that I wrote:

Charlie Charlene in Denver Watchdog

She's ex-military. Nickname was Charlemagne then shortened to King. Because she's tall and broad she has never felt feminine. She has brothers and she's had to fight for everything all her life. Her father told her she'd never make a good wife in an attempt to keep her serving him. But she took off for the military and tried not to look back. She became a SWCC and knew Arden's brother and that's how she came to Colorado.

It's dated 3-14-22. Yikes! I promise I'll write fater!

I owe a debt of gratitude to George R.R. Martin and his character, Brienne of Tarth, for influencing my shaping of Charlie and Sir Mariel both. So, thanks, George!

Meanwhile, I can't believe this is a wrap-up for Mountain Division! Or...at least it was SUPPOSED to be a wrap-up. I don't wanna leave these guys. So I'm not going to. We're just gonna keep on keeping on in Lyons, focusing on the bodyguards and staff of Watchdog, both the ones you know and love, PLUS more of them you haven't met yet. So, I'll just keep going from there starting with Book 7—*Shadows on the Mountain*.

What do you say? Want to come along with me?

xoxo

Olivia Michaels
February 9, 2026

ACKNOWLEDGMENTS

As always, this is for my Lovelies. Thank you so much for reading, not just my books, but these little afterbits that peek into my life.

For the usual suspects—Trinity, Caitlyn, Bella, Riley, Kris, Anna, Kat, Misha (oh, Maaaary!), Susan, Elle, Becca, Ophelia, Jeff Clown-car, Cori, Carrie, Julie, The Librarians of Colorado, and Mike and Carol (I love you both so much).

And special guest star, my ever-patient, ever tolerant, nothing-at-all-like-Maddie-I-pinkie-swear assistant, Amber. God, you poor thing.

FOLLOW OLIVIA

Follow me to catch my latest releases at:

Newsletter:
https://oliviamichaelsromance.com/

Amazon:
https://www.amazon.com/author/oliviamichaelsromance

BookBub:
https://www.bookbub.com/authors/olivia-michaels

Facebook:
https://www.facebook.com/oliviamichaelsauthor

Instagram:
https://www.instagram.com/oliviamichaelsromance/

Want more? Come be one of Olivia's Lovelies on Facebook. I can always use another ARC reader or two...

https://www.facebook.com/groups/639545290309740/

ALSO BY OLIVIA MICHAELS

Watchdog Security Series

More Than Love

More Than Family

More Than Puppy Love: A Christmas Novella

More Than Paradise

More Than Thrills

More Than Words Can Say

More Than Beauty

More Than Rumors

More Than Secrets

Watchdog Security Series Box Set, Books 1-3

Watchdog Security Series Box Set, Books 4-6

Watchdog Security Series Box Set, Books 7-9

Watchdog Protectors

In Susan Stoker's Special Forces Operation Alpha

Protecting Harper

Protecting Brianna

Protecting Sylvie

Watchdog Mountain Division

Bear On The Mountain

Timberwolf On The Mountain

Lion on the Mountain

Blizzard on the Mountain

Thunder on the Mountain

Avalanche on the Mountain

Shadows on the Mountain

Free Short Stories

Tell it to the Bees – A Bear and Ellie Short Story

Safe With Him — A Camden and Elena Short Story

Thanksgiving on the Mountain

ABOUT THE AUTHOR

Olivia Michaels is a life-long reader, dog-lover, gardener, and a certified beachaholic. When she's not throwing a Frisbee for her fur-baby, harvesting tomatoes, or writing, you can find her playing in the surf, kayaking, or kicking back on the sand and cracking open a romantic beach read.

www.ingramcontent.com/pod-product-compliance
Lightning Source LLC
LaVergne TN
LVHW010644110826
845149LV00014B/2944

* 9 7 8 1 9 5 7 5 3 3 4 1 4 *